A DIRE ISLE

A DIRE ISLE

RV RAMAN

A HARITH ATHREYA MYSTERY

Copyright © 2021 by RV Raman
Cover and jacket design by Georgia Morrissey

ISBN: 978-1-951709-52-5
eISBN: 978-1-951709-78-5
Library of Congress Control Number: Available upon request

First hardcover edition published in December 2021
By Agora Books
An imprint of Polis Books, LLC

www.PolisBooks.com
44 Brookview Lane
Aberdeen, NJ 07747

Also by RV Raman

Harith Athreya novels
A Will to Kill

Fraudster
Insider
Saboteur
Conspirator

CHAPTER 1

The inflatable rubber dinghy careened down the River Betwa, carrying its five occupants inexorably towards the rocks and the forbidding white water beyond. The two boatmen at the rear deftly steered it toward the gap in the rocks as the two other men sitting in front of them held their oars clear of the cold water. The fifth occupant, a bright-eyed girl of sixteen, sat at the bow of the raft, mesmerised by the approaching drop in the river. All five pairs of eyes were riveted to the abrupt descent and the roiling waters beyond.

"Hang on!" Athreya called as his right hand let go of the oar and clenched the taut nylon rope under his legs.

To Harith Athreya's left sat his friend and host, Sharad Sikka. Sharad was a native of Bundelkhand, which Athreya was visiting again after many years. Crouching at the bow in front of the men and tightly gripping ropes with both hands was Moupriya, Sharad's daughter. The boatmen at the rear of the raft watched the swirling waters ahead warily, as if expecting them to throw up a nasty surprise at any moment.

Presently, the raft tilted forward alarmingly as its bow plunged over the drop and buried itself – and Moupriya – momentarily into the churning eddies of the Betwa. The girl's squeal of excitement turned into a gasp and ended in a splutter as a mass of frigid water drenched her from head to toe. It would leave the raft with at least six inches of standing water.

"Hold tight, Mou!" her father called. He had reached forward in anticipation and was clutching the collar of her windbreaker.

The raft bounced and spun dizzyingly as the rest of it followed the bow over the drop and hit the frothy water.

"Row!" called one of the boatmen over the din of the cascading torrent, and four oars plunged into the white water as the raft sought to fight its way out of the eddies.

Ahead lay a sharp bend in the river where it also narrowed considerably. The quickening current surged and leapt over rocks as the river narrowed, forcing the men to give their undivided attention to steering the raft. The boatmen's primary task was to keep it from crashing onto rocks, seen or unseen. This turbulent stretch was – depending on one's perspective – the most thrilling or the most dangerous part of their rafting adventure.

After an interminable length of time, they emerged onto calmer waters beyond the bend of the river. Athreya rested his oar and took a well-deserved breather, letting his tired arms hang limply at his sides. The other three men did likewise, allowing the raft to drift down the river.

Athreya ran his long fingers through his uncommonly fine hair that was revealing its first specks of grey. Except the silvery tuft in the front, the rest of his head was largely black. His fine-haired beard, too, was mostly black, except at the chin where a small patch of silver matched the tuft on his head. Sitting there with his hair and beard dripping water, he looked like a bearded collie that had just had a bath.

After staring at little other than the raging waters, and watching out for submerged rocks, Athreya now lifted his gaze to take in the new vista that greeted him beyond the bend.

The river was broader now. The forest on the riverbank to his right was dense, green and silent. Not a sign of civilization marred the stretch of undisturbed nature. The left-side riverbank, however, was not as thick or verdant as the opposite bank. An occasional manmade structure peeped through relatively sparse foliage.

Ahead, the river widened and split into three arms, creating two islets as its outermost arms veered away from each other. The middle arm of the river cut a narrow, rock-strewn channel for the water between the two islets. The boatmen quietly steered the raft towards the left-side arm that was visibly wider. Not only that, but they were ensuring that the raft drifted as close to the left-side bank—and as far away from the islets—as possible.

That was when Athreya noticed that a sudden quiet had fallen over them and their surroundings. Only the whispers of the river around him intruded. The woods on both banks were silent. Even more so were the two islets looming ahead. There was a curious stillness about them that caught Athreya's attention, stirring his not inconsiderable imagination. There was something about them that didn't feel quite natural.

Several long moments passed in silence as they drifted closer to the islets. Dusk was beginning to fall. The index finger of Athreya's right hand, which seemed to have a mind of its own, traced unseen designs and words on his knee. This was a reflexive action whenever his mind was churning.

Athreya caught himself staring at the larger islet. There was something subliminal about it that was casting a spell over him.

Suddenly self-conscious, he broke out of the trance and looked around the raft. Moupriya was staring unblinkingly at the islet as her fingers crept into the waterproof plastic pouch under her windbreaker to pull out her mobile phone. Sharad seemed ill at ease as his eyes darted from the islet to his daughter. The two boatmen at the rear of the raft had done something peculiar – they had swivelled to their left and now sat facing the left-side riverbank. Their backs were turned towards the centre of the river.

Perched awkwardly, both of them were staring upriver toward the direction they'd come. While Athreya couldn't see their faces, their rigid postures made it apparent that they were tense. It was as if they were averting their gaze from the islets. *Were they afraid to look at it?*

Athreya turned his attention back to the nearing larger islet, wondering what it was about it that had stirred his imagination. His index finger resumed tracing words on his knee.

The foliage on the islet – dark green with patches of brown and black – seemed thicker than the forest on the far riverbank. Thick tree trunks stood on the very edge, reminding him simultaneously of the Amazonian rainforest and the Sundarbans mangroves. The slanting evening sun rays seemed incapable of penetrating or brightening the islet, even as it dispelled the darkness in the woods on the riverbanks.

As he stared, oblivious to whatever else the raft passed on the riverbanks as it drifted downstream, he thought he saw a flicker of white deep in the trees. It was a fleeting impression that lasted less than an instant. Something had momentarily caught the rays of the setting sun. But it had vanished almost as soon as it had appeared.

Athreya continued staring. Some more long moments passed. Just as he began doubting what he had seen, it appeared again – a hazy, translucent patch of whiteness in the gloom that seemed to move among the trees.

At that instant, he heard the sound of a photo being taken. Moupriya—who also had been staring at the islet—had clicked her mobile phone's camera. The sound seemed unnaturally loud in the oppressive silence.

"Mou!" he heard Sharad hiss. "Don't!"

Simultaneously, the raft rocked as the boatmen suddenly

changed their position. Athreya turned. The boatmen were no longer staring up the river. Instead, they were gaping at Moupriya with horrified expressions on their faces.

Ignoring her father, Moupriya raised her mobile phone again, pointing its camera at the islet.

"Madam!" one of the boatmen called, startling Athreya. The shout was laced with indignation as well as fear. "Madam, no photo!"

Such was the urgency and intensity of the shout that Moupriya, who was about to click another picture, paused in the act and looked back in surprise over her shoulder.

"No photos, madam," the boatman repeated fiercely in his limited English. "Bad luck! Bad luck!"

"Moupriya!" Sharad snapped, taking his daughter's full name in exasperation. "I told you not to."

"But, Pa—" the girl protested, only to be cut off.

"No!" Sharad barked. "Put your phone away."

Athreya saw Moupriya's ears redden. Just when he thought that the spirited girl was going to push back, she gave in. She lowered her arm, slid her mobile phone back into the waterproof pouch and zipped it up. Sighs of relief sounded from behind Athreya.

Surprised at the tension and the unexpected display of emotion over a simple picture, Athreya turned towards Sharad to ask the obvious question: why shouldn't Moupriya take pictures? But his words remained unsaid on his lips when he saw that Sharad, normally a stoic man, was agitated. His face conveyed a mixture of embarrassment and ire.

Nonplussed, Athreya turned to look at the two boatmen behind him. They had returned to their earlier position and were sitting stiffly with their backs to the islets and their gazes directed up the river. Athreya now had no doubt that they were avoiding looking – even by chance – at the islet.

"Sorry, Athreya," Sharad said sheepishly, interrupting Athreya's thoughts. "The place is a bit of a bogey for locals. There are some superstitions about it that I'll tell you later."

"Does it have a name?" Athreya asked. "This islet?"

"Yes, it's called … Naaz Tapu."

Hardly had Sharad spoken the name than one of the boatmen protested.

"Sharad Sahib," he uttered plaintively. "Naam mat lijiye, don't utter the name!"

Silence fell, and Athreya turned his attention to Naaz Tapu. They were passing it now. It was no more than a hundred and fifty yards away. The boatmen were still perched rigidly with their backs to it and their eyes fixed on the left riverbank. Moupriya, her young face flushed in excitement was staring wide-eyed at it. Whatever the local tales and superstitions about Naaz Tapu, the girl clearly did not subscribe to them.

Sharad was throwing quick glances at the islet, but his eyes never rested on it for more than a couple of seconds. He, too, was ill at ease.

* * *

An hour later, now back in dry clothes, they were in Sharad's car en route to Jhansi. They had come ashore about a kilometre downstream from Naaz Tapu, where Sharad's car and a small truck were waiting for them. The boatmen had loaded the raft into the rear of the truck and departed with it. Meanwhile, the other three had changed into dry clothes in a conveniently located shack and warmed themselves with cups of masala chai before starting their journey back to Jhansi by road. Every stitch they had worn on the raft, including their shoes, had been drenched, and was now lying as a bundle in the boot of the car.

"Why did the boatmen react so violently to Mou taking a picture?" Athreya asked. "It's just open wilderness there, isn't it?"

"Yes," Sharad replied, "but the locals have their own reasons for fearing the islet."

"*Fearing* it?" Athreya repeated in surprise. "What's there about an islet to fear?"

"Well ... old beliefs. They believe that there is something on the islet that is best left alone."

"What kind of something? A creature?"

"Something resides there," Sharad said cautiously, pointing furtively with his eyes to the back of the driver's head. Apparently, Sharad didn't want to speak openly about Naaz Tapu in the driver's presence. "Something that is ... let's say ... insalubrious."

Athreya guessed that Sharad had deliberately chosen a word the driver wouldn't understand. He continued in the same vein.

"This insalubrious thing that resides there ... what form is it? A carnivore? Some kind of a predator?"

"It's not an animal, Athreya. Something more esoteric ... some kind of a presence."

"An apparition then?" Athreya asked. "A local spirit or a phantom?"

"Apparently." Sharad nodded.

"I noticed that you, too, were averting your gaze," Athreya teased his friend. "Not as much as the boatmen were, but you were not comfortable either."

"I grew up here, Athreya," Sharad explained sheepishly. "As a boy, I heard the stories. When you are young and impressionable, such things embed themselves deeply in the mind. What you saw was the instinctive reaction of someone who grew up with these superstitions. My rational part, of course, doesn't believe in it."

"I'm sure it doesn't," Athreya concurred. "I saw that you didn't prevent Mou from staring."

"But he stopped me from photographing it!" Moupriya interposed petulantly from the front seat of the car. "Papa doesn't believe those stories. Yet, he stopped me."

"I had to, Mou," Sharad responded. "Otherwise the boatmen would go bonkers. You know that. They had told me beforehand that we shouldn't photograph the islet. If we disregard their request – especially this one – they won't rent their rafts to us in the future."

"I take it that there is a story behind this superstition?" Athreya asked. "There usually is a juicy tale behind local beliefs."

"Oh, yes!" Moupriya trilled. "It goes like this—"

"Not now, Mou!" Sharad growled. "Not here."

"Okay, Papa," Moupriya tittered gaily. "I'll tell you later, Uncle. Just remind me."

"Tell me, Sharad," Athreya asked, turning to his friend. "Is this only about tales and superstitions? Or is there anything more concrete that has stoked people's fear?"

"I believe there has been a history of incidents over the past hundred years or more," Sharad said. "They say that men who went to the islet didn't return. Some were found dead. Some went mad. Stuff like that spooks people."

"Over a hundred years or more?" Athreya asked. "Isn't that more in the nature of a legend or a myth? Is it believable?"

"Depends on the person who hears it, I suppose," Sharad answered doubtfully. "Someone like you, who has dealt with crime and death for many years, won't be easily convinced. But few people are like you, my friend. Most people *like* to believe in myths and legends. Especially folks with little education. They are suckers for the supernatural."

"I guess you're right. There isn't a place in India that has long history behind it and doesn't have a ghost story to tell. It's par for the course. We are an old land with a rich supply of myths."

"Maybe."

"You're not sure, Sharad?" Athreya gazed quizzically at his friend who seemed hesitant. "Is there something else? Something more recent?"

Although he asked the question casually, Athreya had a pressing reason to ask it. He had come to Bundelkhand on an inquiry, and was wondering if the myth of Naaz Tapu had any bearing on the subject of his investigation.

"Well ..." Sharad paused for a long moment, and then continued reluctantly. "There was an occurrence two years ago. A young man went to the islet as a part of a wager. He went in the middle of the night. The next morning, he was found dead."

"Dead? Where?"

"There is a place that has a rock ledge and a stretch of sand. That's the best spot to alight from a boat if you want to visit the island. He was found a few feet from the water. His head had been broken, and there were claw marks on him."

"*Claw* marks?"

"So they say."

"How did they locate him? Did someone go searching for him?"

Sharad shook his head. "There was no need. The body was visible from the riverbank."

"I see."

"And," Sharad went on, "there was another event more recently – a few months ago, if I am not mistaken. A middle-aged man who was sane and sensible by all accounts, went there in broad daylight. He was a father of two and a responsible husband."

"What happened to him?" Athreya asked, searching his friend's face.

"He didn't return. He hasn't been seen since."

"Didn't anyone go searching for him?"

"They did. But they wouldn't go very deep into the woods. They found nothing."

"Is it certain that the man actually went to the islet?"

Sharad nodded.

"People saw him – he went by a small raft during daytime. Men saw him tie the raft to a tree at the same spot I mentioned earlier – the one with a rock shelf and a stretch of sand. The raft remained where he had tied it. But there was no sign of him."

"Why would a sensible father of two go to the islet to begin with?"

"He was taking soil samples as a part of a local geological survey. I'm told he was a down-to-earth man who didn't subscribe to the local myths."

"Hmm," Athreya said, frowning. "But why don't they want anyone photographing the islet?"

"They don't want to do anything that could disturb the presence. That's why they don't go to the islet, either. They are afraid that they may provoke it by merely going there."

"And what would it do, if it were provoked?"

"So far, it has stayed on the islet. The locals believe that it doesn't like crossing the water. Provoking it, they fear, may make it cross the water and come ashore. That's not a possibility they want to deal with. There is no telling what the malevolent thing might do once it finds itself amongst living men."

Silence fell over the car as the three of them contemplated what had just been discussed. Tales that were decades old – let alone a century old – were most likely fabrications. But something more recent, especially only a few months old, had to be taken seriously. Athreya had to find out more – it may just have a bearing on his inquiry.

Abruptly, a thought flashed across Athreya's mind as he recalled what he thought he had seen just before Moupriya had clicked her camera in the raft.

"Mou," he asked, "did you see something white among the trees of the islet?"

"You saw it too?" The girl's voice rose in excitement as she spun around in the front passenger seat. Her eyes were alight with exhilaration and her youthful face flushed. "That's what I was trying

16

to get a photo of! It was a fleeting glimpse of white. It looked like a bride's wedding dress, didn't it?"

"A dress?" Athreya asked doubtfully. "I wouldn't go as far as that. I thought I saw a hazy white patch among the trees – twice. I was not sure the first time. But it lasted a fraction of a second longer the second time. What does your photograph show? You managed to get one, right?"

"Nothing!" Moupriya pouted. "Just the islet and the river. See?" She showed Athreya the photograph on her phone's screen. "But I think it was the lady in a white dress!" she insisted. "Others have seen her too."

"Now, now, Mou," Sharad cautioned. "Don't get carried away with all those stories the girls at school used to concoct. A lone bride in the middle of a jungle? Indeed!" He snorted.

"Papa!" the girl disputed vigorously. "I saw what I saw!"

"Okay, Mou. Okay. Let's talk about something else, shall we?"

Moupriya, who had turned around and was facing the rear seat, spun back in a huff to face forward.

"There is no denying it," she declared. "Naaz Tapu is haunted."

"Priya Madam!" the driver gasped, repeating what the boatman had earlier said. "Woh naam mat lijiye!"

"Kyon nahin?" Athreya asked the driver at once.

"It's a bad place, sir," the driver replied in Hindi. "An evil place."

"Why?" Athreya persisted.

"Because bad things happen there. Men who go there don't return alive."

"Are you referring to the young man who went there two years ago and was found dead?"

"Him too. But I was thinking of a more recent incident. The one that happened a few months ago."

"The man who went there during daytime and didn't return?"

"Yes, sir. That's the incident I was thinking about."

"How do you know the story is true?" Athreya challenged.

17

"People can just invent stories. It may just be a rumour."

"No sir." The driver shook his head sadly. "This story is true. Ranvir didn't return from the islet."

"How do you know?"

"Because," the driver said, "Ranvir was my neighbour. His wife still prays every day for his return."

CHAPTER 2

A couple of hours later, Athreya and Sharad were at a popular restaurant in Jhansi's Sadar Bazar for dinner. Athreya had wanted to stage a chance meeting with some of the archaeologists who were working at a nearby excavation. He had been commissioned by the organisation that funded the excavation to make inquiries.

"Something funny seems to be going on there," the managing trustee of the organisation had told Athreya a few days ago. "I'm not sure what, but the little I've heard is unsettling."

After the trustee had shared the sparse details of the "funny business" as he had called it, Athreya had agreed to go to Bundelkhand and stay with his friend in Jhansi. However, he had wanted to first meet the archaeologists socially before the trustee told them the true purpose behind Athreya's visit.

Sharad had agreed to engineer a meeting with the archaeologists. The restaurant they were at was their regular weekend haunt. It was very likely that at least some of them would come for dinner there on a Saturday evening.

Athreya and Sharad had just settled down at their table when a clean-shaven, erudite-looking man in his mid-fifties walked in. Catching his eye, Sharad raised an arm and waved. The newcomer's pleasant face creased into a happy smile, and he strode towards their table.

"Your usual jaunt, Sabir?" Sharad asked shaking the newcomer warmly by the hand.

"Hi, Sharad," the man replied in a pleasant, cultured voice that underscored his erudition. "Yes, the usual break. All well?"

"All well. All well." Sharad waved him to the vacant chair beside himself. "Come join us."

The man flashed Athreya a quick, questioning glance, and when Athreya nodded and smiled back, the newcomer took the seat.

"Meet my friend, Harith Athreya," Sharad introduced the two men. "Athreya, this is Dr. Sabir Baig."

Once they had shaken hands, Sharad continued, "Dr. Baig is one of the foremost archaeologists in India. He is a veritable authority on the history of south and east India, and the entire east coast in between."

"Please don't believe him, Mr. Athreya," Sabir cut in. "Sharad overstates – as usual."

"Do I?" Sharad countered. "You have written, what … nine books?"

Sabir shrugged, his pleasant smile still in evidence on his open face.

"Some of them are reference books and the others textbooks," Sharad continued, addressing Athreya. "He represents India in international conferences. He has appeared in several TV documentaries on the BBC and the History Channel. And he is one of the very few Indian archaeologists who has worked on the Indus Valley civilisation in Pakistan."

"Really?" Athreya asked. "That's very impressive. That makes you an authority, Dr. Baig, at least in my book."

"Thank you," Sabir replied, letting out a chuckle. "Thirty years is a long time, Mr. Athreya. One has no option but to do mountains of work in three decades – not only because of the length of time, but also due to the lack of archaeologists in India. One ends up becoming a so-called authority by just staying in the field and doing what comes one's way. And as far as Pakistan is concerned, I owe that opportunity as much to my religion as to anything else."

"Even so," Athreya countered, watching Sabir downplay his achievements. "It *is* impressive. But I am intrigued, Dr. Baig. You say there aren't enough archaeologists in India?"

"Unfortunately not. It's not a career of choice for the overwhelming majority of our students. A tiny number do take up archaeology out of passion, but many who end up here do so because they found nothing else. When your last resort becomes your profession, it's not likely that you have the aptitude or the interest to pursue it seriously. As a result, those who come here by choice tend to do much better than the others."

"Why isn't it a career of choice? Because it's not well-paying? Or because there aren't enough job opportunities?"

"Both. Most end up as lecturers or join a government agency like the Archaeological Survey of India. Some others join museums or restoration projects. There are very few private sector opportunities in this field. You know what government pay scales are like – you can barely make two ends meet.

"And unlike other government sectors, we have no leverage, either. People who work in public transport, electricity or water supply, law enforcement, or even waste collection can twist the government's arm by striking. Who would care if archaeologists went on strike? Nobody would be inconvenienced. They wouldn't even notice. We have no leverage, whatsoever. We archaeologists have to find our reward in our work."

"Indeed," Athreya agreed. "I'm ashamed to say that I never paused to think about this. Archaeology is as much a science as any other. It deserves better. What drives you, Dr. Baig? Personally,

I mean. What has sustained your interest for thirty years?"

"Archaeology is about solving mysteries, Mr. Athreya," Sabir replied, warming up with passion. "Mysteries of the past; mysteries that are sometimes thousands of years old. You have very little to go by – bits of pottery, rusted iron, tarnished bronze, fragments of stone sculptures and the like. You have to juxtapose these artifacts with history, literature, poetry and unconfirmed tales and rumours. Only then can you make some sense of it. Yes, there is some good technology too – carbon dating, magnetometry, sophisticated scanners, etcetera. But piecing it all together is still a human's job."

"You would need to use both logic and imagination, I guess."

"Exactly!" Sabir's face glowed with unexpected pleasure. "It's a thrill that is not unlike reading a detective novel."

"I can relate to that," Athreya enthused. He was beginning to like Sabir. "You don't know which piece fits where in the puzzle, and you don't even know if a piece is important or not. I assume ninety percent of all you do is slogging and grunt work? Just like police or detective work."

"Absolutely right! As a result, it requires a lot of resources."

"And that is where the JBF comes in," Sharad interrupted, "The John Bates Foundation has been a godsend for Sabir. It's a not-for-profit foundation set up by the American billionaire, John Bates. The JBF supports several scientific areas including archaeological expeditions."

"A recent development, I take it?" Athreya asked.

"In India, yes," Sabir nodded. "Through his foundation, Mr. Bates set up the Sarah Bates Archaeological Institute – the SBAI – in memory of his late daughter. Sarah Bates is said to have been passionate about archaeology, and she was an Indophile to boot. She had spent three years here before dying in a car crash back in the US. She was just twenty-nine.

"A month after her death, Mr. Bates set up the SBAI. It's a not-for-profit organisation that promotes archaeology in India with very generous funding. I work for them. It's such a pleasure to be able to afford the tools and technology we require, Mr. Athreya."

Athreya had already heard this from the SBAI's managing trustee, but he heard Sabir out.

"How far is your expedition from Jhansi?" he asked.

"Not far from where we went today, Athreya," Sharad answered. "It's right on the riverbank. Sabir is the deputy director of the dig."

He paused as a shapely young woman with glossy black hair and a purposeful stride entered the restaurant and stood looking around as if searching for someone. She was busty, broad-framed and about 5' 7" with an intelligent face and quick eyes. The clothes she wore, though by no means expensive, were carefully chosen and elegantly worn.

Sabir raised his arm and waved to her. Her wide lips curved into a spontaneous smile as she acknowledged Sabir's wave. She made her way to their table, her gaze taking in Sharad and Athreya. Her sharp eyes studied Athreya for a moment – long enough to make a quick assessment, but not so long as to appear impolite.

"Adhira Khatri," Sabir introduced her as she slid into the chair beside Athreya. "She is the one who holds the purse strings – our finance person. She is also the person who ensures that everything runs smoothly both at the dig and the base."

"That's Dr. Baig for you," Adhira chuckled. "Always courteous and chivalrous, even if it means exaggerating. I am just the accountant and the admin person rolled into one – the only person in the team who is not an archaeologist or a technician. And I'm almost always at the base as I seldom have work at the dig."

"The dig and the base," Athreya echoed. "Sounds like fun. I assume the base is where you stay?"

"That's right," Adhira nodded. "We also have our office, labs and stores there. It's a renovated hotel with the pretentious name of Asghar Mahal."

"Asghar Mahal?" Athreya mused. "Sounds like a heritage build-ing."

"Heritage, my foot!" Adhira snorted. "It was built no more than twenty years ago, though it looks a hundred years old. A failed resort to which the SBAI give a second life because of its proximity to the dig."

"Sounds like an interesting place," Athreya remarked.

"Come over sometime," Adhira suggested immediately. "Are you interested in archaeology?"

"I think so. But honestly, I wouldn't really know until I spent some time at a dig. Haven't had the opportunity so far. From what Dr. Baig says – that archaeology is about solving mysteries – I find my interest kindled."

"Like cracking mysteries, huh?" Adhira grinned amicably. "Me, give me certainty any day. But please do come over. I'd love to have some company other than archaeologists. Does tomorrow work for you?"

Athreya glanced at Sharad. Adhira's invitation would give him the opportunity to meet the other archaeologists.

"Sure," Sharad said. "I can bring him over."

"Excellent!" Adhira said. "Come for lunch. The dig will be closed, tomorrow being Sunday. But you can see a lot of archaeo-logical junk at the base and also meet the others. We usually have a long, relaxed lunch on Sundays with a lot of beer." She turned around and summoned a waiter. "Talking of beer, I'm in the mood for a vodka-tonic. Anyone else?"

Two minutes later, all of them had placed their orders.

"Don't you need to check with Mrs. Markaan before inviting us?" Sharad asked Adhira when the waiter had left. "We don't want to barge in." He turned to Athreya and explained, "Mrs. Markaan the head of the expedition – the 'dig director', so to speak."

In response, Adhira let out one more of her snorts.

"More a headmistress than a dig director, I'd say," she growled.

"No, Mr. Sikka, I don't have to check with her. I am quite free to invite my guests to the base if I wish to. And with both Dr. Baig and I inviting you, she'd better not have a problem."

"Now, now, Adhira," Sabir cautioned. "There is no call for that."

"Isn't there?" she countered. "We are governed by her 'terms of employment' and the non-disclosure agreement. Nothing in either of them prohibit inviting guests."

"I hope we won't be—" Athreya began but was cut off by Sabir.

"Oh, please do come, Mr. Athreya," he reiterated Adhira's invitation. "Don't let what Adhira said give you second thoughts. MM – that's what we call Mrs. Markaan – may be a disciplinarian and may run the dig with an iron fist, but she isn't so bad as to ban social visits. She might have had an objection if you were a rival archaeologist or an antiques dealer."

"Or an antiques thief or their fence," Adhira added carelessly with a frivolous chuckle. "She sees them everywhere."

"In her defence, Adhira, there has been a spate of thefts from digs, museums and even temples. Bundelkhand has had more than its fair share."

"Is that right?" Athreya asked, his interest piqued. The conversation was becoming more interesting by the minute.

"Unfortunately, it's true," Sabir nodded, training his frank, open gaze on Athreya. "There was recently a theft in Orchha, which is not very far up the river. And another near Khajuraho. The Jhansi fort hasn't been immune either. As the dig director, MM is quite justified in being concerned."

"Haven't any of the thieves been caught?" Athreya asked.

"Once a theft happens," Sharad said before Sabir could answer, "the stolen article vanishes astonishingly quickly. I suspect there is some sort of a network operating here. The antique is passed swiftly along a chain from one person to another, and it travels hundreds of kilometres overnight. Even if you catch the suspected thief, the stolen goods are no longer on him or anywhere close by."

"And there has been a spate of such thefts?"

"At least a dozen that I know of in Madhya Pradesh and Uttar Pradesh. Sabir and Adhira may know of more. I believe the network of antique thieves call themselves the Bronze Runners."

"If there are so many successful thefts," Athreya reasoned, "isn't it possible that insiders are involved?"

"There, you touch a raw nerve," Sabir said. "Some believe that is indeed the case—"

He broke off as the waiter returned with their drinks. They sat in silence while he served the drinks and offered ice. Once he left, Sabir resumed.

"As I was saying, some people believe that insiders must be involved. How else can the success rate be so high? Apart from one instance in Gwalior three months back, there have hardly been any unsuccessful robberies. All thefts seem to be well-planned operations. And this is not limited to the Bundelkhand area. There are reports from across the country – Allahabad, Pune, Agra and Jaipur, and elsewhere."

"There was the case of a jewelled dagger belonging to an erstwhile Nizam," Adhira added. "A priceless piece. It was stolen from a museum in Hyderabad recently. Within twenty-four hours, it was being sold in Lucknow. That's how quickly it travelled."

"How do you know that it was being sold in Lucknow?" Athreya asked.

"The Nizam's dagger was recognised when the seller – a fashionable-looking lady – tried to sell it to an American who was known to be a peddler of stolen antiques. Plainclothesmen happened to be following him when this lady turned up to meet him."

"Was she apprehended?"

"Unfortunately not." Adhira shook her head. "She gave them the slip, but not before she lost the dagger – the American tried to run away with it. His luck ran out."

"They caught the American but the seller escaped, eh?" Athreya mused, "If they saw her, they must have her description."

"Medium height, chubby and attractive, with long black hair. Was elegantly dressed in an expensive-looking saree with an ethnic print and in heels. Could easily have been taken for a modern, chic socialite. Two witnesses saw her, I believe. They have been on the lookout for her for the past six months. No luck yet."

"So," Sabir interposed, "coming back to what we were discussing, MM is quite justified in being apprehensive about strangers. All members of the dig here, except Adhira and Dr. Korda – whom you will meet when you come over – have been hand-picked by her. If any theft happens at our dig, it must be an outsider. Adhira and Dr. Korda have been appointed by the JBF. The rest of us are employed by the SBAI."

Athreya remained silent. In his experience, the culprit was more often an insider than a stranger. The majority of the crimes he had seen in his career had been committed by people who knew the victim well or had legitimate access to a stolen article. That all the members of her team had been hand-picked by Mrs. Markaan was of little assurance. However, there was no call for him to voice that thought now.

"I suppose you take precautions to ensure that valuable items are well protected?" he asked instead.

"You mean put under lock and key?" Sabir asked. "We will once we have something of value to protect."

"What do you mean?" Sharad cut in. "You guys have been digging for months now."

"Yes, but we haven't found anything of great value yet," Sabir replied a shade unhappily. "Mostly pottery, broken sculptures and rusted tools – none of which is unique or has intrinsic value."

"Are you disappointed?"

"Well, to some extent. Let me hasten to add that what we have found is a neat little site. But it hasn't added much to the body of knowledge we already possess. It is similar to other sites in the

Bundelkhand area. No thief would be interested in our finds."

"And that," Adhira chuckled a tad unkindly, "has MM riled. She desperately wants to find something valuable or interesting. This dig was her idea – she wouldn't want her first dig at the SBAI to be a washout."

"Is that so?" Sharad asked. "I wasn't aware of that."

"Adhira is right," Sabir chipped in. "MM insisted on this dig against several people's advice—"

"Including yours," Adhira cut in.

"Including mine," Sabir acknowledged. "But that's water under the bridge. If we aren't finding anything of value here, we must cut our losses and move on. We don't want the JBF to lose confidence in us."

"Well," Adhira piped in again, "MM has been looking mighty pleased the last few days." She smiled coyly. "There *must* be a good reason for it," she ended cryptically.

"Adhira." Sabir admonished lightly. "You don't want to get fired like Madhav, do you? Respect the NDA, will you, please?"

For a moment, Adhira seemed to consider a repartee, but thought the better of it. She raised her arm and summoned the waiter again.

"Anyone for seconds?" she asked. "Madhav be get here in ten minutes. Enough time for another drink."

The conversation moved on to more innocuous topics. Sharad, who had fallen silent at the news that nothing of value had yet been found at the dig, stirred and began talking again. Sabir, too, seemed to relax, and Adhira went on chatting in her carefree way.

Looking at the open expression on her face and her merry, toothy smiles, Athreya felt that she was a likeable person. Though she was easy-going, her intelligent face and quick eyes suggested that she could be competent when she chose. He imagined it would be difficult to pull the wool over her eyes.

He also found himself wondering what kind of a person Mrs.

Markaan was. It was amply clear that she was not liked and was considered some kind of a despot. Why had she been pleased over the past few days? Had they at last found something of value at the dig? It appeared that the NDA – the non-disclosure agreement – prohibited the members of the dig from talking about certain things. And who was this Madhav who had been fired – presumably by Mrs. Markaan – for breaking it?

As if on cue, a well-built man in his mid-thirties walked into the restaurant. He was about six feet tall and sported a stubble which, to Athreya, seemed to be the permanent kind that many young men, including popular cricketers, seemed to prefer. Some kind of a designer stubble. They never really shaved, preferring a trimmer to a razor.

Catching sight of Adhira, he made his way to their table. Adhira and Athreya slid one seat over toward the wall to make place for the newcomer to sit.

"A drink before we go?" Adhira asked after introducing him to Athreya as Madhav. She didn't offer any more details.

"Sure," Madhav agreed enthusiastically and took the seat next to Adhira. "How are you, Dr. Baig? What's the news from the dig?"

"Trying to get me fired, Madhav?" Sabir chuckled. "*I'm* not going to break the NDA."

Madhav grinned. "Well, you can always come and stay with me if MM kicks you out."

Madhav turned out to be as jovial and carefree a person as Adhira. He spoke casually about all kinds of trivialities and even joked about his casual relationship with Adhira. On her part, Adhira didn't seem to mind. It seemed to be an open secret that the two were having a fling.

Except for small contributions now and then, Sharad and Athreya were largely content to listen. The ebullient Adhira and Sabir, who had relaxed further, shared the bulk of the chatting with Madhav. The three of them seemed to get along very well.

Presently, Sabir excused himself and rose, saying, "I need to catch up with a friend at another table." He gestured towards a wiry man with close-cropped hair sitting at a table across the room. "Do you know Mr. Jagan?" he asked Adhira and Madhav. "He's quite an expert on Bundelkhand artefacts."

Adhira and Madhav glanced at Jagan and shook their heads.

"Maybe I'll introduce him to you sometime. Quite an interesting chap."

"Sure," Adhira replied. "Some other time. Madhav and I need to go now."

Once Sabir left, Adhira and Madhav finished their drinks and rose to go. They walked away, followed by Sharad's gaze, appearing content and happy in each other's company.

"Interesting pair," Sharad said. "Always good company. Attractive lady, isn't she? Plus, she's a very sharp woman, Athreya. Despite all that gaiety and light-hearted banter, she doesn't let the grass grow under her feet. She's a woman of the world; someone I'd take seriously despite her apparent levity."

CHAPTER 3

An hour later, they were back in Sharad's house. They sat on cane chairs on the lawn in the front of the house, under the clear, starry Jhansi sky.

"Let me tell you why I came down to Bundelkhand," Athreya began in a low voice. "You have been very understanding in not asking questions despite engineering this meeting for me with the archaeologists."

"Well, I figured you'd tell me when the time comes," Sharad replied with a smile. "Tell me only what you are comfortable sharing. No need to go into confidential details unless you want to."

Athreya nodded and leaned forward towards Sharad.

"A few days back," he began, "I got a call from an acquaintance by the name of Liam Dunne. He is one of the trustees of the JBF, and the managing trustee of the SBAI. He expressed concern about some recent developments – 'funny business', as he calls it.

"He has been hearing whisperings of financial irregularities at the dig. I won't go into the details at this point, but it appears that Dunne has sufficient reason to be worried.

"He is also concerned about what Adhira and Dr. Baig mentioned today – theft of antiques from digs, museums and temples. Mrs. Markaan is very troubled by that, and fears that her dig might become a target of the Bronze Runners."

"But they haven't found anything of value," Sharad protested. "That's what Sabir said."

"Yet, Mrs. Markaan is apprehensive about strangers. She handpicked every member of the team. She also seems paranoid that information about their finds might leak out. That's probably why she introduced an NDA."

"Ah!" Sharad exclaimed. "*That* explains it. Leaked information about a valuable find could reach the Bronze Runners. If that happens, the dig could become a target. She's trying to nip it in the bud by putting in an NDA that prevents even a scrap of information from leaking out. And to show that she meant business, she had to fire Madhav when he broke the NDA."

"Tell me more about this infamous NDA that all of you are trashing."

"Though she is the head of the dig and the executive director of the SBAI, Mrs. Markaan is insecure. Her control over the team is through the NDA. I've seen it; it's a draconian agreement. As you would have guessed from what Sabir said, the NDA prohibits a range of 'unauthorised activities'. You can get fired for speaking to another team member about what you found today, let alone speaking to outsiders like you and me."

"Seriously?"

"Yes. Mrs Markaan doesn't have the technical wherewithal to command the respect of her team members. Everyone believes that Sabir Baig is far more competent and knowledgeable than her. Even though she is senior to him by five years.

"Sabir had all but become the executive director of the SBAI. All that remained was the formal appointment order. Then, Mrs. Markaan somehow entered the picture. And the next thing you know she has replaced Sabir as the head of the SBAI.

"Sabir was livid. He considered turning down the deputy director offer. But where else would he get such a lucrative offer? More important than the salary is this: where in India would an archaeologist get so much resource to work with? The JBF's annual budget for the SBAI is five million dollars, not counting capital equipment and additional funding for major digs. That's thirty-odd crore rupees, Athreya. Where in this country do a handful of archaeologists get to work with that kind of money?

"To cut the story short, Sabir decided to stay. Most believe that it is only a matter of time before the JBF trustees realise their mistake and remedy it. If this dig doesn't go well, it won't bode well for Mrs. Markaan."

"It will help Sabir's cause, won't it?"

"I guess so. But that does not necessarily imply that Sabir wants the dig to be a washout. He has professional pride invested in this too."

"And Madhav?" Athreya asked. "Why specifically did she fire him?"

"Madhav is a bit of a smart aleck who finds it difficult to take orders. He would observe his own timings and wouldn't always tell Mrs Markaan where he was or what he was doing. But as he was one of the smarter members in the team, she had tolerated him.

"But all of a sudden, she felt he was up to something but she wasn't quite sure what. He seemed to be asking too many questions of the other team members. She invoked the NDA and fired him.

"They were all stunned that she actually fired someone for violating the NDA. They had assumed that it was an empty threat."

"But you weren't taken in by the NDA excuse, were you?" Athreya asked. "There's something more to this business."

"Well, she came to consult me in a professional capacity before firing him – she wanted a lawyer's opinion on what her options were. She wasn't very forthright about her concerns, but I got the impression that she suspected Madhav of something."

"What specifically?"

"She didn't say. I sensed that he was getting too nosey for her liking."

"Considering her obsession with stolen artefacts, could she have suspected him of being a part of the antique theft network?" Athreya asked. "The Bronze Runners?"

"That thought did cross my mind." Sharad nodded. "It's quite likely."

* * *

The next morning, after a slow and sumptuous Sunday breakfast, Sharad took Athreya and Moupriya to see one Habib Mian. Half an hour later, they found themselves at a timeworn but renovated haveli outside town, where an old man greeted Sharad and Moupriya warmly and showed impeccable old-world courtesy in welcoming the "mehman" in Athreya.

Clad in a white pajama-kurta and topped by a black, velvet topi, the seventy-five-year-old Habib Mian was the very picture of traditional hospitality from bygone days. He insisted Athreya take the best chair available in the office and partake of chai as he apologised profusely for his inability to offer anything more substantial, now that God had deemed it fit to recall his dear wife to Himself.

The haveli they now sat in, he said ponderously, speaking exclusively in a mix of Hindi and Urdu, was owned by a patron of art, who traced his lineage back to one of the royal families of Orchha. The patron had spent a considerable sum in restoring this heritage building and had moved a part of his family's art collection here. It was now a private museum that admitted only people with genuine interest in Bundelkhand's art and history, and was not open to tourists.

"Apart from being highly knowledgeable about Bundelkhand's history," Sharad interposed when the old man paused, "Habib Mian is the ultimate authority on local tales and legends. Unlike some historians who rely mostly on written texts, Habib Mian derives a part of his knowledge from word-of-mouth stories passed on from generation to generation. This, of course, is in addition to the usual written texts that all historians study.

"This uniqueness is, in part, due to his origins. As a young man, Habib Mian was a tourist guide for many years. That was how his love for history was kindled, and it was this love that drove him to seek formal education at an evening college. He would be a tourist guide by day, and a student at evenings and nights when he studied history and debated it with his teachers and fellow students."

The old man's self-deprecating smile, humble as it was, failed to hide his apparent pride in his modest origins.

"There is no local tale, legend or rumour that Habib Mian has not heard a dozen times or more," Sharad went on. "There is no better person to tell you about the islet." Sharad turned to the old man. "Habib Mian, my friend here is interested in the story behind Naaz Tapu."

"Ah! Naaz Tapu," the old man purred, stroking his white beard. "A lovely story, and a heartbreaking one too. But mind you, it is a real story – with real people and a real tragedy. Do you know, Athreya Sahib, why the islet is called Naaz Tapu?"

"Let me guess," Athreya replied. "If I am not mistaken, 'Tapu' means island or islet. And 'Naaz' means pride."

"Good guess," the old timer chuckled. "But only partially right. Yes, 'Tapu' means islet. But the 'Naaz' in this name comes from the name of the heroine in this tragic tale. Her name was Naazneen, and she was as beautiful and charming as the name suggests."

He rose from his chair and opened a cupboard. From it, he took out a framed painting the size of an A4 size paper, which was wrapped in red satin. Slowly, and with loving care, he unwrapped it and showed the painting to the visitors.

Athreya's breath caught in his throat, and he heard Moupriya let out a soft exclamation. The painting was of a hauntingly beautiful woman, probably in her early twenties. She was perched on a high stool and was looking out of the frame with large, light-grey eyes and a half-smile. Her pale skin seemed to glow. Above her exquisitely shaped nose and lustrous eyes were two graceful eyebrows. Fine brown hair cascaded down her shoulders. The overall expression on the face was that of supressed sorrow.

Whether the lady had really conveyed that impression in real life, or if the sorrow was the painter's creation, Athreya didn't know. But there was something enigmatic about the lovely face.

"Naazneen." The old man took the name with affection before continuing in a mix of Hindi and Urdu. "This is the exquisite Naazneen after whom the islet is named; the girl who won the hearts of everyone who had the good fortune to see her; the woman whose suitors included the rich and the mighty. She lived not far from here, but about a couple of centuries ago."

"Light grey eyes," Athreya said. "They must have been very rare in this part of the world."

"They were," Habib concurred. "Very rare indeed. They still are."

"What a captivating woman," Athreya whispered, his gaze lingering on the striking face in the painting. "I'm surprised I've not heard about her before or seen her picture before."

"That's because there are no paintings of her outside this building, except perhaps in one or two other private collections," Habib replied.

"Really?" Athreya's eyes snapped to Habib. "Such a beautiful woman and such an exquisite painting. I find it hard to believe that there are no pictures of it."

"You will understand once I tell you Naazneen's story. The king ordered that all paintings of her be destroyed, and all reference of her be removed from the official history of this region."

"Destroyed?" Athreya was aghast. "Why?"

"I'll tell you the tale at the end of our tour," Habib Mian replied and re-wrapped the painting. He rose and returned it to the cupboard. "I don't want the story to distract you from the rest of the museum. But before we start, I have two requests to make – please don't touch any exhibit, and please don't take photographs."

Over the next hour and half, they were conducted through a dozen rooms or more – some dedicated to specific areas of Bundelkhand and some to specific periods of time. Orchha, Gwalior, Jhansi and Khajuraho had rooms of their own, as did pre-Mughal, Mughal and British periods.

All of them focussed on the royalty and nobles, and detailed their lives – what they wore, how they lived, what arts and crafts they patronised, what weapons they wielded, what cutlery they used, etcetera. Paintings, finery, weaponry, chinaware, brassware, scrolls and books strung together an intimate story.

Moupriya, who would be studying history in college, asked a dozen questions in each room, which Habib Mian answered with delight and indulgence. Rarely did he have such an enthusiastic and inquisitive visitor to the museum as Priya Beti. Sharad beamed proudly at his daughter as Athreya tried to absorb as much as he could from the conversation between two people who were sixty years apart in age.

At the end of their tour of the haveli, they reached a small room that was locked.

"The contents of this room are special," Habib said as he unlocked it. "Like the painting you saw in the office, there are some here that don't figure in recorded history."

As soon as Habib Mian switched on the light, Athreya found himself face-to-face with a life-sized painting that dominated the wall opposite to the door. It was a painting of Naazneen in which she was wearing a white bridal gown.

The expression on Naazneen's face was the same as the one Athreya had seen in the small painting in Habib's office – a hint of suppressed sorrow and a smile that concealed more than it revealed. And, as in the other painting, her face was hauntingly beautiful.

The overall effect of this larger painting was vividly striking. Coming upon it suddenly, especially with Naazneen's light grey eyes at the same level of his own, it took Athreya's breath away for a moment. The intricate embroidery on the silk-and-satin gown was of different pastel shades that blended with the white base material. The folds and the fall of the robe had been captured skilfully by the painter. There was no doubt that it was a fabulous work of art.

After examining Naazneen's finery and surroundings, Athreya's gaze returned to her face, where it stayed until Habib broke the silence.

"Naazneen was the eldest daughter of a minister in the Orchha kingdom," he said. "As you can imagine, there was no dearth of suitors for her. But it was one of the princes of the royal family of Orchha who won her heart.

"Kunwar Vanraj Singh Dev, the youngest of four sons was an accomplished and handsome young man. In addition to weaponry and combat, in which all Rajput princes were proficient, he was knowledgeable in several arts. But what he loved the most was music – an interest he shared with Naazneen."

Habib turned and gestured towards another large painting on the wall to their left.

"This is Kunwar Vanraj Singh Dev," he said. "Like Naazneen's, his paintings, too, were destroyed at the king's orders, and his name removed from history books."

The painting showed Vanraj in ceremonial attire including a turban, coat, cape and sword belt. He seemed to be in his mid-twenties, with a youthful face in which were set intelligent and kindly eyes. A strong jaw and firm lips under a carefully groomed moustache completed the picture of a handsome young prince.

"The two met often," Habib went on. "Sometimes openly to enjoy music, sometimes clandestinely in the royal gardens – and love blossomed. At times, they would sneak away to meet on the islet that is now known by Naazneen's name. But wherever they went, they couldn't escape the eyes of the king, which were everywhere.

"At first, the king assumed that it was a casual affair royals have from time to time. It gradually dawned upon him that Vanraj's interest in Naazneen was more serious. Soon, Vanraj began saying to his mother that he intended to make Naazneen his wife. Word eventually reached the king's ears.

"But you see what the problem was, don't you, Athreya Sahib?" Habib asked.

"Yes," Athreya replied, his eyes still on the young prince's painting. "Naazneen was a Muslim and Vanraj was a Hindu."

"Indeed. For the royal family, that was an unacceptable situation. There was no question, the king decreed, of Vanraj Singh Dev *marrying* Naazneen. He began pressurising his vizier – Naazneen's father – to send the girl away from Orchha, never to return. The ignominious alternative he offered his minister was that Naazneen become a concubine.

"But Vanraj was not to be denied. His heart was set on Naazneen, and his mind was made up. He would make her his legally wedded wife and give her the stature and privileges that went with it. She would be second to none. Even as the king considered various possibilities, Vanraj quietly made preparations and planned to marry Naazneen in secret and present the king with a *fait accompli*.

"The queen was supportive of Vanraj but didn't have the standing to confront her husband. What she did, however, was to support Vanraj's clandestine plan by getting her royal maids to prepare Naazneen for the wedding. The bridal gown you see in this painting of Naazneen was made by the queen's personal seamstress.

"She also gave Naazneen a minor fortune in gold and jewels,

knowing full well the untold problems the young bride would have to face, and the obstacles she would have to surmount – at least till such time that the king accepted the marriage. For that, she would need her own private wealth.

"And so it came to pass that Vanraj and Naazneen were secretly married by a Hindu priest. No sooner had they taken their vows than the problems the queen had foreseen began. Vanraj's eldest brother, the crown prince, had learned of the wedding. Considering it an insult to the king and a blot on the royal family's honour, he sent his men to kill Vanraj and abduct Naazneen.

"Even as Vanraj's men fought off the attackers, the newlywed couple fled with Bhola, Vanraj's trusted bodyguard, and a dozen men. But such a large group would leave tracks that could be followed. The only way to avoid it was to take to water. They entered the Betwa and made for the islet.

"But as I had said earlier, the king's eyes were everywhere. Before long, the pursuers reached the islet. They heavily outnumbered the would-be defenders. They weren't prepared for what followed.

"From the thick woods came a hail of arrows – too numerous to be shot from a dozen bows. Caught on open water, the pursuers fell quickly. Those who escaped the arrows and reached the islet fared no better. Some were never seen again while others turned up as corpses with crushed heads or mauled flesh.

"Bhola, Vanraj's bodyguard – a man over seven feet tall and with prodigious strength – was said to be behind the crushed skulls. Bhola's dog – a monstrous Mastiff the size of a pony – was believed to have inflicted the mauling. Whether this was truly the case, we will never know. But what is true is that a dozen defenders killed the entire contingent of attackers.

"Enraged, the crown prince sent his army to the islet. It is said that then Naazneen invoked something that is in the realm of conjecture. Some claim that her family had a history of sorcery.

"Just as the crown prince's army was about to depart for the islet, his wife and two children fell ill. Nothing that the healers and hakims did revived them. As they lay cold and still at death's door, the queen asked the crown prince to recall his army. As soon as he gave the order, the three unmoving figures began stirring.

"Seeing this, the king intervened and issued his decree – Vanraj, as his name suggested, would be the ruler of the forest. But *only* the forest that covered the islet. No more. That would be his prison for life. If he or his wife were to step off of the islet, their lives were forfeit. The king ordered a round-the-clock vigil to be set up around the islet to ensure that the couple stayed on it.

"Vanraj and Naazneen were never seen again. Whispers had it that the effort to invoke ancient magic had taken Naazneen's life, or at least, destroyed her body. If she still lived, they said, it was only as a spirit. Bereft, Vanraj joined his beloved in the spirit world, leaving Bhola and his gigantic Mastiff to defend the islet, which they do till this day."

Athreya let out a long breath when the old man fell silent. It had been a captivating story, and Habib Mian had told it well. Athreya now understood why the king had ordered all paintings of Naazneen and Vanraj be destroyed, and had their names erased from history. The crown prince, who presumably succeeded his father to the throne, would have ensured that the order was followed. Of course, that was only if the story Habib had narrated was true.

"Habib Mian," Athreya asked aloud, "how much of this is fact and how much is conjecture?"

"Till the couple fleeing to the islet, the story is certainly true. It is also true that the attackers were beaten back. But Naazneen's invocation of sorcery is conjecture, as is the suggestion that the couple joined the spirit world. It is up to each person to believe or not."

"And the destruction of Naazneen's and Vanraj's paintings? And erasing their names from recorded history?"

"True. There are several oblique references to the order. There are songs that mention it, too. The story that I told you has been preserved in poetry and songs. Despite the king's order, a few paintings survived. These paintings were hidden by Naazneen's father, the vizier. He sent them out of Bundelkhand, where one of his other daughters – Naazneen's sister – preserved the memory of Naazneen and Vanraj. It is also true that Vanraj and Naazneen were never seen again."

"Habib Sahib," Moupriya said in a hushed voice. "There are reports of Naazneen and Vanraj being sighted even now."

"So there are, Beti," Habib agreed. "Over the past century and a half, Naazneen, still in her white bridal dress, is said to have been sighted walking through the woods of Naaz Tapu. But there is nothing to indicate that these reports are true. Imagination is a powerful thing, Priya Beti. People often see what they want to see."

"And Vanraj?" Moupriya asked. "The descendants of his followers still invite him to weddings. They lay a table for him at the wedding feast. They say that he sometimes comes and partakes of the food."

"Yes, Beti. Some families believe this legend. They take it as Vanraj's way of thanking those of his followers who didn't return from the islet. Some people even claim to have seen a young man in regal attire attending weddings and sampling food. But I have not come across any proof that confirms this belief."

"So," Athreya asked when Moupriya fell silent, "is it this fear of Bhola and his Mastiff that keeps the local people away from Naaz Tapu?"

"That, and the belief that Naazneen and Vanraj roam the islet in spirit form. Naaz Tapu is considered their domain, their inviolable sanctuary. They brook no interference."

CHAPTER 4

An hour later, they were on the road again, heading towards Asghar Mahal, which the archaeologists from the SBAI called "the base." Sitting in the front passenger seat, Moupriya was talking excitedly about Habib Mian's story. She had wangled a promise out of the old man to allow her to return to the museum in a few days and spend as much time as she wanted. Delighted at the interest the girl was taking in Bundelkhand's history, he had willingly agreed.

"Is this the same road we took yesterday?" Athreya asked Sharad when Moupriya paused her chatter.

"Yes," Sharad replied. "This is the road we took yesterday after rafting."

"Then, we should be passing Naaz Tapu on our way, right? Or is it further down the road from the base?"

At the mention of the name, the driver threw Athreya a disconcerted glance in the rearview mirror.

"Oh no," Sharad responded, avoiding the name. "The islet is very close to the base. You have an excellent view of it from the base. Didn't you notice a brightly-coloured building on the riverbank that we passed yesterday? That was the base."

Athreya shook his head. "Did we pass one? I guess my attention was on the islet."

"That's right! What with the boatmen fretting about Mou taking photos, you must have missed it."

A little later, they turned off the highway into a mud road. Presently, they came to a long, single-story building painted in an alternating pattern of red, yellow and white. Here and there, bright patches of orange stood out. It looked very much like a restored heritage building. The windows, doors, sunshades and every part of it was modelled after the havelis and other old buildings Athreya had seen in Bundelkhand.

The car stopped at one end of the building in front of a pair of large double doors under a wide portico. On the red wall over the doors was a large name saying "Asghar Mahal." The same name, written in Hindi, decorated the wall to the left of the double doors. Only one was open, and beside it sat a grandly whiskered security guard. He rose from his chair and gazed inquiringly at them as they got out of the car.

From where Athreya stood after, two wings of the building ran away at right angles. The one to his left was longer and was about two hundred feet long. The shorter wing must have been a little more than half that length. Both were pierced at regular intervals by grilled windows.

On the top of the building, along its entire length, ran a parapet wall that was painted in a different pattern of orange and white. Large bougainvillea plants, each with a different shade of flowers, rose here and there between windows. Athreya could see no entrance to the building other than the one under the portico.

Stepping past the portico to his right, Athreya peered to see what lay behind the building. A ways behind, the ground sloped downward. Beyond it ran the Betwa.

"Ah! There you are!" he heard a familiar voice say. "I heard a car and thought that it must be you guys."

He turned to see Adhira striding out of the door with a wide, welcoming smile on her lively face. She was dressed in a pair of slacks and a kurti. A sleeveless sweater over the kurti kept her warm.

"I'm afraid we are a little early," Sharad apologised.

"Oh, that's fine," Adhira said, putting an arm around the girl. "Hi, Mou. Welcome to the base. First time here?"

"Yes, Aunty," Moupriya smiled and nodded.

"Aunty, gosh! I feel like I'm a hundred years old, Mou. You are welcome to call me by my name. If that's difficult, let's settle for 'Didi,' okay?"

"Yes, Adhira Didi," Moupriya quipped at once with an impish grin.

"Welcome, Mr. Athreya, welcome Mr. Sikka," Adhira continued, walking up to the two men and shaking hands with a firm grip. "You've been here before, haven't you, Mr. Sikka?"

"A couple of times," Sharad replied.

They walked through the open door into a large rectangular room that looked like the lobby of a boutique hotel. Sofas, chairs and a couple of low tables occupied the space in front of them. To their left was open space with a long counter running along the far wall. Opposite the entrance, near one end of the counter, was another pair of double doors.

They went through and found themselves in a large quadrangle bounded on all four sides by rooms. Two long wings and two short ones enclosed the rectangular open space. It must have been almost a hundred and fifty feet long and sixty feet wide. A covered walkway ran along the entire inner perimeter of the building.

The half of the quadrangle that was closest to them was covered by a large square lawn. At the centre was a circular canopy with several chairs and couple of tables. In the other half was a smaller square that was paved. In it, lying strewn, was an assortment of pottery, sculptures, stoneware and similar items. It seemed to be some sort of an outdoor workspace where excavated artifacts were cleaned and sorted.

Stooping among them was a tall, bearded man who looked like a medieval monk. He was clad in a flowing, one-piece robe that resembled a monk's habit. The grey garment's long, loose sleeves ended above his wrists. His feet were enclosed in a pair of heavy boots. In one hand was clutched a brush and in the other, a fragment of ceramic.

"That side of the building," Adhira said, pointing to the long wing at the far side of the quadrangle, "comprises eight rooms. That's where we stay – our bedrooms, if you will. Seven rooms are occupied. Mine is second from the right arm."

Adhira gestured to the other long wing that ran away to their left.

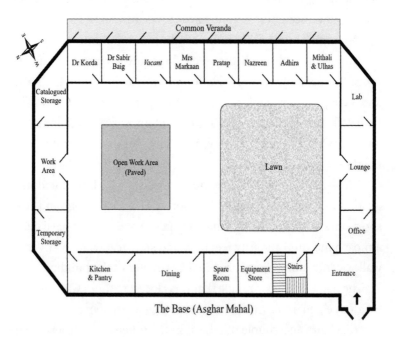

The Base (Asghar Mahal)

"This side houses the dining room, pantry and a few other facilities, including the stairway to the roof. This wing," she indicated the short walkway at the end of which they were standing, "has the lab, the office and our lounge. That opposite wing beyond the paved square is primarily a workplace that includes storage areas."

"Looks like a pretty comfortable place," Athreya said. "Lots of open space and air. At the same time, it's a nice, self-contained establishment. Looks like you have all that you need. Is the entrance the only way in?"

"Yes, but all the eight rooms in the far wing open out into a common veranda, which in turn, opens out to the riverbank. As long as the occupants of the rooms keep their veranda doors locked from inside, the entrance is the only way in or out."

"I would think that you would keep it locked, except when you sit outside at the back."

"Which is not often," Adhira replied. "We prefer to relax on the lawn or in the lounge. It's much safer. You're more at ease when you know that you are in a closed space where no stranger can walk in."

"Don't monkeys bother you?" Moupriya asked. "I saw some on our way here."

"Funnily enough, they don't. I'm not sure why, but some locals claim it's because of the islet in the middle of the river. Apparently, the monkeys avoid it. My own suspicion is the crackers and air guns the workers use drive away the pesky creatures. We don't want them carrying away the artifacts we've worked so hard to unearth."

"By islet, are you referring to Naaz Tapu, Didi?"

"Yup." Adhira glanced at Athreya and Sharad. "Shall we go to the lounge? There is beer waiting for us."

They walked down the covered walkway along the short wing and turned to enter the only door that pierced the wall. Just as they were about to step in, Adhira almost collided with a thin, bespectacled lady with short, curly, reddish-brown hair and a ruby nose stud. She was clad in a crumpled pair of slacks and a sweatshirt that bore half a dozen stains and discolorations. A stained pair of gloves covered her hands up to the elbows.

"Oh, I'm sorry, Adhira," the lady exclaimed. "I was in a hurry to freshen up and change before our guests arrived." She broke off on seeing the visitors and exclaimed again. "Oh! I'm so sorry. Give me fifteen minutes, and I'll be with you. Welcome to the base!"

She hurried off towards the wing that housed the bedrooms.

"That is Mithali, our chemist who doubles up as a part-time paramedic," Adhira explained as they gazed after the slim figure hurrying away. "A nice girl and very hard worker. See, she's working on a Sunday morning, too. Did you see the chemical stains on her clothes? Most of the time, she forgets to wear her apron until it's too late. As a result, she runs through a new set of clothes in a matter of weeks. Her poor husband – Ulhas – goes to Jhansi every month to get her fresh clothes. She'll be back soon, freshly scrubbed."

They entered the lounge, which turned out to be a large and comfortable-looking room. Several chairs and sofas, along with a couple of recliners and easy chairs, offered ample seating. As if that were not enough, two divans with square and cylindrical cushions stood against the far wall. Both the side walls had a door each, which led into adjacent rooms.

"This door," Adhira said, indicating the one in the left wall, "leads to the lab where Mithali and her husband work. Ulhas is the techie among us – he operates our magnetometer, scanners and other scientific equipment. He also doubles up as our IT expert when our computers or mobile phones misbehave."

"This other door," Adhira gestured towards the one in the right-side wall, "leads to the office. That's where I work. Dr. Baig and MM are using it right now for a discussion. Hi, Pratap. I didn't see you."

A man of a little over thirty with long hair and moustache was standing near the closed door, looking at his mobile phone. To Athreya, it seemed that he started a little guiltily at their sudden entrance and hastened away from the door. He pocketed his phone and grinned affably.

"I'm Pratap Yadav," he said as he strode forward and thrust his hand out at Sharad, who was the closest to him. "You must be Mr. Sikka. I think I've seen you talking to MM in Jhansi."

The other two visitors introduced themselves, and Pratap ushered them to the centre of the lounge, waving his arms in a circle.

"Take any chair or sofa you want," he said. "'here are no reservations, except for that high-backed chair, which is MM's throne. It's not particularly comfortable in any case."

"Beer, gentlemen?" Adhira asked as they chose their seats.

"Thank you," Athreya and Sharad said in unison.

"And you, young lady," Adhira said smiling at Moupriya, "are under the legal drinking age, I suspect. Like some juice or soft drink? I'll have a nice mocktail made for you a little later."

"Sure, Didi," Moupriya nodded. "Thanks. Any soft drink would do."

They fell into friendly chatter, and Moupriya asked Pratap about the kind of work archaeologists do.

"It's dusty work, to be honest," Pratap replied. "In the field – which is where we spend most of our time – we are usually digging or, in some way, shifting mud. And when we think we may be close to finding something in the ground, we go on our knees and use trowels and brushes.

"When we do find something, we record its location and bring it to the base, where we clean and measure it. More often than not, it turns out to be a fragment of something – pottery, stoneware, metal ware, sculpture or weaponry. After all that, it may or may not be interesting."

Pratap paused to take a long swig from his beer mug.

"It's tedious work, you know," he continued. "You can go weeks and months without finding anything significant. A lot of grunt work."

"But when you do find something significant," Athreya interposed, "it must be thrilling."

"Yes," Pratap replied a shade unenthusiastically. "That depends on what you find. Nine out of ten times, even interesting stuff might not be as interesting as you had imagined. It's a rare discovery that breaks new ground. But hey!" He grinned suddenly. "It's one way to make a living. I should think that very few professions offer excitement every day."

"I guess you're right," Adhira nodded. "Accounting work – which is what I do – is mostly about tallying numbers and making sure that the books balance to the last paisa. Balancing books, let me assure you, is *not* a particularly exciting job. It's routine work that requires attention to detail." She flashed a quick smile and continued. "Honestly, the only excitement accountants get is when there is malfeasance or embezzlement. If that happens, they are hauled over coals."

"Has that ever happened to you?" Moupriya asked innocently.

"Thankfully not," Adhira let out a full-throated laugh. "Nor do I want it to. I can do without *that* sort of excitement, thank you!"

"Merry, are we?" A sonorous male voice came in through the open door of the lounge.

A moment later, a tall, lean man of about fifty walked in. It was the man they had seen outside, brushing a fragment of ceramic. He was about 6' 3" in height with a lean, cadaverous face topped by a high forehead and a receding hairline. The beard he sported made his long face look even longer.

In the lugubrious face were set a grim mouth with thin lips, and a pair of intense black eyes that were set deep in his skull. Despite the light-hearted remark he had just uttered, there was no hint of a smile on his grave face. At close quarters, he looked even more like a medieval monk than he had from a distance.

"Dr. Korda," Adhira called as she turned to the newcomer. "Come and meet our guests."

Dr. Korda shook hands with solemnity as he laboriously welcomed each person with the grave courtesy that might have befitted a traditional English butler. He spoke each of the three names and looked into their eyes as he welcomed them.

"Harith Athreya," he mused once the minor ceremony was over and they had resumed their seats, nursing drinks. "That's a familiar name. Were you involved with an investigation at the American embassy last year in Delhi? The death of a visiting American diplomat?"

"Yes, I was," Athreya replied. "It was a quiet affair, and my involvement was not made public. How did you know?"

Dr. Korda's thin mouth widened a trifle. Athreya would gradually come to know that this was the closest Dr. Korda ever came to smiling. He was not known to laugh aloud, either.

"One of my friends, a trustee of the John Bates Foundation, was involved in the affair. I wouldn't want to mention his name here as he was one of the suspects at one stage. He spoke highly of you. Very highly. Apparently, the police officer who was handling the case was quite – ahem – clueless until you came."

Athreya smiled and said nothing. Dr. Korda was referring to Liam Dunne. Little did Dr. Korda know that Athreya was here in Bundelkhand at Dunne's request.

"Are you a police officer, Mr. Athreya?" Adhira asked, a guarded expression creeping over her face. Athreya noticed through the corner of his eye that Pratap's head had snapped around to him.

"I've had the opportunity to work with different government departments," Athreya replied pleasantly as he swivelled his gaze towards Pratap. The young man was looking wary now. "I occasionally assist the police, too."

"Some sort of an advisor, was how my friend described you,"

Dr. Korda continued. "He was glad for your involvement. Before you came, matters didn't look good for him. He just happened to be in the wrong place at the wrong time."

"I think I know who you are referring to – Liam Dunne."

Dr. Korda nodded and leaned towards Athreya.

"Are you, by any chance," he asked in a whisper, "here on an investigation?"

"Investigation?" Athreya replied equally softly, arching his eyebrows. He had to be careful now. He didn't want to lie, nor did he wish to expose his hand too early.

"The thefts of antiques and artifacts, you know," Dr. Korda whispered. "I was wondering if that was what brought you to Bundelkhand."

"That would probably be investigated by the Idol Wing," Athreya replied, skirting the issue. The Idol Wing was a unit of the police department that investigated theft of idols, sculptures and other historical artifacts from temples and other places. "Rest assured, they haven't hired me."

"Now that you are here, though, you could perhaps ..." Dr. Korda left the sentence unfinished.

"Oh, no. I'm sure the Idol Wing is quite up to handling it. Adhira and Dr. Baig were telling us yesterday that your dig is not really at risk. You haven't yet accumulated enough valuable artifacts to attract the thieves' attention."

Dr. Korda threw a quick, unreadable glance at Adhira before leaning back in the sofa and answering.

"Well ..." he began and paused to take a few leisurely sips from his beer mug. He seemed to be a man who considered every word before he spoke. After a few moments, he continued. "Well, that is strictly not true, but Adhira was right in giving you that impression. There has been a very recent development, of which we do not speak outside the base. That's as much as I can say for now."

As an awkward silence fell, Adhira changed the topic.

"Would you like to walk down to the river?" she asked. "It's a very pretty view, and the water is nice and clean. We can take our beers and stroll down. We'll be back in fifteen minutes, by which time the others will have freshened up and joined."

"A good suggestion," Dr. Korda agreed and drained his mug. "I need to get out of my work clothes and take a shower. Why don't you go down to the river? I'll join you back here in fifteen minutes."

Soon, the three visitors and Adhira strolled out of the entrance with drinks in hand. They turned left and went around the corner of the building.

As they passed the third window, a voice called out. "Adhira," the dry female voice asked, "can I see you for a minute?"

"Right now, Mrs. Markaan?" Adhira asked, walking up to the window and peering in. "I was just going to show our guests the river."

"This won't take long," the voice replied curtly. "Ask them to go on ahead. You can join them in ten minutes."

As Adhira threw Sharad a helpless glance, he nodded encouragingly.

"I know the way," he said. "You finish your work and come."

With a frown, Adhira turned back the way they had come. The three visitors continued on their way to the river.

Soon, they stood about a hundred feet behind the building, at the top of a gentle slope that ended at the river a few hundred feet away. Shrubs and bushes dotted the ground along with a few small trees. An occasional stump of a tree stood out like blot on the landscape.

"This area was cleared of large trees to give an unobstructed view of the river from the veranda of the resort," Sharad said. "That was done when the resort was still operational."

Shrubs and bushes gave way to rocks and boulders as the slope approached the river. Straight down from where they stood was a wide shelf of flat boulders that jutted out into the water, which flowed from their right to the left. Beyond the water lay Naaz Tapu, still and silent. The waters of the Betwa had acquired a light tinge of blue and green as they reflected the woods on the islet and the sky above. Not a bird was to be seen.

The three visitors threaded their way, first through the shrubs, and then among the grey boulders, as they approached the river. Presently, Athreya and Moupriya reached the shelf of rock and stood staring silently at Naaz Tapu a couple of hundred yards away across the water. Sharad had fallen behind, having to take a call on his mobile phone.

As had been the case the previous day, a palpable stillness lay over Naaz Tapu. Thick foliage and grey shadows concealed whatever secrets the islet held. Athreya's mind went back to the sad tale of Naazneen and Vanraj that Habib Mian had narrated. His mind's eye saw attackers converging on the islet in small boats even as a hail of arrows flew at them from unseen archers hidden among the trees. He sensed that Moupriya, too, was thinking of the unfortunate couple.

Minutes passed in silence. There was nothing to be said. The two of them were taking in Naaz Tapu with eyes made wiser by Habib Mian. Presently, a faint movement appeared at the edge of Athreya's vision. He was so focussed on the islet, and so indistinct was the movement, that at first it failed to register on his mind. Then, when the movement grew more apparent, he noticed it and turned his face towards it.

There stood a woman whom he had not noticed earlier, even though she had been standing there for several minutes. Her back was towards them. She might have been sitting on a low rock at the edge of the water, behind a large boulder, looking out at Naaz Tapu. Now, she had risen, and was standing less than ten yards away. She had made no sound.

She was a slender young woman dressed in a light grey kameez that extended down to her knees. Below it, her white churidar and bare feet were visible. Her soft brown hair fell elegantly down her slim shoulders as she stood there, silently contemplating the islet at a distance.

At a soft sound from Athreya that had escaped him unwittingly in surprise, her pale face turned towards him, and she stood motionless, regarding him solemnly. Still, no sound came from her. Athreya stared back at her, captivated for the second time that day.

The exquisitely shaped nose, the small mouth, the graceful eyebrows and, above all, the light grey eyes made Athreya's heart leap. There was a dreamy quality to her hauntingly beautiful face that was hard to miss. It seemed to Athreya's imagination that sad memories of some personal tragedy lurked behind the grey pools that were her eyes. Her disconcerting gaze seemed to be able to peer into his mind.

It was the same face he had seen in the paintings that morning. The only difference was that this face was a couple of years older. And the face was not smiling.

He heard Moupriya gasp. At the sound, the strange lady's gaze shifted unhurriedly from Athreya to Moupriya. Athreya realised that, like him, Moupriya hadn't noticed the woman earlier. It was as if she had silently materialised beside them.

"Naazneen!" Moupriya whispered.

CHAPTER 5

"Adaab arz hai," the strange woman greeted, bending gracefully forward and lifting her right hand to her face in a typical salutation. Her eyes flickered from Athreya to Moupriya as she continued in a soft, cultured voice. "Aapko mera naam kaise pata?" How do you know my name?

Seeing that Moupriya was too stunned to return the greeting, Athreya did so.

"Adaab," he replied and went on in Hindi. "I'm sorry, we didn't see you. I hope we didn't interrupt you. We didn't mean to intrude upon your privacy."

"You didn't." The lady smiled, and her eyes softened. It was the same enigmatic smile that he had seen in the paintings. It seemed to conceal more than it revealed. "I was not doing anything in particular."

"Were you studying the islet?" Athreya asked.

"Yes. It's a special place for me."

"Special?"

"I grew up here. The islet reminds me of things I must not forget."

The woman spoke unhurriedly and in a measured manner.

Clearly unnerved, Moupriya turned suddenly and ran towards her father, who was still on the phone call.

"Excuse me," Athreya said to the lady. "I must go."

He turned and hurried after the girl. He didn't want her to panic and run into the base. She might do something that could jeopardise his discreet investigation.

"Khuda hafiz!"

The lady's parting words floated after him. A few moments later, he looked back over his shoulder at her. She was gazing after him unperturbedly, with a now-familiar half-smile. When he looked back again after half a minute, he couldn't see her. The spot where she had stood was blocked by foliage.

"What happened?" Sharad asked as Athreya caught up with Moupriya. He was off is phone and had an arm around his visibly agitated daughter. "Mou won't say."

"We met a lady at the river," Athreya replied. "Mou got frightened. It's okay, Mou," he said to the girl. "It's probably not what you think it is."

The girl blinked distressed eyes at him.

"I know it took both of us by surprise," Athreya continued. "But think back with a calm mind, and you'll realise that it's probably a coincidence."

Moupriya took a deep breath and nodded resolutely.

"Yes, Uncle, you're right. That was silly of me."

"What—" Sharad began when his daughter cut him off.

"It's okay, Papa," she said tersely. "Let's drop it, please? I'm already feeling silly."

"Sure, Mou." Sharad cast a quick, inquiring glance at Athreya and dropped the matter. "You want to return to the river or to the lounge?"

"Let's head back to the lounge," Moupriya said firmly.

A few minutes later, they were entering the lounge when Adhira emerged from the office.

"Back already?" she asked. "Too cold? It does get chilly by the water. But don't—"

The rest of what Adhira said didn't register for Athreya. All thoughts were driven from his mind by the sight in front of his eyes. Sitting on a divan, with her legs curled up under her and the half-smile playing on her lips, was the lady they had met at the river.

How had she gotten there ahead of them without his seeing her? He had left her by the river and returned to the base first. And he was certain that she hadn't passed him.

The woman uncurled and stood up from the divan. Leaving her leather sandals on the floor, she came forward on bare feet and stretched out her hand to Moupriya.

"I'm sorry if I startled you," she said in impeccable English. It was the same calm, melodious voice Athreya had heard at the river. "I thought that you had called me by my name. But thinking back, you probably used another name that was similar to mine. I am Nazreen Vaziri, one of the archaeologists here."

Moupriya, her mouth hanging half open in astonishment, took Nazreen's extended hand and shook it. A pink flush crept up her face, and she looked at Nazreen sheepishly.

"I'm sorry, Didi," she said. "I made a fool of myself. I didn't mean to offend you. I'm Moupriya."

"Nice to meet you, Moupriya. Don't worry, I'm not offended."

The light grey eyes seemed to suggest that their owner understood why Moupriya had reacted the way she had. Looking at Nazreen, Athreya decided that she must be in her late twenties. But for some reason, her eyes seemed too experienced for a person of that age. They gave the impression of having witnessed a great deal. Her manner of speaking also conveyed more than a modicum of patience and wisdom – there was neither impulsiveness not frivolity in it.

As Athreya studied her, she turned her disconcerting gaze toward him. The half-smile was still in evidence as she waited for him to speak. He introduced Sharad and himself, which she acknowledged solemnly before returning to the divan on bare feet. Athreya noticed that her step was soundless.

Just then, Mithali returned to the lounge with a sturdy, bearded man aged a little over thirty. Freshly bathed and groomed, Mithali was dressed in a pair of jeans and a pullover. All evidence of chemicals had vanished. Her short, curly, reddish-brown hair was a little tousled, but she didn't seem to care. The ruby nose stud glinted in the afternoon sunshine.

"Ulhas, my husband," she introduced the well-built, bearded man with her, who would easily top six feet in his socks. The broad-shouldered man's muscular arms ended in large hands that had surprisingly long fingers; longer than Athreya's.

"Good afternoon, sir," Ulhas said as he shook Athreya's hand with a strong grip. "Welcome to our little world, where we live more in the past than in the present. First time to Bundelkhand?"

"Technically, no," Athreya answered. "But basically, yes. The last time I came here was many years ago, and I don't recall much of it other than the inside of buildings and some vague memories of the Orchha cenotaphs."

"Bundelkhand has a lot of history," Ulhas said. "I hadn't known any of it before coming here, apart from a vague notion that Bundelkhand was a region in Central India."

"You are not an archaeologist, I gather."

Ulhas shook his head.

"No sir, I'm not. I'm here as a technologist. I operate the electronic equipment like scanners and the magnetometer." He paused to flash a sheepish grin. "While I have worked at archaeological digs before, I am a bit of a dunce when it comes to history. I've never been good at remembering dates and names."

"And you, Mithali?" Athreya asked, turning to her. "Have you worked at digs before?"

"Oh, yes," Mithali adjusted her black, large-framed spectacles on her nose rather self-consciously. "I'd rather do this than work in some chemicals factory. It's so much more exciting here."

"That's nice." Athreya smiled. "Nothing like it when you enjoy your job. Pratap was telling us how boring field work could be."

"Oh, digging and shifting dirt wouldn't be my idea of excitement either," Mithali said uncertainly, glancing at her husband for tacit support. "It's only after the artifacts are discovered and washed that they become interesting to me. Each one is a sort of a mystery – a little mystery that is gradually revealed through chemical tests and scanning. Isn't that so, Ulhas?"

Her husband nodded encouragingly as he towered over her.

"I believe you are also a sort of paramedic for the team?" Athreya asked.

She blushed and adjusted her spectacles unconsciously, perhaps out of habit.

"Only due to the absence of someone more qualified. My father is a doctor, you see. My sister and I used to help out at the clinic quite often. All of us in my family have a smattering of medical knowledge. I'm terrified that I will make some mistake." She flashed another diffident glance at her husband. "Ulhas says that half-baked knowledge could be worse than no knowledge."

"You're fine, Mithali," he assured her. "You only hand out OTC medicines and patch up scratches and cuts. You're fine. And a great help to the rest of us, you know."

Mithali smiled happily at her husband's words.

"Do the people here fall ill often?" Athreya asked.

"Quite frequently," Mithali nodded. "They work long hours out in the open and inhale a lot of dust. Someone or the other has a sniffle every week. And they get scrapes, cuts and bruises often. Everyone here needs attention at least once a month."

"Everyone except our Nazreen," Ulhas quipped scratching his beard with large hand. "She never falls ill, and never gets so much as a scratch herself."

"Really?" Athreya asked.

"Yes," Mithali nodded. "But then, she's a local, accustomed to this climate. She seldom needs to wear sweaters or jackets. She's quite at home here. Oh, I forgot to ask you," she exclaimed, turning to her husband, apparently remembering something suddenly. "Did the shop have T-shirts in my size yesterday? I'm afraid I've ruined another, Ulhas. I'm sorry."

"Yes," Ulhas replied. "I picked up two. You really must remember to wear your apron, Mithali."

"I will. I'm sorry. I'll wear it *before* I wear my gloves." She turned to Athreya and gave him a watery smile. "I'm so absentminded, I always forget to wear my apron before starting work at the lab."

"Good afternoon, Mr. Athreya," a cultured male voice interrupted. "I see that you have met our own dear Florence Nightingale."

It was Sabir Baig. He came up and shook hands as he smiled fondly at Mithali.

"Really, Dr. Baig," Mithali protested, going pink again. "I'm hardly a Florence Nightingale. An untrained nurse masquerading as a doctor is more like it."

"Regardless, Mithali is our Mrs. Helpful. Anything she can do for you, she will."

"That, I wholeheartedly concur with," Ulhas grinned, bringing a pleased smile to his wife's thin face.

"Stop, you two," Mithali griped good-naturedly. But her happy smile betrayed her pleasure at her husband's praise. "Shall I get you some more beer, Mr. Athreya?"

"Yes, thank you."

Athreya glanced around the lounge as Mithali went to fetch beer for him. Everyone other than Mrs. Markaan seemed to have joined them. They were merrily chatting and laughing – Adhira was narrating some scandalous gossip to Moupriya as the latter

tried hard to supress her giggles. Nazreen, with a half-smile playing on her lips, listened quietly. Dr. Korda, Sharad and Pratap were
in conversation in another part of the lounge. Pratap was laughing at Sharad's joke as Dr. Korda – who had shed his monastic
robe – looked on gravely. Beside Athreya, Ulhas was imitating a
shopkeeper he had met in Jhansi the previous day, much to Sabir's
amusement. All in all, they seemed to be a happy and jovial lot – all
except Dr. Korda, who probably was incapable of displaying mirth.

Athreya wondered how Mrs. Markaan would fit into such a
breezy bunch. From what he had heard about her, she seemed an
authoritarian and humourless woman. Maybe, what he had heard
was just bellyaching on the part of a group that resented its boss's
control and the discipline she enforced. He should not form an
opinion without meeting her.

As if on cue, a small-built, bespectacled lady walked into the
lounge. Her sparse, grey-streaked hair was bound up into a tight
little bun at the back of her head. The frail-looking lady, who must
have been pushing sixty, was the shortest of the group – a couple of
inches shorter than Mithali and over a foot shorter than Dr. Korda.

Her stern visage, thin-lipped and humourless, was at variance
with all the others in the room except Dr. Korda. The beady eyes
behind her glasses swept the room and paused on Sharad for a
moment before going on to Moupriya. She didn't seem pleased at
seeing a giggly young girl at the base.

It was not that she frowned or displayed annoyance in any obvious way. It was just the lack of friendliness in the eyes that gave
Athreya that impression. There had been unmistakable interest in
the eyes when they had rested on Sharad. The interest evaporated
as soon as she noticed his daughter. A moment later, her eyes met
Athreya's, and she held his gaze as she assessed him.

At her presence, the buzz of conversation died and laughter
ceased. It was as if someone had unexpectedly done something
obnoxious in the midst of a party. But the pause was for only for a

moment or two. As if suddenly conscious of it, Adhira and Sabir began speaking simultaneously.

Adhira resumed her narrative, but with markedly less levity than before. Moupriya, who had caught Mrs. Markaan's cold glance, found her giggles had disappeared. Sabir turned to Athreya and began talking about some triviality.

She approached Sharad, who stepped forward and met her with a professional smile. After all, Athreya mused, she was his client. She had consulted him at least once. Sharad beckoned to his daughter and introduced her to Mrs. Markaan. To her credit, the old lady hid her irritation and even offered the girl a smile.

After a brief period – just long enough not to seem rude – the girl excused herself and returned to Adhira, with whom she seemed to be getting along. Sharad glanced in Athreya's direction, and the later excused himself and went towards his friend.

"Welcome, Mr. Athreya," Mrs. Markaan said in a dry voice that seemed curiously devoid of emotion. "I hope you are having a good time."

"Yes, I am," Athreya responded. "Thank you. You have a lively little group here."

"A little too lively at times. But Sundays are when they can let their hair down, I guess. More than half of them are young people, as you can see. They need their entertainment. I can't expect them to be like me – I have no interests outside archaeology and history. I'm happy spending my Sunday reading and writing."

"This is a nice, comfortable place, I must say. Even if it is a little far from civilization."

"Yes, we were lucky to find something of this standard so close to the dig. Nazreen being from here helped."

"Nazreen helped you find this place?"

"She comes from the Orchha area, although I must confess that I don't know where exactly her people live. She was my student, you know, and a very bright one at that. One of the best I've had.

She knows the history of this region like the back of her hand."

"I heard you hand-picked your entire team?" Athreya asked.

"I had to. What with so much antique theft taking place, one must be sure."

As Athreya had been talking to Mrs. Markaan, Adhira and Pratap had lifted a large ice chest between the two of them and were now carrying it out of the lounge. Nazreen and Mithali followed them with trays of glasses, mugs and food.

"We are moving to the lawn, Mr. Athreya," Mithali said breathlessly as she passed him. "The winter sun is very pleasant. Those who prefer the shade sit under the canopy. Come when you are ready."

"We'll come now," Mrs. Markaan preempted. "Shall we, Mr. Sikka?"

Athreya chose to sit in the shade under the canopy. He was looking for a chance to chat with Nazreen, but she opted to take a walk on the lawn. Once again, she was barefoot. He took a chair next to Sabir, while Sharad struck up a conversation with Ulhas. Mrs. Markaan and Dr. Korda – now smoking a curved pipe – sat in the sun just outside the canopy's shade. Adhira and Pratap stood smoking a little behind them, while Moupriya listened to Mithali's description of the work she did.

Hardly had five minutes passed before Mrs. Markaan called from the edge of the canopy's shadow.

"Dr. Korda tells me that you assist the police with investigations, Mr. Athreya," she said loudly enough for everyone to hear. "What kind of investigations?"

"Different kinds, Mrs. Markaan," Athreya replied. "I'm not a specialist in any one area. The police sometimes call me when they want an external opinion."

"You investigate homicides, thefts, disappearances and that sort of thing?"

"That's right."

"How about financial fraud?" she queried. "Embezzlement, misappropriation of funds, etcetera?"

You could hear a pin drop. Everyone had stopped sipping their drinks or puffing their cigarettes. Dr. Korda's face seemed to have frozen. Adhira stood rooted to the spot where she stood, oblivious of the smoke curling up into her eyes. An expression of disapproval had gathered on Sabir's face. Only Nazreen seemed unaffected as she kicked her feet in the grass a little distance away.

"Are you referring to scrutinising books of accounts and financial transactions to see if money has been diverted?" Athreya asked.

"Exactly," Mrs Markaan replied.

Athreya had to tread carefully. What Mrs. Markaan was touching upon was a part of Athreya's brief from Dunne. He opted to give the answer he had initially given Dunne.

"That's best done by accountants and auditors, Mrs. Markaan. Finding evidence of defalcation and economic offences is a specialised activity that is usually done by forensic auditors."

It seemed to Athreya that the group silently let out its collective breath. There was no discernible sound, but Athreya felt the tension ebbing.

"Do you know a forensic auditor, Mr. Athreya?" Mrs. Markaan persisted.

Athreya rose and went to where Mrs. Markaan was sitting, taking the chair next to her. Dr. Korda, who had been sitting on her other side, stood and walked away.

"Yes, I do," Athreya said in an undertone. "I know an experienced lady who lives not very far away – in Gwalior, actually."

Mrs. Markaan contemplated Athreya's face for a long moment.

"Tell me," she asked at length, "what brings you here?"

When Dr. Korda had asked him a similar question a short while ago, Athreya had chuckled. But not now. He wondered why two senior members of the expedition seemed to think that he come to Bundelkhand in a professional capacity. He was certain that Dunne wouldn't have spoken to Mrs. Markaan yet.

"Well," Athreya said noncommittally, "Sharad Sikka is an old friend. He has been asking me to come down for a while now."

Giving no indication whether she believed him or not, Mrs. Markaan rose and made her way to the office. Every pair of eyes followed her. Talk again ceased. Adhira lit another cigarette as Dr. Korda sat brooding in a chair. Mithali looked confused. Ulhas and Pratap tried to look unconcerned. After a minute, Sabir excused himself and followed Mrs. Markaan.

Conversation resumed as Adhira shook herself and went around asking if anyone wanted refills. She seemed determined to have a good time, and not let Mrs. Markaan ruin the Sunday afternoon. People resumed their conversations.

By the time Sabir returned half an hour later, Mrs. Markaan's discordant remarks had faded from minds, and cheer had returned to the gathering. Beer had stoked light-hearted banter and unrestrained laughter.

Sabir was carrying two pieces of jewellery when he returned, which he held up for all to see when he reached the canopy.

"These are the finds," he called out. "A bracelet and a ring."

Most people turned and stared, their alcohol-befuddled brains taking that extra second or two to comprehend the significance of what Sabir had said. In those few moments, Nazreen moved quickly and took the bracelet. Pratap took the ring and began studying it along with Ulhas.

"Is this what you were referring to?" Athreya asked Dr. Korda as he and the others gathered around Nazreen. "You had mentioned that there was a recent development."

Dr. Korda nodded gravely at the bracelet.

"It's a valuable piece, as you can see," he said. "MM found it a few days ago and has been keeping it under wraps. The ring is not as valuable."

"Are these the only things she found?"

"I don't know," the tall man replied with a thoughtful frown. "MM is playing this one close to her chest."

"Where did she find them? I know it must have been somewhere at the dig, but where exactly?"

"I don't know that, either." Dr. Korda pulled at his pipe and blew out a thoughtful cloud of smoke. "Until now, only Sabir and I had seen the bracelet and ring. MM hasn't shown them to anyone else. If she has found something more, she hasn't shown us. I'd be interested to know what Nazreen makes of the bracelet – she knows Bundelkhand very well, you know. A veritable expert."

Athreya brought his attention back to Nazreen, who was studying the bracelet closely. Turning it over in her hand, she studied the intricately constructed ornament that was about two inches wide and studded with rubies and emeralds. Over the thin gold bands that formed the base of the bracelet, slender gold strands resembling vines had been wound. At regular intervals, the gold vines wound themselves around flowers that they themselves seemed to have sprouted. Nestled inside each flower was a gem. Embedded securely among gold petals, the rubies and emeralds formed an alternating pattern of red and green.

Nazreen scratched the gold with a fingernail at several places and studied the craftsmanship and the style with which the bracelet had been constructed. She then held it in sunlight at arm's length and examined the pattern the gems made. She brought it back close to her face and looked at the gems closely.

"What do you think?" Sabir finally asked.

"This was not made in Bundelkhand," Nazreen replied in her calm, unhurried manner. "My guess is that this came from the south, perhaps somewhere near Mysore."

"How old?" Sabir asked.

"Difficult to say. It's an eighteenth-century design, but the piece could have been made later, too. Goldsmiths often copy old designs, and an antique finish is not difficult to achieve."

Nazreen handed the bracelet back to Sabir and took the ring from Pratap. The ring seemed to be plain gold band with carvings on its outer surface. She studied it for half a minute, handed it to Sabir and moved away. As the others crowded around Sabir, waiting for their turn to handle the pieces of jewellery. Athreya fell into step with Nazreen.

"You said that the bracelet wasn't made here," he said. "But it was *found* here, wasn't it?"

"Yes, but one doesn't necessarily follow the other. A lot of trade took place between different kingdoms. Not only within the Indian subcontinent, but also with other countries – Persia, China, Southeast Asia, Central Asia and other places. Kings and nobles had jewellery and art collections that included many foreign pieces. Take the Salar Jungs for instance, a noble family under the Nizams of Hyderabad. They had an enviable collection."

By this time, they had gone out of earshot of the others who were bunched together under the canopy.

"I wonder where Mrs. Markaan found it," Athreya mused aloud. "From what I've heard of the artifacts found at the dig, the bracelet doesn't fit the pattern."

"It doesn't," Nazreen agreed, her voice dropping a notch.

She stopped walking and turned to face Athreya. Her face had grown solemn.

"We have made a serious mistake, Athreya Sahib," she said in an undertone. "A dangerous one. Markaan Sahiba believes that others don't know where she found the bracelet. Maybe, others don't. But I do."

"Where did she find it?" Athreya asked, suddenly realising that he, too, was speaking in hushed tones.

"At a place that must not be violated," she replied. "A place that we locals know better than to intrude upon and desecrate. She disrespected our long-held customs in the guise of being an outsider and disturbed what must not be disturbed. I repeatedly warned her against it, but she wouldn't listen. Now, we will have to face the consequences."

"Where was the bracelet found?" Athreya asked again, although he already knew the answer.

Nazreen gazed disconcertingly into his eyes for moment. He felt that she knew that he knew. Yet, she answered his question, but in a whisper. The expression on her face was a mix of remorse and determination.

"Naaz Tapu."

CHAPTER 6

The next morning, Athreya was eating a late breakfast at the Sikkas' house. Athreya was unhurriedly digging into Mrs. Sikka's famed alu parathas while Moupriya had temporarily devoted her entire being to consuming the waffles her mother had made for her.

"So, what did you think of the people you met yesterday?" Sharad asked his daughter.

Half a minute passed before the girl could empty her mouth sufficiently to articulate a response.

"I don't like MM," she stated with the undimmed clarity of youth. "But Adhira Didi and Mithali Didi are very nice."

"Why don't you like Mrs. Markaan?" her mother asked.

"She's not a very nice person, Ma. She didn't like my being there, you know. It was very obvious. Also, she's perpetually frowning, as if she was ticking off someone or the other. A difficult person to please, I think. You know, Ma, she didn't smile even once? It was clear that nobody there liked her. They just put up with her because she is the boss. You know what Adhira Didi said about her?"

"Never mind what Adhira said," Mrs. Sikka interrupted smoothly. "It's not nice to gossip. You seem to have hit it off quite well with Adhira."

"Oh, yes! She's great fun. The stories she tells!"

"What were you two talking about?" Sharad asked. "I saw you giggling away."

"I can't repeat most of it here," Moupriya suppressed a giggle as she recalled something Adhira had said. "Did you know that she is an exercise freak? Works out for two hours every day."

"And guzzles gallons of beer after that?" Sharad chuckled.

"Papa!" Moupriya chided. "That's her business. Anyway, she was saying that whatever she eats goes straight to her hips."

"What's wrong with her hips?" Mrs. Sikka demanded. "She's an attractive woman, if you ask me – curvaceous and pleasing. She's much better looking than the skinny models and the size zero actresses in movies. It's not healthy, I tell you. This size zero nonsense—"

"As I was saying," Moupriya interrupted hurriedly before her mother could expound on skinny celebrities, "Adhira Didi and Mithali Didi are good fun. I only wish that Mithali Didi would be more confident of herself. They all say nice things about her, you know. She's quite a good chemist and very helpful."

"I hope her health is okay?" Mrs Sikka asked. "She's so thin and pale – almost anemic. She needs to go out in the sun."

"Overworks herself," Sharad explained between mouthfuls. "That's what both Sabir and Korda say."

"Dr. Korda," Moupriya shivered involuntarily. "He spooks me. There's something dark and melancholy about him. He *never* smiles. His bony face looks like a skull wrapped in skin, and his eyes are set *so* deep inside his skull. You know who he reminds me of, Papa?"

"Who?" Sharad asked.

"A combination of Saruman from *Lord of the Rings*, and Count Dooku from *Star Wars*."

"Both characters are played by the same actor, Mou," Athreya chipped in. "The late Christopher Lee. He also played Dracula – one of his famous roles."

71

"Really?" Moupriya asked. "Come to think of it, Saruman and Dooku *do* look alike. Anyway, Dr. Korda gives me the creeps." She shivered again.

"Who else did you meet?" her mother asked, moving the conversation away from Dr. Korda.

"Dr. Baig – he is a nice man. Very pleasant and gracious. Quite a gentleman, as Papa says. There were some others I didn't speak to – Mithali Didi's husband, for one. And I avoided Pratap."

Moupriya returned to her waffles in a determined sort of way. Athreya waited for a few moments to see if she would talk about the one person she had missed, possibly deliberately. When a few moments passed, and Moupriya refused to look up from her waffles, a faint smile appeared on Athreya's face.

"And Nazreen?" he asked. "What did you think of her?"

"Who's that?" Mrs. Sikka asked to Moupriya's obvious relief. "Someone new at the dig?"

Athreya looked up in surprise.

"I don't think she's new," he said, glancing at Sharad. "I thought she's been there from the beginning. In fact, she's a local."

"That's what Sabir and Korda said, too," Sharad drawled. "But I had never seen her before. Everyone at the dig comes to Jhansi often, except perhaps Mithali. I've been to the dig a few times and to the base a couple of times. But I've never met Nazreen."

"I've not seen her, either," Mrs. Sikka agreed. "Describe her," she instructed her husband.

Athreya watched Mrs. Sikka as Sharad described Nazreen. Moupriya too, was watching her mother.

"A pretty local girl in her late twenties?" Mrs. Sikka mused. "With grey eyes? How come I've never heard of her before? I know several Muslim families here. No grey eyes that I can recall. Are you *sure* she's a local?"

Even as Sharad nodded, Athreya added, "She is. She told me herself that she grew up around here."

"*Grew up* around here!" Mrs Sikka exclaimed as she set down her water glass with a thump. She seemed affronted that a beautiful girl had grown up around Jhansi without her knowing about it. "Impossible," she declared. "Well-dressed *and* well-to-do, you say? I would know of her."

"Maybe, she isn't from Jhansi proper," Sharad suggested.

"Maybe, maybe," Mrs. Sikka nodded distractedly. "I'll have to find out."

With that, Mrs. Sikka returned to her breakfast and attacked her alu paratha with vengeance. Athreya turned his gaze to Moupriya, who had been listening to the conversation silently.

"So," he asked, "what did you think of Nazreen, Mou?"

"She seems to be a nice person," the girl replied in a small voice. "Doesn't speak unless she absolutely has to. And her voice is quiet and soft when she does. But still …"

Moupriya left the sentence unfinished.

"But still?" Athreya prompted after a couple of moments.

"I … I am afraid of her, Uncle," the girl finished in a whisper.

"Afraid?" Mrs. Sikka's eyebrows shot up. "Why would you be afraid of a beautiful woman?"

"It's the way she looks at you … and the way she smiles. She *knows*. I feel as if she can read my deepest thoughts. Like I wouldn't be able to hide anything from her."

Just then, Sharad's phone rang. He glanced at it and looked at Athreya in surprise.

"Korda!" he exclaimed. "Why is *he* calling?"

Sharad picked up the phone and took the call.

"Good morning, Dr. Korda … yes, sure. Please go ahead. Yes, we can talk. Okay … okay … when? This morning?" He glanced at Athreya. "Yes, he is here with me … can I call you back in a minute?"

Sharad hung up and turned a grim face to Athreya.

"Mrs. Markaan," he said, "is missing."

* * *

As soon as Dr. Korda had announced that Mrs. Markaan was missing, Athreya and Sharad had risen from the dining table and adjourned to the study to call Dr. Korda back. Now, with the door closed, they resumed the conversation.

"*Missing*?" Athreya asked. "Can you elaborate?"

"She seems to have gone out somewhere but nobody knows where to," Dr. Korda replied.

"When did she leave?"

"That's the trouble. We don't know when or where. She's an early riser and is usually up and about by the time the rest of us come out of our rooms. She usually takes a cup of tea at around 6:30 a.m. and is at breakfast by eight.

"Today she did neither. When she hadn't turned up by 9 o'clock, Adhira knocked on her door to ask if she was unwell or if she needed any help. But there was no answer. She knocked several times in vain. She then tried calling Mrs. Markaan on her mobile, but it was switched off. The land line in her room also rang without an answer."

"Did you check with the security guard?" Athreya asked. "I believe there's only one way to get in or out of the base."

"He hasn't seen her, either. And the funny thing is that both the project vehicles are still here."

"There are no other vehicles that she could have taken?"

"None. The two bikes – Pratap's and Ulhas's – are here, too."

"Maybe, she's gone out on foot. You could wait for some time and see if she returns. It's just about 10 o'clock now. Perhaps, she's walked to the dig."

"The same thought occurred to me, so I sent Pratap to the dig. She hasn't been there, either. The security guard at the dig is quite positive. But, as you say, we too thought it best to wait awhile. But that's when Nazreen discovered something strange."

"What?"

"MM's room door was locked from the inside, but the rear door that leads to the common veranda was unlocked. Shut, but unlocked. Nazreen went into the room. MM, of course, wasn't there. She might have left in a hurry through the back door and the veranda."

"Why do you think she left in a hurry?"

"Well … actually, we don't know. Just conjecture, I suppose, because she seems to have gone out wearing her flip-flops rather than her shoes or leather sandals. She usually wears shoes when she goes out. Except to Jhansi, when she wears leather sandals. Most of us use flip-flops only in and around the base."

"When was the last anyone saw her?"

"Around 11 pm, just before she turned in. Adhira and Mithali were strolling on the lawn when Mrs. Markaan stepped out of her room briefly. Ten minutes later, they saw her room light go out."

"If she had come to Jhansi," Athreya asked, "where do you think she might be headed?"

"I can think of only two places – Mr. Sikka's or the museum."

"The government museum?" Sharad asked.

"Yes."

"It wouldn't have opened yet. Would you like me to go over there and check?"

"If you can, Mr. Sikka," Dr. Korda replied. "That would eliminate one possibility."

"No problem. We'll do that right away."

"Dr. Korda," Athreya asked as they rose. "Something more seems to be troubling you. What is it?"

"I'm not sure, Mr. Athreya. I guess I'm just a little uncomfortable. I can't understand why Mrs. Markaan chose to go out of the *rear* door of her room. The only reason could be that she didn't want the security guard or anyone else knowing that she was going out.

"She's taken her torch with her. That suggests that she went out when it was dark. She's gone out all alone, Mr. Athreya. All alone in the dark, that too through the rear door. I can't imagine why."

* * *

Fifteen minutes later, they pulled up outside the closed gates of the government museum, where the security guard informed them that the museum was shut for the day – closed every Monday, in fact. After a protracted conversation, Sharad convinced him that they were not visitors who had come to see the museum. They had instead come to meet one of the administrators on business. As the guard reluctantly let them enter, Sharad asked if he had admitted an elderly lady earlier in the morning.

"No, sir," the guard replied. "Only two people have come in so far, apart from the sweepers and the janitorial staff. Both of them are officers who work here. Both are men."

As they entered the main door of the museum, they saw a familiar figure.

"Madhav!" Sharad greeted the well-built man in his early thirties, "what are you doing here?"

"Hello, Mr. Sikka," Madhav replied. "Didn't you know? I work here, now. After MM fired me, I've taken up a stop-gap job so that I can be near Adhira."

"What do you do here?" Sharad asked.

"Catalogue artifacts and some other miscellaneous work. The museum recently received a fresh batch that needed to be classified and catalogued. It's a temporary job. It's very difficult to get a proper job in archaeological circles after you get fired so publicly…"

"Speaking of MM," Sharad went on, "is she here?"

"Nope."

"I was wondering if she came in here earlier in the morning."

"Nobody is here other than me and one other staff member. This is a government office, Mr. Sikka, and it's closed to visitors on Mondays. People will start coming only now."

"You're sure she isn't here, Madhav?" Sharad asked.

"Well, *I* haven't seen her. Most offices are still locked. Why would MM come here, anyway?"

"To meet someone, perhaps."

"Well, she would certainly not come to see *me*." Madhav let out a coarse, humourless laugh. "Not after what she did to me. And if she comes here to see someone else, she wouldn't tell me."

Madhav's responses were factual and quick; given with a dead-pan face. Athreya had expected him to show more surprise that they were looking for Mrs. Markaan at the museum so early in the morning. Yes, he had asked why she would have come there. But the question was posed in a matter-of-fact way, with no attendant surprise.

"When was the last time you saw her, Madhav?" Athreya asked.

Madhav frowned as he tried to recollect. "A couple of weeks at least. As you can imagine, I'm not very keen on meeting that virago."

"Madhav," Sharad asked. "Can we have a look around to see if she is here?"

"You can certainly try, but they won't let outsiders wander about in the building."

Sharad smiled and laid a hand on Madhav's shoulder.

"They will," he said, "if we go around with *you*."

Madhav shrugged.

"Okay," he replied. "If we do see her, I'll walk away – I don't want to talk to that vicious woman. But my guess is that you're wasting your time. She isn't here."

Fifteen minutes later, Madhav was proven right. Mrs. Markaan was not at the museum. They thanked Madhav and returned to their car. As they were driving to the base, a thought gnawed at the back of Athreya's mind.

Why had Madhav not been surprised at their searching for Mrs. Markaan at the museum? And so early in the morning? And on a Monday, when the museum was closed? Surely, it was an unusual thing to do, and would have caused any reasonable person some surprise.

* * *

Athreya stared in annoyance at the open door of Mrs. Markaan's room. The narrower door at the far side of the room—the one that led to the common veranda—was shut and bolted from inside. He had hoped that the archaeologists would have left the room untouched and in the same state they had found it. Apparently, they had not.

"Nazreen opened this door after she entered the room through the veranda door," Dr. Korda said in response to Athreya's question. "I realise now that we should have left it as we had found it. But then, we did not realise that something could be wrong. We were just looking for MM."

The time now was around 11 am, and there was a strong sense that something was amiss. Mrs. Markaan's phone still went unanswered. Between the two of them, Dr. Korda and Adhira had called everyone in and around Jhansi with whom Mrs. Markaan could have had any sort of business. They had also searched the rooftop terrace of the base and had combed the dig and its vicinity for a second time.

Dr. Baig, clad in khaki cargos and an off-white cotton shirt with two pockets, stood beside Adhira with a worried expression on his erudite face. The crisis had robbed him of his usual gentlemanly courtesy. Athreya had learnt that the khaki cargos and the off-white shirt were his work uniform at the dig. From his left shoulder hung a brown rucksack containing his tools. Covering his feet were lightweight, brown canvas shoes.

He had left for the dig on the dot at 8.30 am, as was his unvarying routine. He was apparently a man of very regular habits, which included a work day that began at 8:30 a.m, and ended at 5:30 p.m. On learning that Mrs. Markaan had still not returned to the base, he had hurried back from the dig a few minutes before Athreya and Sharad had arrived at the base.

Towering beside Dr. Baig was Dr. Korda, back in his grey monastic robe. On his feet were thick-soled leather boots that added an inch or two to his already formidable height. The boots were predominantly black, but with two wedges of brown leather near the heel. His normally lugubrious expression had turned positively sepulchral in the aftermath of Mrs. Markaan's impromptu departure. He had remained at the base, awaiting Mrs. Markaan's return or, at least, some word of her.

Dr. Korda now scratched his beard thoughtfully at Athreya's implied censure, as he went on in his sonorous voice.

"I realise that we should have left the room untouched," he said with a hint of embarrassment. "And I apologise for not having done that. In retrospect, it seems to be the obvious thing to do. Unfortunately, we can't go back in time to correct it. Let me, with Adhira's help, try and itemise the changes we have made to the room from the time we found it unlocked.

"While the rest of us were standing inside the quadrangle and fruitlessly debating what actions to take, Nazreen went through her own room to the veranda, and tried Mrs. Markaan's veranda door from the outside—"

"What made her do that?" Athreya asked.

"I'm not sure. I suggest you ask her. As I was saying, Nazreen tried Mrs. Markaan's veranda door and found it open. She entered the room. As far as I know, she didn't touch anything. She came straight to the front door of the room and opened it, startling the rest of us in the bargain. For a moment, we thought it was Mrs. Markaan opening her door."

"How was the front door before she opened it? Was it locked? Bolted? Where was the key?"

"It was bolted from the inside," Dr. Korda clarified. "There are two bolts – a vertical one at the top, and a horizontal one in the middle just under the handle and the lock. The horizontal bolt had been shot from the inside. The vertical bolt was not. As far as the lock was concerned, it had not been turned. The key was on the table, where it still lies. As far as I know, nothing else was touched in the room." He turned to Adhira and asked. "Anything to add?"

"No, nothing really except that we opened the closet and the bathroom door. Nazreen entered the bathroom to see if MM was there. She didn't touch anything in the bathroom apart from the door."

"Did you or Nazreen touch anything the room?" Athreya asked.

"Well …" Adhira frowned as she tried to remember. "I opened the closet doors, but I don't think I touched anything inside. We may have moved a few things on the table to see if MM had left a note. I think Nazreen picked up the room key to check the room number on it. It was MM's room key. That's all, I think."

"And then, one of you must have shut the veranda door and bolted it from the inside, I presume?"

"Yes … yes." Adhira reddened in embarrassment. "I should have remembered that, I'm sorry. Nazreen did that."

"Why did you shut the veranda door?"

"Why?" Adhira seemed a little bewildered. "Because it opens out to the riverside, where we don't have a security guard. Anyone could walk into the room if we leave it open."

Athreya nodded and entered Mrs. Markaan's room. It was a large one, furnished with a double bed, a set of sofas around a low table, a chest of drawers, a desk and three chairs. A red-and-green fresco adorned the white ceiling, while three rustic-looking wall hangings decorated the walls. Two windows pierced the walls next to the two doors, one offering a view of the riverside and the other a view of the quadrangle.

Two pairs of shoes and a pair of leather sandals stood in a neat line along one wall. A suitcase lay flat and closed on a granite ledge in a corner. The partially open closet doors showed clothes neatly stacked beside other personal items. On the table were some papers and books. They had once been neatly stacked and arranged but had recently been moved around. A wooden holder held several pens and pencils.

The room was a picture of order and method. That such an organised and tidy lady should take off on her own in the darkness was indeed a surprise.

"How do you know that she has taken her torch?" Athreya asked.

"It's always in the right corner of the desk against the wall," Adhira said, pointing to a corner of the desk. "Always in the same place so that it's easy to locate in the darkness when the power goes off."

"Do you have power outages often?"

"Quite often. A couple of times a day, at least."

"Was there one last night?"

"I don't know. Once I'm asleep, I couldn't say. I'll ask the others if they noticed."

"Anything missing, as far as you know?"

Adhira shook her head. "But I wouldn't really know if any of her personal items are missing."

"What about her handbag or purse?"

"The handbag is in the closet. I didn't open it."

"Good thinking."

Athreya walked around the room, studying the floor, the carpet and the chairs. At length, he came to a halt between the veranda door and the window next to it.

"The curtains are closed," he said. "Was this how they were?"

"Yes. At least when I entered the room."

Athreya pulled out his camera and took several pictures of the room, covering its entirety from at least two angles. He then opened the veranda door and stepped out.

The veranda, which was about ten feet wide, stood six or seven feet above the ground outside. Close to where Athreya stood, a broad set of steps led down to the ground. There were narrow steps at both ends of the veranda, too. He walked the length of the veranda and found that all the other doors – seven of them – were shut, and all the windows curtained.

He stood at the top of the broad steps and let his imagination run free. He stood still for a long moment, sometimes with his eyes shut, sometimes open, and tried to take in with all his senses, the veranda and the riverside it overlooked.

At length, he turned to Adhira and spoke in a low voice.

"Does anyone outside the dig and the base know of Mrs. Markaan's sudden departure?" he asked.

"No, I don't think so," Adhira replied.

"Not even a friend? Say, an erstwhile member of the expedition?"

Adhira didn't reply. There was no need to. Athreya knew the answer.

"I'm going to walk about a little bit," he said at length. "Can you bolt the veranda door from the inside and lock the front door using the key? It's important that we leave everything in the room exactly as it is. We mustn't touch anything. If this becomes a police case, the room and whatever evidence it contains must remain as uncontaminated as possible."

"Okay," Adhira said in a small voice, nodding simultaneously. "Will you return through the main entrance once you are done?"

"Yes."

Athreya went down the steps as his imagination took flight. A dozen yards from the bottom step, he halted and looked around absently, taking in the foliage, the tree stumps, rocks and the thorny bougainvillea climbing up to the rooftop terrace at irregular intervals. Without realising it, he picked up a stick and began scratching the ground with it. His right hand seemed to have acquired a mind of its own.

He took in the silence and the stillness around him, wondering why not a single leaf was stirring in such an open place beside a flowing river. His imagination perceived the nature around him as some kind of a collective being; a formless presence that was holding its breath. Something had happened here that was out of the ordinary.

As far as Mrs. Markaan's sudden departure was concerned, a dozen possibilities floated past his mind's eye as he stared unseeingly at the river with glazed eyes. He knew instinctively that each of them was plausible under different sets of circumstances. But it was too early to judge the possibilities; premature to make any sort of assessment. What he knew was miniscule. There was a lot more he had to discover.

He knew what he had to do next – he had to retrace the path to the river that he had taken less than twenty-four hours earlier. And he had to deal with whatever he encountered there. With an effort, he reined in his imagination and brought his mind back to the present.

As he did, he realised with a start that he was holding a stick and drawing something on the bare ground with it. He dropped the stick and stared at what he had drawn.

It was a rough sketch of a bracelet.

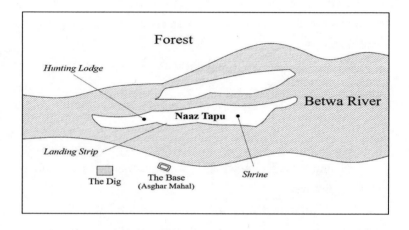

CHAPTER 7

Athreya went down the slope leading to the Betwa, following the faint path that threaded its way through the foliage. As he approached it, silence gave way to the muted whisper of the flowing water that was occasionally augmented by the soft sounds of water lapping over the rocks. The sun was bright in the near-cloudless sky, and yet, the islet across the water seemed to be holding on to its shadows. The clean, crisp air by the river felt invigorating, urging him to hasten to the river.

Presently, he came to the wide shelf of flat stone that jutted out into the clear water, which seemed a little bluer today. He stepped onto it and surveyed the vista before him. Green and thick, Naaz Tapu lay about two hundred yards before him, stretching away on both sides, up and down the river. To his right, at the very edge of the water, a clutch of boulders rose a few feet from the shelf of flat stone.

As he reached the water, a brown head came into view. She was sitting there on a narrow ledge.

"Aaiye, huzoor," she said without rising or turning. The voice was cultured and courteous. "Adaab arz hai."

"Adaab," Athreya responded. "I thought I might find you here."

"I have been waiting for you," she said. "It was only a matter of time before you came here."

"Contemplating the islet today, too?"

"It is our past, present and future. I told you, it's close to my heart."

"Why so? I know that you said that you grew up here. But why the special connection with the islet?"

"It's mine, Athreya Sahib. It's mine in ways you do not know. But you didn't come here to talk about that. You came to talk about Markaan Sahiba's nocturnal venture, didn't you? Have they finished calling everyone they know in Jhansi?"

Athreya knew she was referring to the people at the base. "I think so."

"And they are none the wiser to Markaan Sahiba's whereabouts, I suppose."

"Correct," Athreya confirmed. "Do you know where Mrs. Markaan went?"

"Don't you, Athreya Sahib?"

Nazreen turned her head to look at him. He experienced the now-familiar unsettling feeling as the light grey eyes – unperturbed and knowing – alighted upon him. How much did those deep, grey pools see? Instinctively, he tried to make his face expressionless. With a start, he realised that the eyes were the same colour as the centuries-old stone shelf he was standing on.

"None of the vehicles are missing," he said, not answering her question. "The security guard saw no outside vehicle come to the base either. How far could she have gone on foot?"

"Did they ask if the guard heard an engine or a motor?"

"Should they have?"

"There are other modes of transport, Athreya Sahib. Adhira has probably not told you yet, but Markaan Sahiba rented a rubber raft two weeks ago. Adhira is the one who released the deposit for it."

"Raft?" Athreya echoed. "Are you saying that Mrs. Markaan

could have gone by the river?"

"Couldn't she have?" the lady countered, still sitting on the rock ledge, half-hidden from Athreya's view. "I would wager that the security guard heard the sound of an engine or a motor in the darkness. If he could pinpoint the time he heard it, you will gain valuable information."

"Where is the raft kept?" Athreya asked briskly, trying to suppress the growing confusion over how Nazreen knew so much.

"A hundred yards or so upstream." She gestured unhurriedly to her right. "There's a tongue of water that cuts into the riverbank. That's where it is moored."

"Show me." Athreya swung to his right and prepared to stride across the rock shelf.

But Nazreen stayed where she was, remaining completely composed. She didn't even rise. She turned her face away from Athreya and resumed her contemplation of the islet across the water.

"There is no need," she said. "I just checked. The raft is not there."

"We'll initiate a search for it. Can you describe it?"

"I can do better. I will show it to you."

Athreya blinked rapidly. His suspicion was confirmed. One of the possibilities his mind had imagined was taking shape. His fears were about to be realised. But above all, he was conscious that Nazreen was becoming increasingly unfathomable. How did this woman know so much?

"Show me," he said, turning to face the river.

Nazreen rose gracefully from her perch and moved soundlessly towards him. The slender lady was dressed as she had been the previous day, but in different colours. She now wore a pale green kameez and a bottle-green churidar. Her brown hair fell to her shoulders. Once again, she was barefoot. She was carrying her sandals in her hand.

For the first time, Athreya realised that she was wearing no jewellery. Not even an ear-stud, ring or a chain around her neck. She halted next to Athreya and turned to face Naaz Tapu. Her eyes narrowed as she gazed into the distance and raised a graceful arm to point toward the islet.

"Can you see it?" she asked. "The raft is grey and green in colour with a grey beading."

Athreya gazed at where she pointed, but he could discern little. He tried for fifteen seconds, in vain. Without taking his eyes of the islet, he lowered the backpack he was carrying and his fingers searched for the zip to open it.

"You see where the edge of the islet goes inwards?" she queried. Athreya nodded. "Look a little to its right. There is a thin strip of brown earth."

Focusing his eyes on the place she had indicated, Athreya saw the strip a few dozen yards long. To its left was thick green foliage and near its right end a cluster of flat grey rocks, not unlike the shelf he was standing on. His fingers found the backpack zip and began opening it.

"Yes, I see it," he said. "But I am not sure I see a raft."

"Concentrate on the grey rocks to the right of the strip. The raft is on top of the rocks. It blends in with the rocks."

Suddenly, Athreya saw it. The outline of a symmetrical shape of the raft grew apparent among the naturally disordered rocks. And as he trained his gaze on it, it grew clear. Yes, a raft was visible, now that he knew where to look for it.

"Mrs. Markaan went to Naaz Tapu in the middle of the night?" he asked as he pulled out a leather case from the backpack. "Whatever for?"

"I'm sure you'll find out, Athreya Sahib. Is that a pair of binoculars you are carrying?"

Athreya clicked open the leather case and pulled out the field glasses he had borrowed from Sharad.

"You came prepared." Nazreen's half-smile widened in appreciation as she took the binoculars. "Then, this isn't unexpected."

"Not after what you told me yesterday."

Nazreen stood motionless and studied the islet through the binoculars. A minute passed in silence. Then another. Eventually, she took the field glasses off her eyes and gave them to Athreya. Without a word, he put them to his eyes and studied the brown strip, the rocks and the raft. The strip of earth was narrow, muddy and wet. And the raft seemed to be tied to a stake driven into the rock shelf on which it was resting. It seemed smaller than the dinghy he had gone rafting in the previous day. It had a small motor at its rear, which had been raised so that it wouldn't touch the rock shelf.

"See anything else, Athreya Sahib?" Nazreen asked. "At the very edge of the strip where the foliage begins. There's a narrow path between two trees. Look at the path just where it disappears behind the trees."

Athreya fiddled with the focus adjustment to bring into sharp focus the spot she had indicated. He stared at the path and the trees that shrouded it. He could see nothing amiss.

"Look for a speck of blue," she said, as if instructing a child. "On the path just were the tree trunk cuts it off from view."

"Yes!" Athreya exclaimed. "You have uncommonly sharp eyes. It's a small blue object … it seems to be caked in mud."

"Yes, it is caked in wet mud from the strip. Can you make out what it is?"

Athreya stared hard for a minute and eventually gave up.

"No," he said, still peering through the field glasses. "What is it?"

"A rubber flip-flop."

Athreya whipped the binoculars from his eyes and stared at Nazreen. She had the same expression she had had the previous day when she had spoken about Mrs. Markaan exploring Naaz Tapu – a look of grim remorse.

"Markaan Sahiba's flip-flops are blue."

* * *

The small motorboat carrying three passengers and the boatman slowed to a crawl as it approached the brown strip at Naaz Tapu's edge. Nazreen stood erect at the bow, perfectly balanced and calmly looking ahead at the islet with clear grey eyes. She might have been going there for a picnic. Behind her, Athreya sat on the forward plank that spanned the breath of the boat. On the rear plank was Dr. Korda in his grey monastic robe and heavy boots. Behind him, operating the motor and the rudder, was the distinctly uneasy boatman, eager to turn tail at the slightest excuse. Nothing would induce him to step ashore onto the islet.

It had taken considerable cajoling and a handsome exchange of cash for the boatman, who lived a couple of kilometres downstream, to agree to the trip to Naaz Tapu. He had declared that he would not set foot on the cursed islet under any circumstances. No sane local would do so, he had avowed.

But the only other local on the boat showed not the slightest trace of apprehension. To all appearances, Nazreen held no fear of the islet. Her benign half-smile and tranquil gaze betrayed no apprehension as she calmly directed the boatman to the rocks on which the rubber raft was resting. They were to alight on the rock shelf because Athreya had issued specific instructions that nobody was to step onto the mud strip.

As soon as the rock shelf was close enough, Nazreen leapt from the boat and landed lightly on a rock. She caught the rope Athreya threw to her and pulled the boat until its side touched the rock. Athreya alighted gingerly, while Dr. Korda remained seated in the boat, awaiting Athreya's instructions.

Asking Nazreen to stay where she was, Athreya shot a video of the rock shelf and the rubber raft and followed it up with a series of photographs from different angles. Nothing seemed out of the ordinary. The rubber raft had been pulled up from the water and tied to a stake driven into the rock.

The rock shelf, which was dry except for Nazreen's and his tracks, held no clues to Mrs. Markaan's nocturnal excursion. The rubber raft was empty. Its hinged motor had been swivelled inwards so that the propeller stood clear of the rock underneath. A visual inspection of the raft yielded nothing, and Athreya refrained from touching any part of it.

The rock shelf ended about ten feet from the raft and gave way to the squelchy strip of brown mud. On one side of the rocks was the mud strip, and on the other was water. There was no way to reach the rest of the islet from the rock shelf without crossing the strip, which at its narrowest was over ten feet wide.

A single track of footprints snaked across the strip from the rocks to dry ground at a point where the strip was about fifteen feet wide. The footprints – if the marks could be called that – were large depressions in the watery mud that were roughly the shape of the sole of a shoe, boot or some other footwear. Athreya knew from experience that the prints on squelchy mud tended to be much larger than the feet or footwear that caused them.

Water oozing out under the pressure of the foot distended the print in all directions as it gushed out. In addition, feet often slipped and slithered on the spongy, slippery surface before they gained purchase. This lateral movement further expanded the print.

Besides, watery mud was too runny to retain any markings, including those of soles. As a result, such prints were often useless for identification purposes.

Athreya stood at the edge of the rock shelf and completed his camerawork before studying the prints. He noticed at once that the spacing of the prints was uneven. They were closer together at some points, but wider apart at others. That was understandable, as confidence was often low when walking on slippery and unreliable surfaces. People tended to take shorter steps when they were uncertain. And as their confidence grew or fell, they lengthened or shortened their stride.

He also saw was that most of the prints extended a few inches backward down the slope, towards the river. This too was to be expected, as the strip sloped upwards from the water to the dry ground. When a foot was placed on it, it would slide back a little before gaining purchase. But what did surprise him was the how much they had slid back. Perhaps the water content in the mud here was high. He would know when he himself walked on the strip.

What was amply clear was that there was only one set of tracks. And the prints were wider towards the dry ground and narrower towards the rock shelf. Clearly, someone had walked from the rock shelf to the dry ground. A single track also meant that the track-maker had not returned.

If Mrs. Markaan had made these tracks, she hadn't returned to the rock shelf. Which meant that he would have to cross the mud strip in search of her.

"If you don't mind getting your trousers wet," Nazreen said, as if reading his thoughts, "we can get into the water and cross the mud strip at the other end – the far end from here."

"How deep is the water?" Athreya asked.

"Three feet. We will walk a dozen feet from the shoreline."

Once again, Nazreen seemed to be extraordinarily well informed about minute details. Athreya did not comment on that. Instead, he agreed to get into the water.

He followed Nazreen who unhesitatingly stepped into the water, knowing exactly where to place her feet. Dr. Korda watched them mournfully from the boat. He seemed content to sit there till he was required.

Water oozed out from under Athreya's foot as he trod the mud, and his feet slid back before gaining purchase on the firmer mud under the watery top layer. He found he was taking shorter strides than usual as he walked uncertainly up the slope.

Nazreen, on the other hand, seemed entirely at home. Whether there was real contentment on her face, or if it was just his imagination, he didn't know. But she went across the squidgy strip as if she were sauntering across a lawn. When she reached the edge of the strip and stepped on to firmer ground, she walked to where Mrs. Markaan's tracks were and halted, waiting for Athreya's instructions.

By the time he caught up with her, thick sticky mud was clinging to the edges all around his borrowed rubber flip-flops, and some of it had annoyingly found its way between his toes. He longed to wash his feet and rid himself of the unpleasant feeling.

As soon as he caught up with her, he saw the blue rubber flip-flop. It lay about a yard from the edge of the mud strip where Mrs. Markaan's tracks ended. Once again, his camera went to work before he knelt and studied the mud-caked footwear. It looked as mud-caked as the ones he was wearing. There was little doubt that this one had traversed the mud strip.

It was the common hawai chappal found by the millions in every part of the country. The base was bright blue in colour, and the two rubber straps were of a darker hue of blue. It lay with its heel pointing towards the mud strip and the toe pointing up the faint path snaking between two protective tree trunks that seemed intent on preventing the path from going further into the islet.

"This is Markaan Sahiba's chappal," Nazreen said. Her voice seemed loud in the stillness of the islet.

"Sure?" Athreya asked.

Nazreen nodded.

"It's broken," she whispered. For the first time, Athreya thought he detected an edge of anxiety. "Did something happen here that made Sahiba break into a run? She seems to have fled into the woods."

One of its two straps had snapped as if it had suddenly been yanked with force. The straps of such flip-flops usually gave way at the base, where it frayed more than in other parts. But this strap had broken midway, near the high point of its arch. That would have taken considerable force. Athreya found himself agreeing with Nazreen. She seemed to miss very little.

Leaving the broken flip-flop where it lay, Athreya rose and made as if to go forward up the path. But a light hand on his shoulder restrained him.

"I will go first," Nazreen whispered. "You shouldn't. Follow me closely, and don't wander away into the woods."

Athreya found himself nodding mutely.

Nazreen walked forward slowly, following the path as it squeezed itself between the two unwilling tree trunks. With alarm, Athreya found that his flip-flops were making loud squelchy noises, while Nazreen walked soundlessly three feet ahead of him.

Hardly had he gone a dozen yards when he felt the atmosphere thicken. It grew darker. The air seemed pregnant with moisture and had grown heavier. The trees were crowding closer around him and their branches were bearing down upon him. Oppressively, disconcertingly.

Creepers, wrapping themselves around tree trunks like possessive serpents, wound their way upwards and outwards, filling the spaces between tree trunks and darkening them. The sky was not visible from under the canopy of leafy boughs and vines, even though the sunshine was bright.

The ground was thick with foliage and fallen leaves that rustled testily as Athreya's feet disturbed them. He had already lost sight of the path that had been faint to begin with. His nose picked up smells he did not recognise.

His fertile imagination went berserk and began weaving mental visions from the tale of Naazneen and Vanraj that Habib Mian had narrated. Bhola appeared in his mind's eye, standing over seven feet tall and carrying an iron mace. As did his monstrous dog with its massive fangs, sharp claws and a dripping maw. An inconsequential question flashed across Athreya's mind – was it a Mastiff or a hound?

Above all, it was the deathly silence and the eerie stillness of the islet that unnerved him. He had no option but to place his faith completely and unreservedly in the strange lady whom he was following. He stepped onward.

As soon as his imagination-fuelled visions ebbed, he found himself confronted by an old enemy – claustrophobia. The closely-packed foliage bearing down upon him and the near-absence of sunlight made him feel as if he were in a tomb. His breathing had grown laboured and an acute restlessness had seized him. His heart was thudding in his chest. Panic flared.

His subliminal fear of closed spaces had returned to haunt him.

He knew from experience that the only way to counter the growing anxiety was with logic. The fear was entirely imagined, he told himself. He could walk out of the woods any time he chose and feel the sunlight and the breeze on his face. The airlessness was an illusion – there was enough air here to last him for ever. As he battled his unfounded panic, the rational part of him resolved that he would not allow his fears to show to his companion.

Then, suddenly, relief came in an unexpected form – they came upon Mrs. Markaan. She was lying face down on the ground with one hand outflung and the other bent under her chest. A blue, mud-caked flip-flop dangled from her left foot. Her right foot was bare. The back of her head had been crushed as if she had been struck from behind by a large, blunt weapon.

Mrs. Markaan had met a violent death.

Athreya's panic vanished in an instant. Instead, his blood ran cold when he saw the last of the injuries. The back of her shirt had been ripped open by three claws that had cut deep into her flesh. And on her exposed arm were fang marks from a giant jaw.

CHAPTER 8

Twenty minutes later, Dr. Korda was back at the base and on the phone. He called the police at Jhansi and conveyed to them all the details Athreya had given him. When Athreya and Nazreen had informed Dr. Korda about their discovery, the boatman – with his eyes perilously close to popping out of his head – had been extremely eager to take Dr. Korda back to the base.

As soon as Dr. Korda got ashore, the boatman had whipped out his mobile phone. Within fifteen minutes, the news of yet another death at Naaz Tapu was swirling in Jhansi, rapidly acquiring embellishments by the minute. By the time a constable ran into the police headquarters with the exaggerated tale, rumour had spread that Bhola and his gigantic dog had been seen killing an old lady who had desecrated the islet.

Dr. Korda's call corrected the story, and within half an hour, the police were on their way by road along with a forensic team and a doctor. Separately, a police motorboat was churning its way to Naaz Tapu.

Back at the islet, Athreya and Nazreen were alone, waiting for the police and for Dr. Korda to return. Knowing that it would be at least an hour or two before they did, Athreya returned to the body and stood beside it. His long, fine hair fell over his face as he stooped, making him look like a weeping willow bending over the fallen body. The silver patch in his beard stood out in the gloom.

He crouched beside the body and examined it without touching or moving it. He studied the crushed head, her outflung arm, her feet, and the claw marks on her back.

He then went a couple of yards away and knelt beside the torch, which Nazreen confirmed was Mrs. Markaan's. He examined the torch without touching it, and photographed it.

When he rose and pushed his hair back, he found that his perspective had changed. The mystic thoughts and perceptions that had earlier been stoking his imagination had vanished. As had the claustrophobia. Cold reality had sunk in. He decided to make a survey of the islet with Nazreen.

But two minutes into the woods, he had lost all sense of direction. The restlessness returned as he found himself in the dark, airless jungle with trees and creepers crowding around him.

"It's best not to wander around the islet needlessly," Nazreen said in her calm, understated manner. "If there is anything specific you want to do or see, I can help you."

"I'm told there is an old hunting lodge somewhere on the islet. Do you know where it is?"

Nazreen nodded.

"It's close by, but it's basically a ruin. It was built over three hundred years ago and has not been used for at least two hundred years."

"Have you been there?"

Nazreen favoured him with silence and an inscrutable glance.

"Why do you wish to see it?" she asked.

"You said that Mrs. Markaan had taken the bracelet from Naaz Tapu. I was wondering where on the islet she might have found it. Separately, I had heard mention of the hunting lodge, and wondered if it was there that she found it."

"Very likely," Nazreen said. "She has been digging around the lodge for the past few days."

Keeping his face expressionless, Athreya wondered how Nazreen knew this. Had she come here in the past few days? Had she seen it for herself?

He broke off his chain of thought when he sensed Nazreen studying him silently. Not prepared to return her gaze, lest she somehow found out what he was thinking, he turned away as if he was inspecting the woods around them.

"Which way is the hunting lodge?" he asked.

"This way." Nazreen stepped past him and began threading her way through the dense foliage. "Stay close to me. You don't want to get lost here."

Already lost, Athreya followed her, thankful that she was wearing a light coloured kameez that stood out against the darkness of the forest. Whenever he looked around, he did so hastily, so that he didn't run the risk of losing her. The foliage was so thick, and the forest so gloomy that he could easily lose sight of her in a few seconds. Because of the closely-packed trees, they couldn't go in a straight line even for a dozen feet. Nazreen had to wind her way around the tree trunks and the bushes.

Five minutes later, he suddenly found himself face-to-face with an ancient stone wall that disappeared into the leafy branches above and into the creeper-clad tree trunks on either side. He was surprised to see that the vines had left the stone wall alone.

"This is the side wall," Nazreen said in an undertone. "If we follow it, we'll come to the entrance."

"Let's do that," Athreya whispered.

They came to an arch in the wall. The opening was about six feet wide and ten feet high. No gate or door barred their passage through the arch, which was made entirely of grey stone that had darkened with age. A stone-paved walkway ran inwards from the arch, to what seemed to be some sort of a building beyond a court-yard.

Five rectangular holes, which once were a door and four win-dows, stared back at him from across the courtyard. No wood or iron had remained for two centuries. Little could be seen of the in-terior of the building. The courtyard, which was curiously devoid of shrubs, was covered in knee-high wild grass, which had also broken through the cracks and gaps in the walkway.

On the unpaved ground to the right of the walkway was an ir-regular depression in the ground ringed with freshly-turned earth. The shallow excavation stretched from the walkway to the outer wall on their right.

"So, this is where Mrs. Markaan found the bracelet and the ring," Athreya mused aloud. When Nazreen didn't react, he went on in an undertone. "This just seems to be a hole in the ground. No sign of a chest or chamber or any sort of receptacle here. Is this usual for archaeological finds?"

Nazreen shrugged her shoulders and remained silent as her eyes studied the small excavation with displeasure. After a minute, she looked up.

"I'm going into the lodge," she said, her voice just about carry-ing to him. "Want to come?"

Athreya nodded and followed her through the doorway into a large, square room with a high roof. The stone floor had warped and become uneven with age, and the plaster between the stone blocks comprising the walls was crumbling. Three more doorways opened into other rooms, which were darker than the one they were in. At the far left corner, narrow steps led upwards, while sim-ilar steps led downwards at the far right corner. In another corner lay a small array of digging tools, which Nazreen inspected grimly.

"I wish Markaan Sahiba had heeded my advice," she said rue-fully. "She would have been alive today."

"You believe she was killed because she came to Naaz Tapu and excavated around the hunting lodge?" Athreya asked.

"Can you offer any other explanation, Athreya Sahib?" she countered in a matter-of-fact way. "Every life is precious, even that of a woman who was not liked by the ones she spent her day with. But she needn't have died."

"Why was she disliked?"

"It's not right to talk ill of the dead, huzoor."

"Did you dislike her, too?"

Nazreen nodded in the gloom.

"The others at the base, too?"

"Everyone had his or her reason to dislike her. Unfortunate, but true."

"Nazreen," Athreya said, "this will now become a murder investigation. We need to find out who killed Mrs. Markaan. We need everyone to talk. We don't have the luxury of not speaking ill of the dead. If we are to avenge her, we *must* know. You understand, don't you?"

"I do, Athreya Sahib … perhaps more than you realise. Injustice is not new to me. But let some time pass before we talk about it. Justice and vengeance will gain their rightful place in time. Let the day pass. We found her dead not more than an hour ago."

"The details can wait. But with time, the trail also grows cold. Isn't there anything you can tell me now?"

Nazreen sighed and remained silent. The sigh was the first expression of emotion he had heard from her. The silence continued as they stood in what appeared to be the hall of hunting lodge. Just as he began feeling that she was not going to say anything more on why the people at the base disliked Mrs. Markaan, Nazreen spoke.

"Many people believe that Markaan Sahiba did them a bad turn," she said. "She fired one man on a flimsy pretext. Another feels she usurped the position that was rightfully his. Young people who have worked with her have seen her take credit for the work that they have done. There are whispers about financial irregularities too – real or imagined.

"Markaan Sahiba is – was – high-handed in dealing with workers and others who are less fortunate than her. Take the workers who would have worked here at the hunting lodge, for instance. She brought them from another state to work at the dig so that they have no knowledge or fear of local myths. She is likely to have terrorized them into silence. It's going to take some effort to find out who she got to work out here. She was not a good woman, Athreya Sahib. But she didn't deserve to be killed."

"And the bracelet?" Athreya asked. "You said that she desecrated the islet by taking the bracelet, and that led to her death. Then, is the legend of Naaz Tapu true?"

"Is history true, Athreya Sahib? Or is it the lies of the one who wins? Were the heroes of the past truly heroes? Or were they villains? Where does one draw a line between history and legend?"

She broke off and looked up as if she had heard something. She listened intently for a moment and turned.

"We must leave now," she said. "The police will be arriving shortly. We must meet them at the landing strip."

Without waiting for a response, she started out of the hunting lodge. Athreya followed in silence. Nazreen walked faster than she had on the way there. Just as they reached the landing strip, they saw the boat making its way from the riverbank to the islet, carrying half a dozen passengers.

"Please do me a favour, Athreya Sahib," she said as they waited for the boat to draw near. "Try not to have people desecrate the islet any more than necessary. Especially the hunting lodge."

* * *

The sky had darkened by the time the police brought Mrs. Markaan's body on a stretcher to the rock shelf behind the base.

Athreya, who had been waiting there with the archaeologists, stepped forward as they laid the stretcher on the rocks. He knelt beside the stretcher and uncovered Mrs. Markaan's right hand, which was half-clenched in a curious way. While the ring finger and the little finger were clenched and were touching the palm, the other three fingers were unclenched.

Athreya shone a torch and studied the hand for long moment before trying to unclench the two fingers. But rigor mortis had set in. The police doctor, who had been watching over Athreya's shoulder stepped forward to help. Shortly, the fingers were pulled back and the whole palm became visible.

On the palm was a semi-circular, maroon-and-purple mark.

"What could have caused this?" Athreya asked.

"Something hard must have pressed against the palm with force," the doctor said. "It must have been hard and thin – some kind of a semi-circular metal object, perhaps. About three inches in diameter. See, the skin is bruised all along the semi-circle, and torn in two places where small ridges in the object dug deeper into the palm."

"Could she have been clenching it when she fell? Could the impact of the fall have caused the bruise?"

In response, the doctor shone his torch on the middle and index fingers. A thin blue mark ran across both of them.

"Possible," he said. "I am not sure, but if these two fingers were clenched, I think the mark on them would be on top of the mark on the palm."

Athreya looked up and scrutinised the women gathered around for a brief moment. He then zeroed in on Adhira.

"Can I borrow your bangle, Adhira?" he asked. "I want to confirm a suspicion."

He took the gold bangle from her and held it over the semi-circular mark on Mrs. Markaan's palm. It fit very well. He rose and held out the bangle for others to see.

"Dr. Baig, Nazreen," he said, "you studied the bracelet Mrs. Markaan had found. Was it approximately the size of this bangle?"

"Yes," Nazreen replied at once. "It was more or less the same diameter. But it was considerably wider. This is a single-strand bangle, while the bracelet was almost two inches wide."

"She's right," Sabir confirmed. "Adults' bangles don't vary much in size. The diameter would have been roughly the same."

"And a two-inch-wide bracelet would be wide enough and hard enough to make the marks we saw on the deceased's palm," added the doctor. "It fits almost exactly. She must have been clutching the bracelet when she fell forward. The force of the impact when her hand hit the ground would have been adequate to cause the bruises."

Athreya returned the bangle to Adhira and went around to the other side of the stretcher. There, he uncovered Mrs. Markaan's left hand, which was unclenched. He shone his torch on it and pointed silently to the ring finger. On it was a plain gold band with a carved design on it.

"She wore it!" Nazreen hissed.

"Is that the ring MM found along with the bracelet?" Sabir asked in disbelief.

"I have a photo of the ring on my phone," Dr. Korda's deep voice answered. "Let's compare it with the one on her finger."

It was identical.

"Strange," Dr. Korda rumbled as he put away his phone. "The old lady was wearing the ring and clutching the bracelet when she was attacked. The bracelet was taken from her, but not the ring. I wonder why?"

"Perhaps because her left hand – the one the ring was on – was trapped under her chest when she fell," Athreya suggested.

"But this makes no sense!" Sabir exclaimed. "None of it makes any bloody sense! MM took the bracelet and the ring to the islet? That too, in the middle of the night? Whatever for?"

"When we answer that question, Dr. Baig," Athreya answered, "We will be close to solving the case."

* * *

Athreya followed Inspector Bhupinder Singh Deo as the latter made his way to the entrance of the base to speak to the security guard. Inspector Bhupinder had been the last person to return from Naaz Tapu, and by the time he had left the islet, darkness had fully descended. He had seen off the police wagon carrying the body, asked the police doctor to wait and approached Athreya apologetically.

"I've heard a lot about you, Mr. Athreya," he had said. "It would be a privilege to work with you. However, until I get the clearance from my DCP, I can't let you participate in the investigation."

"I understand, Inspector," Athreya had said.

"I would be happy to have you with me when I interview witnesses and suspects. What I can't do is to let you lead an interview. I don't want someone telling the DCP that a civilian is leading the investigation."

"That's fine. I'll stay silent. If I have a question, I'll check with you before asking. Is that okay?"

"Yes, thank you. I'm sorry. You know how these things are at the department—"

"Don't worry, Inspector. No need to apologise. Shall we begin?"

"Yes, sir."

Bhupinder nodded and strode briskly to the entrance. Soon, the clean-shaven, energetic young police officer in his late twenties faced two security guards, who had thrown crooked salutes to the man in uniform.

"Why are two security guards here?" he began in Hindi.

"Madam told me to call him in early, sir," the guard with a

luxurious moustache said, gesturing to the other man, a stub-ble-chinned youngster.

"Which madam?"

"Adhira Madam, sir."

"Why?"

"She said that you might want to speak to him immediately."

"Why?"

"He was on duty last night, sir. When … when Markaan Mad-am was … you know."

Bhupinder turned to the younger guard. "Were you on duty last night?"

"Yes, sir."

"What time is your shift?"

"Eight to eight, sir. It's seven o'clock now. That's why they asked me to come early."

"Where is your post when you are on duty? At this entrance?"

"Yes, sir. This is the only entrance."

"Do you sit inside or outside?"

"Mostly inside, sir. I go out every hour to patrol the building."

"Do you shut and lock the entrance when you do that?"

There was a momentary hesitation. "Yes … yes sir."

"Always?" Bhupinder persisted.

"Dekhiye, sir." The guard grew shifty-eyed and shuffled his feet. "The front door squeaks loudly when it is bolted. That sometimes disturbs people when they are sleeping. We've been scolded by Markaan Madam about that in the past."

"Okay. What exactly do you do when you go on your rounds?"

"I shut the door but I don't bolt is unless I expect to be away for more than five minutes."

"That's what I do when I am on night duty, too, sir," the other guard said. "But there is no fear of intruders here. And it's so silent that we'd hear it if the door is opened when we are away."

"Would you also hear any vehicle that comes here at night?" the inspector asked.

"Of course. At night, we can hear every single vehicle that goes on the main road. There is no question of a vehicle coming here undetected."

Bhupinder turned to the younger guard and continued. "Did you hear any vehicles or engines last night?"

"Many from the main road, sir. Before eleven o'clock, there are vehicles on the main road every few minutes. Sometimes more often. After that, it is less frequent. The traffic starts again at about five o'clock in the morning."

"I don't mean vehicles on the main road. I'm interested in anything that came closer."

"No vehicle came here, sir. I am sure of that. But I think a car came somewhere there." He pointed to the north. "It must have turned in from the main road. But I am not sure."

"What is in that direction?" Bhupinder asked.

"Where they are digging."

"Digging?" Bhupinder seemed puzzled.

"I think he is referring to the dig," Athreya suggested.

"Of course." Bhupinder said. "Thank you." He turned to the guard. "What time was that?"

"Around eleven o'clock, sir."

"Okay. Did you hear anything else?"

"Yes, sir. I heard a different kind of an engine. The sound was not the same as trucks, cars or motorcycles. It sounded … different."

"Can you describe it?"

"It was … it was," the guard struggled for a few moments. "… different."

"What else can you tell me about it?"

"It came from another side, sir. From the river."

"The river? What time was that?"

"1:25 am, sir. I looked at the time on my mobile."

"That's very precise. Are you sure?"

"I looked at the time, sir." The guard was unshakable in his belief.

'Did you go out to investigate?"

"Yes, sir. I went around the corner and till the veranda at the rear of the building. I could hear the engine for a short while, but I couldn't see anything. Then the sound stopped."

"Was the moon out?"

"Yes, sir. Half-moon. But the river is too far to see at night. Trees and shrubs are in the way. I hurried back to the entrance as I had not bolted it."

Another ten minutes of quizzing elicited nothing new. Athreya and Bhupinder walked back to the spare room next to the dining room, which had been converted into a temporary office for Athreya and the inspector. Just as they were walking in, a soft voice hailed Athreya from the lawn. It was Nazreen.

"Now that you have heard what the guard had to say," she said as Athreya joined her, "I have something to tell you. I saw a light from my window last night. Someone was carrying a torch and walking among the foliage behind the building. I watched the light move towards the river."

"What time was that?" Athreya asked.

"A little after midnight," Nazreen said in an undertone. "More than an hour before the guard heard the engine at the river."

* * *

In the temporary office, Athreya found the police doctor talking to the inspector and showing him the photographs he had taken with his digital camera. As Athreya closed the door and pulled up a chair, the doctor briefed Bhupinder about the bracelet marks on Mrs. Markaan's palm and the fact that she had been wearing the ring when she was killed.

The time of death, the doctor said, was difficult to pinpoint, as at least twelve hours had elapsed after death when the doctor had viewed the body. His best estimate, before doing a post mortem, was that death occurred sometime between midnight and 4 am. That, the inspector remarked, fit in with the security guard's testimony that he had heard an engine at the river at 1:25 am.

When the discussion turned to the wounds on Mrs. Markaan, the doctor and the inspector—both locals— grew uncomfortable and edgy.

"I suppose there is no doubt that death was caused by the blow to the back of the head?" Athreya asked.

"None, sir," the doctor replied. "The skull was crushed and the brain tissue underneath was mangled. Death would have been near-instantaneous."

"What weapon could have caused such an extensive wound? The entire rear part of the skull seemed to have caved in. An iron rod, or even a hammer couldn't have done that. This wound seems to indicate a very broad, very blunt weapon,"

"That's right, sir," the doctor concurred grimly. "I'll have to confirm during the post mortem, but the initial impression is that the wound was inflicted by a single blow, delivered from the back and above. As you say, the skull has caved in and has taken the shape of a crater. It must have been a large and heavy weapon that was swung with extraordinary strength."

"A shallow bowl-shaped crater," Athreya mused aloud. "What does that say about the weapon?"

The doctor's unease grew further, and he shuffled his feet as he answered haltingly.

"That is what troubles me, sir. Such a broad, shallow bowl-shape would require the weapon to be spherical … like a metal ball at least a foot across. What kind of weapon would that be?"

"I can think of one such weapon, doctor," Athreya said. "An

archaic one. A mace."

"A mace?" Bhupinder's consternation flared. "Good lord! How—"

"One moment, Inspector," Athreya interrupted. "There is one more aspect that needs clarification – the angle at which the blow was delivered." He turned to the doctor. "You said that the blow came from the back and from above. How far above?"

"I'll have to measure that during the post mortem, Mr. Athreya," the doctor mumbled miserably. "But my initial impression is that it was delivered more from above than was from the rear. At least forty-degrees from the horizontal … perhaps more … sixty degrees."

Athreya whistled softly.

"Sixty degrees from the horizontal! Even allowing for a two-foot long shaft from the grip of the mace to the ball, it would have required a very tall man to deliver the blow! A very tall man with prodigious strength."

"Bhola," the inspector growled. "Vanraj and Naazneen's bodyguard. The giant with a mace."

CHAPTER 9

There was a knock at the door to the office a few moments after the doctor had left. Still dressed in his work clothes, Dr. Korda stooped as he entered the doorway. Seeing him come in from the darkness outside, Athreya recalled Moupriya's comparison of Dr. Korda with the ominous characters Christopher Lee had played onscreen. There indeed was a baleful air about this tall man.

"I've just had a chat with Liam Dunne, Mr. Athreya," Dr. Korda said in his baritone voice. "I need to have a word with you."

"Who is Liam Dunne?" Inspector Bhupinder asked.

"One of the trustees of John Bates Foundation," Athreya answered. "It's the philanthropic trust that funds this archaeological project."

"He is also the managing trustee of the Sarah Bates Archaeological Institute, the organisation that employs most of the archaeologists here," Dr. Korda added. "I have a message for Mr. Athreya from him. As you and the inspector are working together, I thought I might deliver the message in his presence."

"Certainly," Athreya nodded. "Please go ahead."

"Mr. Dunne has a request, Mr. Athreya. He would like to engage you to investigate Mrs. Markaan's death. I have instructions to draw up a contract to that effect – assuming, of course, that you agree."

Athreya suppressed a smile. That was convenient. Now, Athreya did not need to disclose the fact that Dunne had sent him to Jhansi in the first place.

"I agree. Did he say anything else?"

"He would like to speak to you at the earliest."

"Now?" Athreya asked.

"If that's possible."

"Go ahead and have your call, Mr. Athreya," the inspector interposed. "Meanwhile, I'll talk to my ACP and DCP. If you are engaged by the JBF or the SBAI, you will be permitted to interview witnesses and conduct an investigation. That will make it easier for us to work together. We can share the workload – especially that of interviewing witnesses. We have dozens of people to interview, and time is short."

Athreya followed Dr. Korda out of the room. Two doors away, the tall man stopped and spoke in an undertone.

"Mr. Dunne wants to speak to you on your mobile. He will call you in a few minutes." He indicated the open door they were standing near. "If you'll go up these stairs to the terrace, you'll not be disturbed. Besides, the signal is the strongest up there. I'll tell him that you are expecting his call."

Athreya went up the stairs to the terrace, wondering why Dunne wanted to speak to him on the mobile. One possibility was that he wanted to discuss matters that he didn't want others at the base to overhear.

The open terrace ran right around the quadrangle with parapet walls running on both the inside and the outside. Bougainvillea of different hues, rising from the ground below, flowered in profusion, creating a riot of colours on the otherwise barren terrace.

Athreya got a panoramic view of the quadrangle from the terrace and wondered how the river would look from it. He began walking along the terrace, making his way to the rear part of the building that overlooked the river. A half-moon was out in the clear night sky, and the temperature had dipped considerably since sunset.

His mind went back to his earlier conversation with Dunne.

* * *

It had been over a week ago when Athreya's phone had rung just as he was preparing to turn in for the night. A Delhi number flashed on the screen.

"Good evening, Mr. Athreya," a male voice with an American accent had said. "This is Liam Dunne. I am not sure if you remember me. We had met in Delhi last year."

"I certainly do," Athreya had replied. "How are you, Mr. Dunne?"

After the initial pleasantries, Dunne had said that he wanted Athreya's help to look into a problem. He had spoken about the archaeological mission in Bundelkhand and Mrs. Markaan, and had explained what he wanted to be done.

"There is something funny going on at our excavation, Mr. Athreya," he said. "I am not sure what it is, but the little I am hearing is unsettling. Three things seem to be amiss."

"Please go ahead," Athreya replied, settling into his armchair.

"I have been having an unusually high number of phone calls with Mrs. Markaan over the past couple of weeks," Dunne began. "We have been discussing a number of matters, which I will speak about one by one.

"The first matter, not to put too fine a point, is that Mrs. Markaan suspects that some financial irregularities are taking place at the dig. She fears that money is being siphoned off in some way, but she isn't sure how. Not being familiar with accounting, she wants me to send over someone who could examine the accounts."

"Did she say why she suspects it?" Athreya asked.

"Not specifically, as she didn't have details. But she has a general feeling that the SBAI's expenses as reflected in the JBF's books are too high. When she and I discussed financial matters on our earlier monthly calls, she got a feeling that the JBF was sending more money to the SBAI than it ought to; more money than the SBAI was actually spending.

"As background, you need to understand how money flows between the two organisations. The SBAI has a permanent advance – an imprest, if you will – with it, from which it spends. Every month, the JBF sends money to the SBAI and tops up the advance. The amount sent is equal to the expenses incurred the previous month. That brings the advance back to the original level. Got it?"

"Yes."

"On the first day of every month, the SBAI sends a fund request to the JBF based on the expenses incurred the previous month. The amount requested is *exactly* equal to the expenses the SBAI has incurred the previous month. The JBF immediately transfers the requested amount. I hope that is clear?"

"Very clear. Please proceed."

"Acting on Mrs. Markaan's suggestion, I did something we don't normally do. I compared two sets of accounts – the JBF's books and the SBAI's books. Once I did that, some discrepancies came to light. The amounts the JBF was transferring to the SBAI were sometimes higher than the expenses reflected in the SBAI's books.

"Of course, it could be due to an accounting error. But it could also mean that someone was siphoning off money as it flowed between the two organisations. If one crore rupees were sent by the JBF, only eighty lakhs were reaching the SBAI's books. Twenty lakhs were going somewhere else."

"I see. Who handles the accounts at the mission?"

"Adhira, the accountant, and Dr. Korda, who is our representative at the dig. Both of them are the JBF's employees. All the others are employed by the SBAI. The reason we put the JBF's employees in financial and administrative roles is to have better control. In this case, it might have backfired. It is not conclusive yet. It needs to be investigated by a forensic auditor."

"If Adhira is the accountant," he asked. "What is Dr. Korda's role?"

"Adhira reports to him," Dunne replied. "Dr. Korda is the direct representative of the JBF there, and is our observer. The observer ensures that everything happens as they are meant to happen. If they don't, he reports back to us. As he happens to be a historian and an archaeologist, he is also the cataloguer of the project. He sorts and catalogues the artefacts that are discovered."

"Does he approve expenses, too?"

"Yes. He approves all expenses above a certain threshold, be they running expenditure or capital outlays. That is to ensure that both the SBAI and the JBF are on the same page on all major matters."

"Are you not certain that financial irregularities are taking place?"

"No. At least not deliberately. There seems to be a gap between the JBF's books and the SBAI's books. That could be due to genuine human error. We don't have chartered accountants at the mission, you know. Adhira has done B.Com. and is the accounts-cum-admin person. At this point, I would like to give her the benefit of doubt."

"And Dr. Korda?"

"Him, too," Dunne said. "He doesn't handle the accounts himself, you see. While he has the overall responsibility, he is not a chartered accountant either."

"Then, Mr. Dunne, you may want to send an accountant to look over the SBAI's books."

"I will, Mr. Athreya. Very soon. As soon as I can spare him.

Now let me go on to the second matter I wanted to discuss.

"About a month ago, Mrs. Markaan began feeling uncomfortable about the frequent thefts that were taking place in museums and archaeological sites. She felt our project was becoming a target. As a result, she decided that she would not publicise any valuable discoveries.

"That, by itself, was fine. However, she began suspecting one employee named Madhav, whose behaviour seemed strange. He seemed to be overly interested in what was being discovered each day. He seemed to be excessively curious about what everybody else was doing, and whether they expected to find an artifact soon. He was roaming around the dig at night when everyone else was at the base, and was poking around the stores at the base when others were at the dig. He also kept very irregular hours and would not say where he had been or was going to be.

"She called me and said that she wanted to fire him. I suggested that she take legal opinion, which I she did. She consulted your friend, Mr. Sikka. Thereafter, she fired Madhav.

"But for some reason, that didn't put her fears to rest. She continued to be apprehensive that our project was becoming a target of the Bronze Runners. She even feared that they might have already infiltrated the project."

"Infiltrated the project?" Athreya repeated. "How?"

"I don't know. Perhaps, she was referring to the workers who work under the archaeologists' supervision. I wanted to mention this to you so that you could bear it in mind during your investigation. Now, let me go on to the third matter – anonymous letters."

"Sorry?" Athreya asked, unsure if he had heard right.

"Anonymous letters," Dunne repeated. "I've received three of them, all personally addressed to me. They are printed on plain white sheets using a laser printer. I am not sure if the printer can be traced."

"They can under certain circumstances. But with so many internet cafes and printing shops around, I wouldn't bet on it. What do the letters say?"

"Many things, but what is common is that they are all against Mrs. Markaan. Somebody dislikes her enough to send anonymous letters to me. And, as they are addressed to me personally, I suspect it must be an insider. My name doesn't appear on any public documents relating to the SBAI or the project. Only an insider would know about my oversight role of the SBAI.

"The letters talk about Mrs. Markaan's incompetence and provide several examples. I hate to say this, but it appears that I may have made a mistake in making her the head of the SBAI. The accusations in the letters seem to have some truth in them. I wish whoever wrote the letters had had the courage to have a private chat with me.

"In addition to incompetence, the letters accuse Mrs. Markaan of stealing credit from juniors. Several examples are quoted. Nazreen had apparently done some outstanding work when she was Mrs. Markaan's student. The old lady seems to have stolen her work and published it under her own name. Other than acknowledging Nazreen's 'contribution' in one place, there is no mention of the young lady. Quite shocking.

"The letters list over half a dozen instances of taking credit for others' work and flagrant plagiarism on Mrs. Markaan's part. The affected parties include Mithali, Ulhas and some others. These accusations, too, I am sorry to say, ring true. We have been able to confirm at least three instances. Nazreen refused to confirm or deny.

"One letter accuses Mrs. Markaan of favouritism. Apparently, she is partial towards Pratap Yadav, who, by all accounts, seems unable to pull his weight. Despite his ineptitude, the letter alleges she gives him endless opportunities – opportunities that should have gone to more deserving people.

"And finally, the letters are full of praise for Dr. Baig and the respect his colleagues have for him. The letters fall just short of actually suggesting that I replace Mrs. Markaan with Dr. Baig. Yet again, nasty and abhorrent as they are, the letters seem to have a kernel of truth."

* * *

Athreya's phone rang, breaking into his thoughts and bringing him back to the present. It was Liam Dunne. Athreya glanced around the terrace, and seeing that he was alone, he answered the call. He summarised the events of the past two days and answered Dunne's questions.

"I've asked Dr. Korda to have a room prepared for you at the base," Dunne said when Athreya finished. "In case you wish to stay there."

"Thank you. That would be useful."

"There is one thing I forgot to tell you the last time we spoke. Mrs. Markaan had been up to something in the past week or two. Something out of the ordinary, but I don't know what it was. She had hardly been going to the dig the past few days. Instead, she was visiting Jhansi often, and she seems to be disappearing to some other place for hours at a time."

"Did she say anything about the islet in the river?"

"The islet with a funny name? The one that has a legend attached to it?"

"Yes. Naaz Tapu."

"No. Why?"

"Did she mention that she was exploring the islet, probably with a couple of workers?"

"No, she didn't! Is that what she's been doing?"

"Apparently. She hired a rubber raft a week or so ago, which she might have been using to get there. She probably believed that the islet was worth excavating. Against pleas and earnest advice to the contrary, she seems to have started digging. What is more surprising is that she let nobody – including her colleagues – into her confidence.

"And to top it all, she seems to have gone to the islet in the dead of the night, at around 1:30 am. That is where I found her dead today."

"Good lord!' Dunne exclaimed. "Oh, my sweet lord! What strangeness is this? Why would she want to do something so bizarre? Christ! I can't believe this."

"Did she tell you about a gem-studded gold bracelet she had found? And a gold ring? Valuable artifacts."

"No! Where did she find them? On the islet?"

"Maybe," Athreya said. "We're not sure yet."

"What about that legend? If I remember right, it says something about the islet being haunted. People who go there don't come back alive."

"You do remember it right. That's exactly what happened to Mrs. Markaan, too. There are some gory details—"

"I just remembered two things Mrs. Markaan said to me a couple of days ago," Dunne cut in. "She told me, *'I've discovered something. I can't speak to you about it yet, but I'll do so soon.'*"

"That may well have been about Naaz Tapu. What is the other thing she said?"

"It's even more ominous. She said, *'I may have made a mistake, Liam.'* I have no idea what she might have been referring to."

* * *

After the call, Athreya went downstairs to the entrance where he and the inspector had spoken to the security guards. A few men, including the two guards, were standing in a group and talking.

Seeing Athreya, one of the guards broke away and came over to him.

"Is Markaan Madam's driver here?" Athreya asked.

In response, the guard hailed one of the men in the group, who turned and hurried towards Athreya.

"Are you Markaan Madam's driver'" Athreya asked him

"Ji, sir," the driver nodded.

"Come with me."

Athreya laid a hand on his shoulder and walked him away and out of earshot of the group. When they had gone about fifty feet away from the building, he halted and turned to the driver.

"I'm told that Markaan Madam had been going to Jhansi often during the past couple of weeks," he said. "Is that right?"

"Just the past week, sir," the driver replied. "She went there three or four days. She had gone to Jhansi the previous week too, but only once."

"Okay. Which days did she go?"

The driver frowned as he tried to recall. "Saturday, Monday and Wednesday mornings. Then on Friday afternoon and Sunday morning."

"Sunday morning?" Athreya echoed. "You mean yesterday?"

The driver nodded.

"Do you work on Sundays?" Athreya asked.

"Quite often. I get overtime."

"Where in Jhansi did Markaan Madam go?"

"Sometimes to the museum, sir. Sometimes to a restaurant."

"The government museum?"

"Yes, sir."

"Who did she meet there?"

"I don't know, sir. I would park the car in the parking lot and she would go inside. When she finished her work and came out, I'd drive her back."

"You never saw who she met?"

The driver shook his head.

"Didn't anyone come out of the museum to see her off?"

"No, sir. Hers was a known face at the museum. The security guards never asked who she was. She has been going there occasionally over the past few months."

"But it was only last week that she went there often?"

The driver nodded.

"Did you see anyone you recognised at the museum?"

"I know one or two sahibs there by sight, sir. And the security guards."

"Nobody apart from that?"

"No, sir."

"Did anyone else from Asghar Mahal also go to the museum?'

"No, sir."

"How long would Mrs. Markaan stay at the museum?'

"It varied. Sometimes half an hour, sometimes longer."

"How long did she stay yesterday?"

"Yesterday? She went to a restaurant, sir. Not the museum."

"Which restaurant?"

"Europa Restaurant. It's near Elite Crossing. She had gone there once before this week," he added. "On Friday. I think she was meeting someone."

"Who?"

"Don't know, sir."

"So, she went to Jhansi five times recently?"

"Yes, sir."

"Okay. Did you overhear her say anything in the car?" Athreya asked. "People often make phone calls from the car."

"She spoke in English most of the time, sir. I can't understand it."

"Do you know who she called?"

"Last week?"

"Yes."

"I don't remember when, but she spoke to that white man once – Dunne Sahib. On Friday, she also made a call to someone in Delhi. I don't remember the name of the person she called."

"Did she take any names that you recognised?"

"Yes, sir. She mentioned Korda Sahib and Adhira Madam. And Madhav Sahib, too."

CHAPTER 10

Athreya and Inspector Bhupinder stood beside Dr. Korda as the robed man addressed the rest of the expedition members gathered in the lounge. In addition to the residents, Madhav was also there – he had come to the base a couple of hours ago. Mithali, her anaemic face almost white in the aftermath of the tragedy, sat close to her husband. Pratap sat next to the couple, tense and fidgety. He was absent-mindedly nibbling at his nails, much to Adhira's annoyance.

Adhira was hunched forward in her chair, entirely composed and in control of herself, listening to Dr. Korda. Beside her, Nazreen looked exactly as she always did – calm and silent, with her tranquil grey eyes on Athreya. Sabir sat next to her, stoic and stone-faced, as Madhav completed the group, playing idly with his mobile phone.

Dr. Korda had just introduced the inspector and had told them that the JBF had appointed Athreya to investigate Mrs. Markaan's death. At the tall man's nod, Athreya stepped forward.

"The first twenty-four to forty-eight hours after death is the most crucial period," he began. "Unfortunately in this case, we have lost the first twenty hours or so. The trail is that much colder now. We therefore need to proceed as rapidly as we can.

"I realise you have had a bad day and a terrible shock. But we can't let another twelve hours go by without starting our investigation. We need to talk to all of you right away. Not just to the people in this room, but also the staff who help you run the base, and the workers who help you at the dig.

"To cover as much ground as possible tonight, the inspector and I have divided up the work between us. The inspector and his team will talk to the staff and the workers, while I speak to each of you in turn.

"To make it easier for you, I'll meet you in the order your rooms are arranged. I will begin with Dr. Korda, whose room is at the far left, and proceed in the sequence of your rooms till I reach Mithali and Ulhas. Finally, I'll talk to Madhav. This way, you will know when you will be required, and can plan your dinner and other activities accordingly. Is that okay?"

Eight heads nodded silently.

"The spare room next to the dining room is where we will have our conversations tonight. The inspector and I will need to trouble you tomorrow as well, but we'll come to that in the morning. However, if any of you wish to talk to me about anything at any time, I am available. I will be staying here in the vacant room between Dr. Baig's and Mrs. Markaan's.

"As you know, the police are dusting Mrs. Markaan's room for fingerprints. They will be taking your fingerprints, too, so that they can compare them with those they find in Mrs. Markaan's room. That's the only way to identify the prints that do not belong to the residents of the base."

Athreya turned to the inspector, who nodded and strode out briskly to commence his interviews of the staff. Athreya and Dr. Korda walked out of the lounge and made their way to the temporary office.

"While we have numerous questions, we have next to nothing in terms of facts and information," Athreya began when they were seated. "I would therefore ask you to talk about everything you heard or saw after dinner last night, which I believe ended at around 10 p.m. Is that right?"

"That's right," Dr. Korda answered in his deep voice. "Let me think a minute. I'd like to make sure that I give you the facts correctly, for whatever they may be worth."

He closed his eyes and stayed still for a couple of minutes. He then opened them and began speaking in a measured manner.

"Dinner finished a little after ten o'clock," he said. "We came out to the lawn thereafter and were strolling and chatting. As far as I can remember, all of us were there at dinner, including MM. I recall her specifically because she didn't have her regular dinner. She had a plate of fruits instead."

"Was that out of the ordinary?" Athreya asked.

"No. She did that often, probably a couple of times a week. Sunday lunch had been late and heavy, as you might recall. On such days MM often had fruits for dinner.

"I must have strolled till about eleven o'clock before returning to my room. As always, Sabir was the first to retire. He must had gone to his room around 10:30 p.m. MM was next; she went five to ten minutes later. I was the third. I remember seeing the time when I shut my room door behind me – it was 11:03 p.m."

"Were the others still on the lawn when you retired?"

"Yes, all the others." He counted them off on his fingers. "Adhira, Pratap, Nazreen, Mithali and Ulhas. Adhira and Mithali were together, as were the two men. Nazreen was walking alone on the grass, barefoot as usual.

"After going to my room, I showered and changed into my nightclothes. I plugged in my mobile phone for charging, took my tobacco pouch and pipe, and went out to the veranda as I do every night."

"What time was that?"

"Around 11:30 p.m. I sat in my cane chair and smoked my pipe for a little over half an hour. Now, let me be a little specific here. My room, as you know, is at the very end of the corridor. I chose that room for the specific reason that I could sit at the end of the veranda every night, smoke my pipe in peace and blow the smoke out of the veranda-end. That way, nobody would be inconvenienced by my smoking.

"When I sit that way, my back is to the rest of the veranda. That is by design. The last part of the day before bed is a time for solitude. I don't want to speak to anyone, and they respect that. I sit there in splendid isolation and ignore anyone who comes out to the veranda behind me. I usually sit there till midnight, when the watchman comes around on his hourly round.

"Last night, the watchman came around at 12:02 a.m. and wished me good night. I emptied my pipe and returned to my room at 12:04 a.m.. I was in bed a minute later."

"Did anyone come out on the veranda when you were there between 11:30 p.m. and 12:04 a.m.?"

"Yes. I heard at least three people, but I don't know who they were. I only know that Sabir was not among them."

"How can you be sure of that?"

"His door is next to mine. I would know if it opened or closed. As it is closest to me, that sound is far louder than the sounds from other doors. Also, Sabir is a man of regular habits. He hits the sack between 10:30 p.m and 10:45 p.m., and is always fast asleep by 11:00 p.m."

"Okay. Did you hear or see anything after midnight? After you returned to your room?"

"I heard the sounds of veranda doors twice, but I can't tell you the times. I suspect it must have been MM's veranda door, as I don't think I would hear the doors beyond hers. I sleep with my windows closed, you see."

"When do you think you fell asleep? I know it's difficult to pin-point."

"I must have dozed off by 12:15 a.m. or so."

"That's useful, thank you. Prima facie, it looks like Mrs. Markaan was in the building till a little after midnight, and might have opened her door twice between 12:05 a.m. and 12:15 a.m. During one of those times – probably on the second occasion – she might have left the building."

Dr. Korda nodded. "If she wanted to avoid everyone, she would have waited for me to return to my room and for the guard to come around at midnight. The coast would have been clear thereafter."

"Is there anything else that might be relevant? Any unusual conversation, gesture, anything?"

"Nothing. I've been thinking about it, but I can think of none."

"How was Mrs. Markaan on Sunday? Anything out of the ordinary?"

Dr. Korda shook his head.

"I believe she went out on Sunday morning. Is that right?"

"Yes. She left at about half-past-nine and returned about two hours later – a little before you and Mr. Sikka arrived."

"Any idea what she went out for? On a Sunday?"

"No idea."

"Can you think of any reason for Mrs. Markaan to go out alone after midnight?"

The corners of Dr. Korda's melancholy mouth drooped further as he shook his head.

"What do the bracelet and the ring have to do with this?" Athreya asked.

Dr. Korda shook his head again, choosing not to speak.

"The legend of Naaz Tapu," Athreya continued. "Do you think there's anything to it?"

In response, Dr. Korda dipped his hand down his neck into his robe. When it came out, it was holding a thin silver chain with a silver cross hanging from it.

"I believe in God, Mr. Athreya," he said, shifting uneasily in his chair. "And in Satan's existence. It is fashionable to say that one doesn't believe in the supernatural. I follow history for a living, and I am interested in all kinds of tales from the past. A historian ignores myths and legends at his own peril.

"One shouldn't speak ill of the dead, but I do believe that MM was unwise in defying a local myth. That too in the middle of the night when God's light is below the horizon."

"You remember the question she asked me on the lawn on Sunday?" Athreya asked, changing the topic. "About an expert to investigate financial irregularities?"

"Yes, I do," Dr. Korda replied gravely.

"Why do you think she asked that question?"

"Frankly, I don't know."

"She chose to ask it openly—in front of everyone."

"Which I thought was in bad taste. It was as if she was accusing one of us of financial misconduct."

"Do you think she was?"

"What can I say, Mr. Athreya? The obvious candidate is Adhira. That's what MM implied. Adhira is the one who manages the money and keeps the accounts. Unless otherwise specified, MM was accusing Adhira. That much was clear to all of us."

"Do you think there has been any misappropriation, Dr. Korda?"

"No!" The reply was emphatic. "One can't go around insinuating without a proper basis. What evidence did MM have?"

"We don't know that, do we?" Athreya answered smoothly. "Whatever knowledge she had, perished with her. Do you think we should have the books examined by an accountant?"

Dr. Korda's face darkened further in suppressed anger. He didn't reply for a few seconds. When he eventually did, it was in a guarded fashion.

"That's, of course, the JBF's prerogative. But that would be a blow to Adhira. It would be tantamount to accusing her. We must be careful in what we do, and we must be sure that we have a sound basis for whatever we do."

"Doesn't anyone else get involved with the accounts? Usually, there are at least two people involved in approving financial transactions."

"MM was the other, and I get involved in transactions above a certain threshold."

"Do you see the accounts every month?"

Dr. Korda shifted in his chair again.

"I don't inspect the accounts regularly. But as the JBF's observer here, I am involved in the requests for funds that we send to the JBF on the first day of every month. Adhira submits the draft fund request to me, and I send the final request to the JBF."

"I assume you verify that the amount requested is based on the actual expenses incurred the previous month?"

"Yes." Dr. Korda's face was wooden.

"Then, you would have to look at the monthly accounts too, wouldn't you? To verify that the amount requested is the same as the expenses incurred."

"Yes. But I look at only the total expenses."

"I further assume that you use the same figure in the final request that you send to the JBF. Right?"

"Yes."

"Does anyone cross check that, Dr. Korda? Just in case you may make a mistake?"

"No."

"Why not?"

"There is no need. Everything is fairly straightforward."

"And the JBF transfers the requested amount the same day?"

"Usually. The next day at the latest."

"One last thing – you had said that you shot a brief video clip of the bracelet. Can you send it to me?"

"Certainly. WhatsApp? What's your number?"

Athreya gave it to him, and the archaeologist sent him the video.

"Thank you, Dr. Korda." Athreya smiled amiably once he received the clip. "Is there anything else you think I ought to know?"

"No." The tall man rose to his full height.

"If you remember anything, please tell me. Any time of the day or night."

Dr. Korda inclined his head in acquiescence and turned to go.

"I will send Sabir in."

* * *

Sabir was back to his usual genial, polite self when he came in to talk to Athreya. The first matter he brought up was Mrs. Markaan's next of kin.

"We don't seem to have that information," he said. "Nazreen says there was a nephew by the name Sandeep in Patna. She has heard MM mention him. You know that she was MM's student in college, don't you? She is the only one here who has worked with MM previously."

"I knew that Mrs. Markaan hand-picked everyone here," Athreya said with surprise. "I had assumed some of them would have been picked based on prior work done together. Isn't that what most of us do? If I find that I work well with someone, I'd like to work with them again. There is often an element of mutual trust between us. I hadn't realised that she had picked all strangers with the exception of Nazreen."

Sabir shrugged and smiled disarmingly.

"Perhaps," he said pleasantly, "the people who had worked with her earlier were not keen to repeat it."

"But Nazreen did," Athreya countered.

"That's probably for a reason. Nazreen knows this part of the world like the back of her hand. She focusses on this area and its history, to the exclusion of everything else. She wouldn't want to be left out of any project that involves Bundelkhand."

"Really? Can she make a career out of the history of one small part of India?"

"Well, it's not all that small, you know. It's one-third the size of Punjab. But I take your point. The fact is that Nazreen doesn't need to build a career. I don't know details, but I'm sure she is pretty well off. You can make out, can't you? She has only two interests in life – Bundelkhand and music."

Athreya blinked involuntarily. Music? That had been Naazneen's primary interest, too.

"Anyway, that's not what you wanted to talk about, I guess," Sabir went on cheerfully. "Should I tell you about my movements last evening? There is nothing much to tell, though."

"Please do."

Sabir repeated what Dr. Korda had said about dinner and the post-dinner stroll on the lawn. The only difference was the time when Sabir had retired. While Dr. Korda had said that Sabir had retired at 10:30 p.m., Sabir said that he had retired ten minutes earlier.

"I went to my room at 10:20 p.m. and went to bed. I read in bed for fifteen minutes, and switched off my light at 10:40 p.m. I must have fallen asleep very soon thereafter."

Sabir said that he was a sound sleeper and had heard nothing after he went to bed – neither the sound of doors nor the regular beat of the watchman's stick as he went around the building every hour.

"I left for the dig at 8:30 a.m. this morning as I always do. Of course, I knew that MM hadn't come to breakfast yet, but I didn't give it much thought. It was only a couple of hours later that I realised the seriousness of it."

When Athreya spoke about the Naaz Tapu legend, Sabir dismissed it out of hand.

"A pile of nonsense," he snorted. "Complete bunk, in my view. Every place with history – *every single place* – has a ghost story or two. As a people, we just love the supernatural. And to this day, we are suckers for it. It's in our blood. The bracelet is just another archaeological find. It's not some religious relic with some obscure, esoteric history. It's a great pity we've lost it."

To Athreya's question regarding the project accounts, Sabir said that he was not involved with it at all. That was something MM, Dr. Korda and Adhira handled between themselves. Like Dr. Korda, Sabir, too, thought that Mrs. Markaan's question about investigating financial misappropriation had been in bad taste.

"My heart went out to Adhira," he said. "But she took it very maturely. Fine girl, Adhira," he finished. "A thorough professional.

"By the way, she wanted to know if she could come in next. If it's okay with you, she and Pratap will switch slots. She has work to finish and can't start on it till she's had her conversation with you."

"Sure. Please send her in."

* * *

As soon as Adhira came in, she took control of the discussion. Athreya gladly let her. In his experience, people tended to say a lot more when they were speaking of their own volition.

"One of the first things you would be looking for is motive," she began with surprising intensity. "After MM's deplorable behaviour on the lawn on Sunday, it is clear that if one person had a very visible motive to get rid of her, it was me. She all but accused me of embezzlement that day. It's therefore important that we deal with that before we speak of anything else."

"I agree," Athreya said. "Go right ahead. I'm listening."

"The first thing I want you to know is this: from before this project began, I have been telling Dr. Korda and Mr. Dunne that I am *not* the right person to be the project accountant. Basically, I am not a finance or an accounting person. I am an *administrator*. I am a person who organises things – I get things done. I don't keep silly books.

"Yes, while at the JBF, I've helped out on occasion with the accounts. But that's *always* been under the supervision of a chartered accountant. If I'm told what accounting entries to pass, I can do that. If I am told to reconcile two stacks of numbers, I can do that too. But to expect me to *completely manage* the accounts of a project that spends tens of crores is unfair. I am not equipped to do that. I am not qualified for it.

"I've done my B.Com. but I hardly paid attention in class. Who did? I studied for exams and cleared them, but I don't understand accounting well. I have *absolutely* no interest in becoming an accountant. What I want to be is an event manager. I am good at organising things, Mr. Athreya! Point out a flaw in how things are organised at the dig or at the base, and I'll willingly own up to it. But, don't blame me if the accounts don't tally."

"You've said all this to Mrs. Markaan and Dr. Korda?' Athreya asked.

"Dozens of times! And to Mr. Dunne, too. But they just postpone the issue."

"Do you expect the project accounts to have errors?"

"Expect?' she echoed. "That's probably putting it rather strongly. Is it likely that I've made mistakes? Yes. I've been saying that for ages. Mr. Athreya, I have nobody here to guide me; nobody to show me the right way of recording certain transactions. I just muddle along the best I can.

"All MM did was find fault with me. She was not like Dr. Baig – he takes the time and effort to guide his juniors. But she would just look down her haughty nose from her high horse and insult me. And then—" She swallowed hard. "And then, she had the gall to accuse me of stealing in front of everyone!"

Adhira stopped speaking, her breast heaving. It had been a passionate speech. Seeing Athreya watching her silently and waiting for her to continue, she seemed to realise that she may have gone overboard.

"I know I mustn't say such things, now that MM is dead," she said in a more measured voice. "But what can I do, Mr. Athreya? Is this fair? It was one thing when all I had to deal with was a nasty boss. But now it's different – I am probably a prime suspect because everyone knows I had a motive.

"I'll freely admit that working here will be easier now. I hope – fervently – that Dr. Baig takes her place. That's how it should have been in the first place. Did you know that Dr. Baig was slated to be the director? MM was nowhere in the picture. All of a sudden, she comes out of the blue and takes the position. Dr. Baig was livid, but thankfully, he agreed to join as the second-in-command."

She stopped speaking and sat back. Athreya gazed back at her. She might or might not be the prime suspect for murder, but she was a good candidate for another role – the author of the anonymous letters. When it became clear that Adhira had said what she had set out to say, he took over.

"I have a question about the fund request that goes to the JBF every month," he said. "I believe you prepare the draft request and give it to Dr. Korda. He then converts it to the final request and sends to the JBF. Is that right?"

"Yes, sir."

"The question I had was this: do you check what amount Dr. Korda enters in his final request? Say, the amount in your draft request is one crore. Do you check that the final request prepared by Dr. Korda is for one crore?"

"No, sir. How can I do that? He is my supervising officer."

"Another question," Athreya went on. "When the money comes in from the JBF, do you check the amount against the draft request you had prepared?"

"Yes, sir. I do. The amount is split into two parts, which come into two different bank accounts – one in Delhi and the other in Jhansi. I total them up and check it against the draft request I had prepared."

"Have they always tallied?"

"Oh, yes." She gave a wry smile. "I may not be a qualified accountant, Mr. Athreya, but I'm not *that* dumb."

"Who decides how much money should go into which bank account?"

"Dr. Korda. He states that in his final request."

Athreya's thoughts were whirling. Here was an apparent gap! What if Dr. Korda was maintaining a *third* bank account without Adhira's knowledge? What if he added twenty lakhs to Adhira's draft request of one crore, and asked for that additional twenty lakhs to be credited to the third account? Adhira would be none the wiser. She would still get her one crore, split between her two bank accounts.

"Let's talk about last night," he said, changing the topic. "Tell me everything you saw and heard after dinner. And everything you did. Between dinner and falling asleep."

Her account tallied with Dr. Korda's, except that she was not sure when Sabir had retired. She confirmed that she and Mithali were strolling on the lawn when Mrs. Markaan had opened her door briefly and looked out.

"What time was that?" Athreya asked.

"About eleven o'clock." Adhira said.

"Do you remember what she was wearing?"

"Who? MM?"

"Yes."

"The loose salwar kameez set she had been wearing much of

the day. It was dark green."

"Hadn't she changed into her nightclothes?" Athreya asked.

"Hey!" She sat up. "You know what, MM usually changed into her nightie as soon as she returned to her room. She must have retired by 10:30 p.m. or 10:40 p.m. But she hadn't changed into her nightie by 11:00 p.m. I wonder why?"

"Why did she open her door? Do you know?"

"Nope." Adhira shook her head. "She just opened it and looked out for a few seconds without coming out. Then closed it."

"Are you sure that it was her?" Athreya asked casually.

"Who else could it be? It was her door, alright."

"What happened after that?"

"Nothing much. Mithali and I walked around for half an hour, and I went to my room and to bed."

"What time did you go to bed?"

"11:35 p.m."

"What happened thereafter? Did you hear or see anything?"

"I was lying awake in bed, thinking of what MM had insinuated. I guess I was upset. I usually fall asleep quickly, and I sleep pretty soundly. But what MM had said was rankling last night. It must have been 12:30 a.m. before I fell asleep."

"You were lying awake in bed for an hour between 11.35 p.m. and 12.30 a.m. Did you hear anything?"

"Oh, heaps! I heard the security guard doing his round at midnight. He strikes his stick on the ground as he goes, you know. Not hard, but enough for you to hear. Then, a little after 12:15 a.m., I heard Mithali's door open, and I saw her pass my window."

"How sure are you of the time?"

"I had just looked at my clock a minute earlier. It had said 12:15 a.m."

"Which way was Mithali going?"

"From right to left. Away from her room. She actually stopped at the left edge of my window."

"Was it open?"

Adhira nodded and went on.

"She returned to her room a couple of minutes later and closed her door. Then, two minutes later, I heard it open again. This time, I didn't see her or Ulhas. After ten more minutes, I heard it close again."

"Okay," Athreya nodded. "What then?"

"Nothing. I think I must have fallen asleep."

"Did you go out to the veranda at all?"

"Nope. Not even once."

CHAPTER 11

Nazreen's interview turned out to be a quick and efficient affair, in which she spoke succinctly and only to the extent required. The entire time, she watched Athreya solemnly with her tranquil grey eyes. Athreya found himself getting accustomed to the gaze that he had initially found unsettling.

She confirmed what the others had said about the post-dinner stroll in the quadrangle, and said that she had been the last to retire for the night. Adhira and Mithali had retired around 11:30 pm, and they had been followed five minutes later by Pratap and Ulhas. Nazreen herself had retired a few minutes before midnight, and had been awake in her room till 12:30 am.

"I heard sounds of doors twelve times between midnight and 12:30 am," she said with precision. "And I saw someone with a torch going toward the river."

"From where did you see that?" Athreya asked.

"My window, which I always keep open. I love nature and the night. Would you like to take down the details?" she asked before Athreya could suggest that she narrate what she saw and heard.

Athreya drew a sheet of paper towards himself and nodded.

"I saw the torch at 12:15 am," she began. "I looked at my clock as soon as I saw it. Someone was shining it and walking away from the building. He or she was about a hundred feet from the veranda when I first saw the light. I could see it for two minutes as it drifted away in the darkness. At 12:18 am, I lost sight of it.

"I heard the sounds of doors twelve times – three times before I saw the torch and nine times after. All the three sounds that came before I saw the torch were from the left. The first one was about five minutes after the security guard passed."

"That would make it about 12:08 am, I presume?"

"Yes. Judging by the loudness, I believe it was Markaan Sahiba's door. I then heard the same door again three minutes later."

"12:11 am," Athreya muttered as he wrote. "Mrs. Markaan."

"A minute later, I heard another door from the left. This door was closer."

"Pratap's?"

Nazreen nodded.

"12:14 – Pratap," Athreya wrote down on his paper.

"That's what made me get out of bed and go to the window. That's when I saw the torch."

"Any idea who the person with the torch could have been?"

"I couldn't make out in the darkness, but from all that we have gathered so far, it might have been Markaan Sahiba. But I don't know that for a fact."

"Okay. You said that you watched the torch till 12:18 am. What happened after that? Did you remain at your window?"

"Yes, I stood at my window, watching and listening. I heard four door sounds in the next five minutes – one from the left, and three from the right. The one from the left was Markaan Sahiba's door, and the ones from the right were Mithali's."

"That was followed by a five-minute gap, after which I heard five more sounds – Markaan Sahiba's door and Pratap's door in quick succession, within seconds of each other. Then Markaan Sahiba's door sounded again within a minute, and yet again after two more minutes. And the last was Mithali's door a minute later. Twelve door sounds in all."

"Did anyone pass your window during this time?"

"No. I stayed at the window for another five minutes, but all was silent. I returned to bed."

"Your testimony is very precise, Nazreen." Athreya commented.

"I have been taught to watch and listen, Athreya Sahib. And to speak only when required."

"A remarkably detailed account, I must say. It would be of much value if I can be sure of its accuracy."

"It's accurate, Athreya Sahib. You may depend on it. Of course, you have only my word for it."

"Did you go out to the veranda at all, Nazreen?"

"No."

"You heard the doors that are close to your room. All the ones you heard are one or two doors away from you. Would you have heard if Dr. Korda or Dr. Baig had opened their doors?"

"My hearing is keener than the average person's, but I don't think I would have heard the doors beyond Markaan Sahiba's."

"Okay. You remember what Mrs. Markaan had said on the lawn yesterday afternoon?"

Nazreen nodded silently.

"Why did she do that?" Athreya asked.

"Because it was her nature, Athreya Sahib. She liked to keep people insecure. She liked to remind them that she had a hold on them. She wanted to be the puppeteer."

"Did she have any hold on you?"

Nazreen shook her head.

"You told me earlier that you too disliked her. But you didn't tell me why."

"Let the past remain the past, huzoor. I am not keen on reviving it."

"Is it something to do with stealing credit for something you had done?"

"You seem to have heard it. Then, why ask?"

"I wanted some details."

Nazreen shook her head. All the time, her unperturbed gaze held Athreya's.

"Whatever Markaan Sahiba did to me has no bearing on the present. It would suffice for you to know that her deceitfulness was not sufficient motive for me to kill her."

"I didn't suggest that, Nazreen."

"I know." Her half-smile widened a trifle. "I wasn't born yesterday, huzoor."

"If you disliked her, why did you agree to work with her?"

"Because the dig is at my doorstep. I would be interested in any project that explores the history of this place."

"You told me that Mrs. Markaan was killed because she went to Naaz Tapu and excavated at the hunting lodge. Do you still believe that?"

Nazreen nodded in silence.

"Have you told anyone that she had been exploring the islet and excavating the hunting lodge?"

Nazreen shook her head.

"About the legend of Naaz Tapu," Athreya asked. "What can you tell me?"

"A lot more than Habib Mian told you, Athreya Sahib. But not now. It is not relevant. Let the past remain the past."

"With all respect, Nazreen, let me be the judge of that."

"No, huzoor. You are an outsider – which is both good and bad. Until I get to know you better, I will not speak of certain matters. If you press me, you will meet only silence. But be assured that when I do speak, I speak the truth."

"Then tell me this: are there other forces at work here that I am not aware of?"

"Likely. I don't know what you are aware of and what you aren't."

"Have you heard about the Bronze Runners?"

Nazreen nodded solemnly.

"What can you tell me about them?"

"Not much. They are around. I sense their presence here."

"Here at this project?" Athreya asked.

Nazreen nodded.

"Is it something to do with the bracelet?"

"I don't know. I honestly don't. I would like to find out."

"Will you tell me if you learn of anything in that regard?"

"I will."

"Where is your house, Nazreen? Where do your people live?"

"It's not relevant. Is there anything else, huzoor?"

She made as if to rise. The interview was over.

"Only this, Nazreen. If there is anything you think I need to know, please come to me. At any time of the day or night."

She inclined her head with enviable grace as she rose.

"Khuda hafiz."

* * *

Athreya was expecting Pratap, instead Madhav walked in.

"Sorry to jump the queue, sir," he said with an apologetic smile. "But I have to get back to Jhansi while the others don't. I hope you don't mind if I finish my discussion a little ahead of schedule."

"Not at all," Athreya replied. "Please sit down." He waited for Madhav to settle in his chair before continuing. "What brought you to the base?"

"Why, MM's death, of course."

"Of course. I was thinking about your feelings that made you come here. You had made it quite clear this morning that there was little love lost between you two."

"Yes, but still … I had worked with her for a few months, you know."

"How did you feel when you heard about her death?"

"Honestly, sir, I can't say that I was terribly sorry. But it creeps up on you. After a while, you get upset with yourself for not feeling the grief that you ought to. I guess the mind then manufactures something akin to regret. That's what brought me here."

"Were you surprised by her death?"

"Surprised, sir?" he asked incredulously. "Shocked!"

"Who told you about her death?"

"Adhira. She called me."

"When?"

"At about five o'clock or so. I came immediately."

"Did you see Mrs. Markaan's body?"

"Yes and no. I was here when the police brought her from the islet, but she was fully covered. I was a ways away."

"Then, you would know about the bracelet and the ring. What did you think about them?"

"I was surprised. I hadn't known about them. She had kept the find a secret. I didn't even know she was exploring the islet."

"Was she?" Athreya asked, trying to sound casual.

Only Nazreen knew about Mrs. Markaan excavating the islet, and she hadn't spoken to anyone about it. How had Madhav known?

"Wasn't she?" Madhav countered. "I might be mistaken, but I thought I heard someone mention it."

"Who? I would like to know more about it. It may be pertinent to the investigation."

Madhav frowned for a few moments and then shook his head.

"Can't remember right now," he said. "Everyone was talking in the lounge. I'm not sure who said it. I'll tell you if I remember."

"Please do." Athreya smiled benignly and went on. "What do

you think of the Naaz Tapu legend?"

"I know we are all scientists here," Madhav said cautiously, "but it's still probably a good idea to not cross local myths. I've never been keen on haunted places, you know. Anyway, what's there in that islet other than trees and some ruins?"

"You just said that Mrs. Markaan found the bracelet there."

"No, no," Madhav said. "That's what I *heard* someone say. I myself have no clue where MM actually found the bracelet."

"I'm sure you've heard all the details about last night. What do you think?"

Madhav shrugged his shoulders and turned his palms upward in an expression of puzzlement.

"It makes no sense, Mr. Athreya," he said in a low voice. "Why would MM want to go to the islet in the middle of the night? Alone? Her death is a complete puzzle. Yes, one could say that the legend of the islet lived up to its reputation. But won't that be tantamount to accepting that ghosts exist? On the other hand, if it had nothing to do with Bhola and his monster of a dog, it is murder."

"Exactly. Any thoughts?"

"Me?" Madhav laughed. "I'm as clueless as the next person."

"Okay. As a matter of routine, we are asking where everyone was last night. Will you tell me about your movements?"

"Certainly." He frowned for a second. "I had dinner with a couple of friends and we hung about till about ten o'clock. After that, I returned home." He grinned suddenly. "Home now is a single room, where I stay as a paying guest with an elderly couple. My room has its own entrance from the outside, so that I don't have to disturb them when I come and go."

"Can I have your contact information, and that of the friends you had dinner with?"

"Sure."

He pulled out a pen and wrote on a sheet of paper Athreya pushed forward.

"I am not sure if you know," Madhav said when he finished writing, "but MM was pretty worried about antique thieves. Apparently, there is a network of them operating all over the place. She had become quite jumpy, in my view."

"Did she speak to you about it?"

"Yes. She wanted to know if I had heard about them."

"Had you?"

Madhav shook his head.

"She seemed to believe that the network had an eye on this project, too. That's probably why she concealed that fact that she had found the bracelet and the ring – she didn't want the thieves to get a whiff of it." He flashed a wry smile. "You know, I think she might have even suspected *me* of being a part of the network."

"Why do you say that?"

"Because of the way she interrogated me and asked about my whereabouts. I didn't take very kindly to it and a sort of friction developed between us. That's what eventually led to her firing me."

"Is that the reason she gave when she fired you?"

"No, but I'm sure that was a part of it. What she did tell me was that I was too inquisitive about others' work, and that I was doing things that were prohibited by the NDA."

His voice dropped a notch as he went on.

"I must confess that I was foolish at times, Mr. Athreya. She overheard me talking about the project over my phone to a friend – an outsider. That is expressly prohibited by the NDA and can invite instant dismissal. She nailed me with that and fired me."

"Thank you for being candid, Madhav," Athreya said. "I appreciate that. Is there anything else you can tell me?"

"'Nothing comes to mind." He flashed a quick smile and rose. "But if I do think of something, I'll let you know."

* * *

The initial part of the discussion with Pratap yielded little by way of fresh information. He didn't remember the precise time when he had returned to his room from the lawn. Nor did he know when he went to bed. All he could say was that he must have retired around 11:30 p.m. and had fallen asleep soon after. He had not been awake at midnight to hear the watchman's rhythmic beat with his stick.

"Did you go out to the veranda after you returned to your room?" Athreya asked.

"No, I was pretty tipsy, you know," he said offhandedly. But his eyes were wary. "After all, it was a Sunday night. I went to bed straight away. I didn't hear or see anything."

"What if I told you that someone heard your veranda door open and close?"

"*My* door?" Pratap exclaimed in indignation. "How did this person know that it was *my* door? It doesn't have bells on it to make it sound any different from the other doors. It could have been *any* door."

"The person is quite sure of it."

"Then he or she is mistaken," Pratap declared. But the guarded look in his eyes didn't go away. "Honestly, you should verify such random claims, Mr. Athreya."

"That's exactly what I am doing, Pratap. Who better to ask than you? Do you suggest that I ask someone else about your door?"

"Oh, okay. I guess not." Pratap seemed to relax slightly. "Did this person see me?"

"No."

"Then?" Pratap challenged with a hint of a smirk. "Really, Mr. Athreya …" He left it hanging.

"Did you know Mrs. Markaan well?"

"I guess so." Pratap looked at his hands as he spoke. "I guess she spoke with me more than she did with the others. She seemed to have taken a liking for me from the beginning."

"Did you know her from before?"

"Yes, to some extent. We met at two or three conferences where both of us were presenting papers. We got talking. She was a knowledgeable lady, you know. Some of the stuff in her papers was very interesting. Quite varied, too. I was surprised at the breadth of topics she covered. I've been following her publications for couple of years now."

"All of it was her own work, I presume?"

"I think so." Pratap frowned in confusion at Athreya. "Why that doubt?"

"Well, one hears of people who take the work done by their juniors and students and pass it off as their own. I suppose Mrs. Markaan was not one such person."

"I think not," Pratap said sharply.

Athreya could see that thoughts were churning in the younger man's mind. Athreya's statement seemed to have triggered something. He let the silence grow.

"It's interesting that you say that," Pratap mused aloud at length. "In some areas, I found her depth of knowledge to be a *little* less than what I had expected. But then, nobody has deep knowledge in every area."

"How did you feel when you learnt of Mrs. Markaan's death?" Athreya asked.

"Sad," Pratap replied immediately. "I was fond of the old lady, you know. She was kind to me. I'm not a very instinctive archaeologist, Mr. Athreya. I'm not like Nazreen or Dr. Baig. I need guidance. MM showed patience with me and taught me things. I'll miss her."

"Would it be fair to say that you were closer to her than the others?"

"Maybe." Pratap shrugged. "She was fond of Mithali too."

"Did Mrs. Markaan ever speak to you about her family or relatives? We need to inform her next of kin."

Pratap shook his head.

"What do you think of the Naaz Tapu legend?" Athreya asked.

Pratap licked his lips unconsciously.

"It's a dark place, Mr. Athreya," he said in a small voice. "I've never been there, and I don't want to go there. Why meddle with things you don't understand? Was MM's death connected to the legend? I don't know. I hope it wasn't."

"If it wasn't," Athreya said in a measured manner, "it must be murder. Murder by another human being."

Pratap paled. He clasped his hands together, perhaps to keep them from shaking.

"I realise that, Mr. Athreya. Either way, it's bad. That's why I've decided to leave this project as soon as I am allowed to."

* * *

By the time Athreya began the conversation with Mithali and Ulhas, he was tired. At the end of a long, taxing day, the repetitive interviews were getting to him. So, when Mithali and Ulhas walked in together, he didn't object to a joint discussion. In any case, they would have thought through what they were going to say and agreed. All Athreya really wanted to talk about was the repeated opening and closing of their veranda door. The rest of it had been discussed and verified multiple times. He steered the discussion in the direction he wanted.

"Adhira told me about what she said to you," Mithali said of her own volition when the discussion got to the veranda door. "I went out on the veranda because I saw a light behind the building. I first saw it from my window. It looked as if someone was going down to the river with a torch."

"What time was this?" Athreya asked.

"I don't know exactly. But it must have been around 12:15. Is that right, Ulhas?"

"Give or take a couple of minutes," Ulhas confirmed, unconsciously clenching and unclenching his large hands. "I didn't see the time."

"I went out, took a few steps, and stopped," Mithali continued. "It occurred to me that it might not be safe to go alone to the river in the dark. So, I watched silently from where I was. After a couple of minutes, when I could no longer see the light, I returned to our room and told Ulhas."

"When she told me," Ulhas added, "I decided to take a look myself. I went out and hung around on the veranda for ten minutes or so, in case the light appeared again. With all this talk about antique thefts, I thought it was worthwhile keeping an eye out. We switched off our room light so that whoever was behind the building couldn't see us."

"Did you see the light again?" Athreya asked.

"No."

"What time did you return to your room?"

"Just short of 12:30 am. I looked at the clock, I remember."

"And after that?"

"We went to sleep."

"When you were out in the veranda," Athreya asked, "did you see anyone else?"

"No." Ulhas turned to his wife who shook her head. "No, we didn't."

"Are you sure? From the evidence I've gathered so far, I think you should have seen *someone*."

"No, sir. We didn't see anyone."

For the next ten minutes, Athreya went over what they had said and confirmed his understanding. He also asked them about what they thought of the Naaz Tapu legend. Mithali was positively scared and spoke animatedly about it. Ulhas thought that it was best to leave such things alone. No, neither of them had never been to the islet, and had no plan of ever doing so. It was an eminently avoidable place.

Did they have any possible explanation for Mrs. Markaan's strange behaviour? No. Had they been fond of the old lady? Not particularly, but after having worked with her for a few months, you did feel sorry for her and the way she had died.

All the while he was talking to the couple, something was gnawing at the back of Athreya's mind. It had bothered him on Sunday, too. For some reason, he was a little puzzled about Mithali's physical movements – the way she moved her limbs, walked and went about doing things. It seemed to him that they were on the slower side. Her arm movements, the way she got up from her chair, the speed at which she walked, her gait, everything was *just a fraction* slower than he would have expected.

What that meant, he had no idea.

CHAPTER 12

The next morning found Athreya at the riverside after breakfast. With him was Inspector Bhupinder. In addition to viewing the riverside and the islet in daylight, they wanted to go out of earshot of the base before exchanging notes from their respective interviews of the previous evening.

"We've learnt nothing new from either the staff of the base or the workers employed at the dig," Bhupinder began after Athreya had briefed him on the interviews of the residents of the base. "There are three kitchen workers who live at the base. They cook, serve food, wash utensils, purchase provisions and food. These three – all men – sleep in the dining room.

"There are two others who clean and wash. They stay with the excavation workers employed at the dig. Apart from them, two local ladies and a gardener come in the morning and leave in the evening.

"The three kitchen workers wound up the kitchen at about 11 o'clock on Sunday night and went to sleep. They heard or saw nothing during the night. They woke up at around 5:30 am."

"They couldn't have gone out of the building without the security guard seeing them, I suppose?" Athreya asked.

"That's right. The workers employed at the dig stay in a dormitory type of arrangement nearby. That building has two doors – one in the front and the other at the rear. Both the doors were locked and bolted from the inside and were not opened during the night."

"How can they be sure?"

"The bolt of the front door screeches. Loud enough to wake the sleepers. The rear door is a little warped and doesn't open or close easily. It needs to be kicked or banged to close properly."

"You verified that yourself?"

"Yes, sir. I'm sure none of the workers could have left or entered the building after it was locked. And all the workers were accounted for during the night. The supervisor does an informal roll call every night when they lock the doors."

"That leaves them out. Were you able to speak to anyone who had worked with Mrs. Markaan last week? Did they go to the islet?"

"Not yet. A reticent lot, these buggers are. They wouldn't tell me who went to the islet with Mrs. Markaan. We'll get to it, sir. Don't worry.

"Coming to Mrs. Markaan's room, we found a number of fingerprints. Most of them, as expected, are Mrs. Markaan's. But there are few others too – Adhira, Nazreen, Pratap, Ulhas and the maid's."

Athreya stopped walking and turned to Bhupinder.

"Pratap and Ulhas?" he asked.

"Yes, sir." The inspector smiled grimly. "I thought you would find it interesting. What is even more curious is that they seem to be *fresh* prints."

"Let me guess, Bhupinder. You found some of them *over* Mrs. Markaan's and the maid's prints, didn't you?"

"Yes, sir."

"Did you also find one of Ulhas's prints over Pratap's?"

Bhupinder's eyebrows rose.

"How did you know?" he asked.

"It seemed likely after yesterday's testimony. Adhira said that she had opened the cupboard, and Nazreen had touched the desk and some things that were on it. But what I am very interested in is this: whose prints did you find on the suitcase?"

"Pratap's."

"And Ulhas's prints? Where were they?"

"On the desk and the back of the chair that was at the desk."

Athreya nodded.

"It begins to make sense'" he said. "The veranda door must have had all their prints, I suppose? Nazreen's and Adhira's prints must have been on the top."

Bhupinder nodded. "We should confront Pratap and Ulhas, sir."

"Not publicly, Bhupinder," Athreya said in a low voice. "Not yet, at least. I don't want to back them into a corner where they become useless to us. I don't think these prints are directly related to Mrs. Markaan's murder. They came about fortuitously due to her unexpected absence. We need to use them to obtain leads to the actual murder, if possible. I'll talk to them privately."

"Okay," Bhupinder nodded. "I'll leave them to you. Here are some more things we found apart from the fingerprints. Firstly, Mrs. Markaan's mobile phone seems to be missing. It was nowhere in the room. We already knew that it was not on her body. Calls to it are not going through – it's not reachable."

"Have you requisitioned her call history?"

"Yes, I have. I hope to get it today or tomorrow. Now, here is something that could be interesting. We opened the deceased's suitcase without moving it. Clothes and papers were arranged neatly in it. Among them, we found a rectangular empty space where something had been kept.

"On the clothes at the bottom of the empty space was a rectangular impression one foot long and nine inches wide. A box of up to six inches in height could have been kept there. We found nothing in the room that matches the empty space and the impression. Whatever it was, it is gone now."

"The suitcase's lock … is it a number lock?"

"Yes!" The inspector flashed Athreya a surprised glance. "Now, the rubber raft at the islet, we found no useable fingerprints. Overnight dew erased whatever prints there were."

"Is the raft still in the same place, Bhupinder?"

"Yes, sir."

"When you move it, please do so carefully. Lift it and move it away. Don't drag it."

"Okay. Why?"

"I want to know if there is anything under the raft – a piece of evidence or even a mark on the rock ledge."

"Why didn't I think of that?" The inspector seemed cross with himself.

"Because you have been very busy, Bhupinder. Meanwhile, I have had the time to dream and let my imagination wander. Nothing may be found under the raft, but it's worth checking. Anything else?"

"One last thing. I've initiated an inquiry in Patna, where Mrs. Markaan is from. I'm trying to trace her next of kin."

"Good, Bhupinder. You have covered a lot of ground. Did you pass on my message to your police doctor?"

"Yes, sir. We'll have the answer tomorrow once he completes the post mortem."

"Excellent. I'll see you later. Someone is waiting to talk to me alone. Call me if you learn anything in Jhansi."

* * *

Athreya sauntered aimlessly by the riverside as the inspector strode back to the base. Five minutes later, as Athreya was passing by some tall foliage, a slim figure materialised beside him.

"Adaab, Athreya Sahib," Nazreen greeted.

She was wearing a pale blue kameez over a dark blue churidar. Except for the colours, her outfit was the same as the previous two days.

"Adaab," Athreya replied. "Reluctant to speak in front of the inspector, Nazreen?"

"I prefer to talk to you and keep my interaction with the inspector and other locals to a minimum. I have something to report to you, but it isn't much."

"I'd like to hear it. But first, I have a question about what you told me yesterday. It's about the twelve sounds you heard from the veranda."

"The door sounds?"

"Yes. I wanted to confirm that you are absolutely sure of what you heard."

"I'm sure, huzoor."

"You are also certain about which doors opened when? Mrs. Markaan's, Pratap's and Mithali's? Are you certain that you identified them correctly?"

"Yes. You can depend on it."

"Thank you. Now, what is it you wanted to tell me?"

"I spoke to the two workers who went to Naaz Tapu with Markaan Sahiba. Over the past two weeks, they excavated at the hunting lodge for five half-days. And as far as they know, nothing was found there."

"Nothing at all?"

Nazreen shook her head.

"But I did learn something interesting," she went on. "On each of those five days when they were digging, Markaan Sahiba disappeared for one to two hours. She seemed to have wandered about the islet."

"It's a very dense jungle, Nazreen," Athreya whispered. "I lost my sense of direction very quickly. How did she navigate alone?"

"With a signal transmitter and a corresponding receiver. The transmitter is at the hunting lodge, and the receiver was with her. All she had to do was to move in the direction where the signal was coming from, and she would return to the lodge. It's common practice in jungles."

"Does that mean that Mrs. Markaan found the bracelet and the ring elsewhere on the islet? Somewhere deeper?"

"That's what I fear."

"*Fear*?" Athreya asked. "Why?"

"The deeper one goes into Naaz Tapu, the greater the peril."

"It's a small islet, Nazreen."

Nazreen turned her unsettling gaze on Athreya.

"It's large enough to hide its secrets from the world, Athreya Sahib. There are different ways to reckon size."

"You know what this means, don't you?"

Nazreen gazed silently at him.

"This means that I will have to go deeper into the islet," he said. She nodded.

"Will you come with me, Nazreen?"

"I will."

* * *

Athreya waited for a few minutes for Nazreen to go out of earshot before pulling out his mobile phone. As he began ambling back to the base, he called a Delhi number. The call was answered after two rings.

"Good morning, Mr. Athreya," Liam Dunne said.

"Good morning, Mr. Dunne. Do you have a minute?"

"Certainly."

"I wanted something from the JBF. I was wondering if you could send it to me."

"From the JBF?' Dunne sounded puzzled. 'What would that be?"

"I wanted copies of the monthly fund requests that you get from this project. The ones on whose basis you transfer money to the SBAI."

"The requests that Dr. Korda sends to me? Certainly. Would you like me to send them along with the copies of the anonymous letters?"

"Yes, please. Can I also get copies of the fund transfers you make in response to the requests? I wanted to see how much was sent to which bank."

"No problem. This is confidential, I take it."

"Yes. Nobody knows that I am asking for these documents."

"I'll have them sent as soon as I get back to office. I'm on my way to a meeting right now. How soon do you need them?"

"As soon as I can get them, Mr. Dunne."

"Getting them to your friend's address by a courier will take a couple of days. Jhansi is not a priority destination from Delhi, you know. Would you like me to send you scanned copies by email instead? You'll get them early in the afternoon. I'll have to do this myself – don't want to let anyone else into it at this stage."

"That would be useful, thanks. I'll message you my email address."

Athreya hung up and called another Delhi number. After briefing the man at the other end of the phone line and explaining when he wanted done, Athreya hung up and sent him several photographs through WhatsApp.

* * *

On returning to the base, Athreya went in search of Pratap. Not seeing anyone in the lounge or the work areas, he went to see Adhira, who was working in her office.

"Has everyone else gone to the dig?" he asked.

"Dr. Baig and Dr. Korda have," Adhira replied. "I also saw Nazreen go – she just walks across. I don't know about the others, but Mithali seldom goes to the dig. Her work is all here. Ulhas goes sometimes, whenever scanning of any sort needs to be done."

"Thanks. I'll check with the security guard."

On querying the security guard at the entrance, Athreya learnt that Pratap had left a little while ago on his bike. The guard was not sure where he had gone, but judging by the fact that he had been wearing his helmet, the guard's guess was that Pratap might have gone to Jhansi. He never wore his helmet when he went to the dig.

Athreya called Bhupinder and told him that Pratap might be en route to Jhansi, and that it might be a good idea to know where he goes and whom he meets. Then, after taking directions to the dig from the guard, Athreya headed towards the dig on foot.

There, he found himself overlooking a large, shallow excavation about a hundred yards long and half as wide. He estimated the depth to be about fifteen to twenty feet. In the excavation were old crumbly walls and pillars, neatly laid out but without any ceilings. The walls varied from three feet in height to about ten feet. Among the walls and pillars were Sabir, Dr. Korda and Nazreen with about a dozen workers.

Just then, Ulhas arrived in a project car, carrying a heavy grey suitcase and a large metal box containing scanning equipment. He easily carried both of them in his long, muscular arms. He looked far more at ease than he had been looking since the discovery of Mrs. Markaan's body. He greeted Athreya with a grin and a quick nod and went down into the dig.

Sabir saw Athreya from a distance and climbed up to the rim of the excavation to greet him.

"What do you think?" he asked Athreya as they stood side-by-side, looking over the dig.

"So neatly constructed," Athreya replied, appreciating the symmetry and accuracy with which the walls and pillars were placed. "They are all laid out in tidy, straight lines. Very geometric, I must say. How old is this?"

"Over a thousand years old. We believe it is from the tenth century – the early part of the Chandela Dynasty."

"Really?" Athreya asked in surprise. "Then why do you sound disappointed?"

"Well, this seems to be an abandoned site," Sabir replied patiently. "For some reason, the builders abandoned it after constructing the foundation and the walls, and after placing a few pillars. That's why there are no ceilings. As you will see, there are very few statues or carvings on the pillars. As a result of the abandonment, this place was never used for any purpose. With no social activity taking place here, there are very few artifacts here to unearth.

"Although it's of a decent size, this dig has hardly added to the body of knowledge of the Chandelas or Bundelkhand. At the end of the day, archaeologists dig for primarily one purpose – to learn something new. We seem to be failing quite spectacularly in that regard."

"I see. Though you are disappointed, you aren't surprised."

Sabir nodded.

"Whatever we know about this region's history suggests that we may not find anything new or interesting here," he said. "That was Nazreen's belief too, which has turned out to be correct."

"Interesting lady, Nazreen," Athreya remarked.

"Isn't she?" Sabir smiled. "Nobody can figure her out, you know. With that amiable expression on her face and her enigmatic half-smile, it's impossible to know what she is thinking. None of us knows anything about her personal life, her family, and such. The only thing I know about her is that she can't suffer fools. But her knowledge of this area is astounding – it's almost as if she had lived in those times!"

Sabir then took Athreya on a tour of the excavation, pointing out the few things of interest. The scale of the building and its layout suggested that it was meant to be a public space of some sort – cultural, civic or religious, Sabir didn't know.

Two hours went by pleasantly, and by the time Athreya looked at his watch again, it was past noon. After another fifteen minutes, he thanked Sabir and began walking back to the base, wondering about an archaeologist's life. It must call for a huge amount of patience, he decided. They had to dig for months to ferret out a small piece of information or insight. And in some cases – like here – months of effort resulted in nothing new. At the end of the two hours, Athreya's respect for archaeologists had gone up several notches.

* * *

Midway between the dig and the base, Athreya's phone rang. It was an excited Bhupinder with fresh information that he had uncovered in Jhansi. Athreya sat down on a rock and took the call as his right hand pulled out a small notebook and a pen from his breast pocket. As he listened to Bhupinder, his pen began scribbling on the notebook with a mind of its own.

"I found out who Mrs. Markaan has been meeting at Europa Restaurant – the restaurant near Elite Crossing," he said.

"Who?" Athreya asked.

"You'll never guess ... Madhav!"

"Madhav?' Athreya echoed. "But he told me that he hadn't met Mrs. Markaan for two weeks."

"Well, he met her as recently as Sunday morning. She went to

Europa Restaurant where Madhav was waiting for her. They spent about twenty minutes talking, after which she left. Five minutes later, Madhav left.

"The pattern has been the same on both the days they met at the restaurant. They arrive separately and they leave separately. Madhav arrives first and leaves last."

"You're sure of this, Bhupinder?"

"Absolutely sure, sir. And at the museum, she has been meeting a man who does not work there. He's an outsider who is not known to the museum employees. But she has been meeting him is a discussion room that is out-of-bounds for the general public."

"A stranger can't just walk into a discussion room and meet another stranger, Bhupinder," Athreya objected. "They must have had some sort of permission."

"Exactly! I'm trying for find that out, but the director of the museum is travelling. He is back tomorrow. But, I have more to tell you."

"Go ahead."

The pen in Athreya's hand was scratching indecipherable marks on the notebook, reflecting the tangled thoughts in his mind.

"I got Mrs. Markaan's call records for the past few weeks," Bhupinder went on. "I haven't gone through it fully, but I had a quick look at the past week's calls. She spoke to Madhav at least twice."

"When was the last call?"

"Saturday evening. The day before they met for the last time at the restaurant. There are calls with some unknown numbers too, which I am trying to identify."

"Can you put in a request for Madhav's call records, too? I think you have sufficient basis now."

"I already have. There is more on Madhav. He has recently acquired a second-hand car – a Maruti Swift. He only had a bike when he was working at the dig. He got the car two days after he was fired."

"Why would a man who has just been fired and has lost his income buy a car?" Athreya mused aloud as the pen in his hand began drawing a car on the ground. "Particularly when it's difficult to get a full time job in archaeological circles after one gets fired publicly? Those were Madhav's very words when Mr. Sikka and I met him yesterday morning."

"Interesting, isn't it? There is more to this man that needs finding out. By the way, I also went to where he rents a room. It's a very convenient place if you don't want people to know when you come and go. The old couple who own the place retire early at nights. And they are also a bit hard of hearing."

"Does Madhav have a tail now?" Athreya asked.

"Yes, sir! I'm going after him now."

"You're not going to confront him right away, I hope?"

"No, no! We don't want him to spook him and make him fly away. Everything we do will be discreet. He won't get a whiff."

"Excellent, Bhupinder. Anything on Pratap?"

"Not yet. I have a tail on him, too. Your call was timely – my man saw him ride into Jhansi and has been shadowing him since. He hasn't yet reported back to me. I'll let you know if we find anything interesting."

Athreya hung up and stared at the last sketch he had drawn in the notebook. It resembled the front part of a suitcase, showing the handle and some scratchings under the handle. The scratchings were difficult to make out, but Athreya knew what he had drawn – it was a three-number combination lock.

* * *

After having a quick lunch at the base—everyone except Pratap was there—he followed Adhira into her office.

"Hi, Adhira," he said. "Busy?"

"Hello, Mr. Athreya." Adhira smiled pleasantly at him. "A lot left to do today, although I started work early. Didn't get much done yesterday, you know."

"Am I interrupting you, then?"

"Oh, no! Not at all. Is there anything specific you needed?"

"I was thinking about what you said yesterday, and wondered if I could help you in any way. I'm talking about your troubles with the accounts. As a first step, I wanted to take a look at the fund requests you prepare for Dr. Korda. Is that possible?"

"Of course." She flashed him a grateful glance. "I could use some help, Mr. Athreya."

She strode across her office and pulled out a box file, which she put on a table and opened.

"Here," she said. "They are filed in this section. Would you like me to take you through them?"

"If you don't mind."

Over the next few minutes, she showed him four draft fund requests that she had prepared and explained the different fields on them. Athreya asked some questions and then pulled the box file towards himself. As he began studying the first request, he looked up at her.

"Can you do me a favour, Adhira?" Athreya asked, in an attempt to send her out of the office on a pretext. "Can you check if Ulhas or Mithali is around, so that I can have a chat with one of them?"

"Sure!"

As soon as she strode out, Athreya pulled out his mobile phone and photographed all the monthly fund requests Adhira had prepared. He also photographed the fund transfer advices from the JBF, which had details of how much money was transferred to the Delhi and the Jhansi banks.

CHAPTER 13

As soon as Athreya saw Ulhas, he knew that the younger man had something to tell him. He came into the temporary office close on Athreya's heels and began speaking as soon as they were seated.

"I'm afraid we've been less than truthful with you, Mr. Athreya," the tall man said, stooping forward slightly as he sat. "We didn't want to get a colleague into trouble, especially when what he did had nothing to do with MM's death. We also didn't want to get into a controversy. I hope you understand."

Athreya nodded.

"As you know, between Mithali and me, we went out to the veranda several times that night. You also know that she saw a glowing torch, which was why we went out in the first place. But what we were not entirely honest about was the question you asked – did we see anybody in the veranda? We told you we hadn't.

"The truth is that we did see someone. Mithali saw him when she stepped out. But as far as we know, he didn't see her."

"Pratap," Athreya said. It was not a question, but a statement.

Ulhas nodded.

"Why didn't she come to tell me this herself?"

"She's afraid, sir."

"If she saw Pratap," Athreya went on, "she must have also seen him enter Mrs. Markaan's room."

Ulhas paled slightly.

Athreya knew what was going through the younger man's mind. Ulhas knew that Athreya suspected that Mithali had seen Pratap on the veranda. But he didn't know for sure if Athreya knew of Pratap entering Mrs. Markaan's room. Ulhas had hedged his bet and waited to see how much Athreya actually knew. Based on that, he would decide how much to tell Athreya.

"Yes, sir," Ulhas confessed. "She saw him enter MM's room. Confused, she returned to our room and told me."

"After which *you* went out," Athreya continued. "You waited for five to six minutes, till you saw Pratap come out of Mrs. Markaan's room and enter his own room."

Ulhas nodded. "Yes, sir."

"Is that all?" Athreya asked. "Or is there more you wish to tell me?"

Ulhas stared at him silently. Athreya rose and went to the door. There, he yanked it open and stepped out in a single motion. He saw Mithali a short distance away down the corridor, hidden partially behind a pillar. She was waiting for her husband.

He caught her eye and summoned her. Caught and with no other option, she reluctantly came to him. Without speaking a word, he ushered her into the temporary office and shut the door. Mithali sat beside her husband and stared at Athreya wide-eyed in fright.

"I am not accusing you or your husband of murder," Athreya said to her. "Please understand that."

Mithali swallowed and nodded. Ulhas was sitting stunned in his chair.

"However, I do not take kindly to being lied to," Athreya went on. "What you did is wrong. Had you lied to Inspector Bhupinder instead of me, the consequences would have been different – we wouldn't be sitting here, chatting. I hope you understand that."

Mithali nodded again. Athreya continued his admonition.

"That you withheld information to avoid controversy, I can understand. But you further assumed that Pratap entering Mrs. Markaan's room had nothing to do with her death. How do you know if that is indeed the case?"

Husband and wife shook their heads in silence.

"Now, before you came in," he said to Mithali in a low voice, "I was asking your husband if he had anything else to tell me. He didn't answer. I thought it best to ask you."

Ulhas and Mithali remained silent. The silence dragged on.

"Well," Athreya asked after a long moment, "would you like to tell me or should I tell you?"

Blood drained from Mithali's face. Her eyes were like that of a trapped deer. Ulhas sat stone-faced.

"What you did, Ulhas," Athreya went on, "wasn't murder. You went into Mrs. Markaan's room to retrieve something. You left fingerprints."

Mithali could no longer hold back. She broke into tears as Ulhas seemed to be in a trance. Athreya sat back and surveyed the couple silently. The only sound was that of Mithali weeping.

Gradually, the sobs subsided, and Mithali looked up after wiping her face.

"I think you already know about MM, Mr. Athreya," she said haltingly. "She takes the work done by her juniors and students and passes it off as her own. She did that to Nazreen when she was a student. She tried to do that to Madhav, but he was too smart for her. This is the reason why nobody wants to work with her again. Once bitten, twice shy."

Ulhas placed a large hand on his wife's arm to comfort her. At the gesture, a silent sob burst through Mithali's lips.

"Mithali and I have been doing this research," he said, taking up the narrative from his wife. "We combined chemical analysis with scanning techniques and came up with a draft paper. Of course, we knew that we had to keep it out of MM's reach.

"But, like a fool, I left it on my desk when I went to look at how a certain scan was proceeding. I needed to monitor it every five minutes. Unfortunately, MM unexpectedly walked in – I thought she was at the dig when she wasn't.

"She just picked up the papers and left. I didn't notice it immediately as I was monitoring a scanner. When I realised thirty seconds later and ran to the corridor, I saw MM with the document in her hand, entering her room."

"When was this?" Athreya asked.

"Saturday. Saturday afternoon."

"We had to take it back before she published it, Mr. Athreya," Mithali piped in, almost pleading. "When I saw Pratap enter MM's room, I figured that the person with the torch must have been MM. I immediately saw an opportunity to retrieve our document. I went back to the room and told Ulhas."

"Both of us then went out to the veranda and down the steps near our door," Ulhas said. "We waited near the broad steps below the veranda that are near MM's door."

"You did that to avoid Adhira or Nazreen seeing you cross their windows?" Athreya asked.

Ulhas nodded and continued his narrative.

"When Pratap came out of MM's room," he said, "I went into MM's room while Mithali stood guard at the steps. I hoped to find it on her desk. Luck was with us. I only searched for a few seconds and found it. I grabbed it and left. We retraced our path on the ground below the veranda and returned to our room in jubilation."

"We were *so* happy, Mr. Athreya," Mithali sniffed. "*So* happy that night, that we opened a bottle of wine Ulhas had been saving up. We had put in *so much* hard work into our research, I can't tell you. Everybody here will tell you that I hardly went to Jhansi all these months. They will also tell you that I have been working very hard.

"*This* is what I was working on, Mr. Athreya. To have it taken away so callously was a heartbreak. I hope you understand now why we took such a big risk. Had we been caught, I don't know what would have happened to us."

"Can I see the document? I would like to test it for fingerprints to verify what you have said. Finding Mrs. Markaan's fingerprints on it would support your story."

"Of course!" Mithali sprang up and overbalanced for a moment. "Shall I bring it now?"

Athreya nodded and watched her as she walked away just a *fraction* slower than her eagerness would suggest.

* * *

After Mithali and Ulhas had gone and Athreya had briefed Bhupinder on the couple's revised testimony, he checked his email to see if Dunne had sent the scanned documents he had promised. He had. As Athreya's iPad was in his suitcase at Sharad's house, he decided to study the documents on his mobile phone's small screen.

First, he opened the images of the draft requests he had surreptitiously photographed in Adhira's office. On a sheet of paper, he wrote down the amounts Adhira had asked for in her last four draft requests.

Adhira's figure

239 lakhs
196 lakhs
177 lakhs

213 lakhs

He then opened, one by one, the scanned documents Dunne had sent and studied them until he found the information he was looking for. These documents were the four final requests that Dr. Korda had sent to Dunne. From the scanned images, he copied the amounts Dr. Korda had requested, writing them beside the corresponding amount Adhira had asked for.

Adhira's figure	*Korda's figure*	*Difference*
239 lakhs	*258 lakhs*	*19 lakhs*
196 lakhs	*196 lakhs*	*--*
177 lakhs	*197 lakhs*	*20 lakhs*
213 lakhs	*227 lakhs*	*14 lakhs*

Three of the past four months, Dr. Korda had inflated the amount by 19 lakhs, 20 lakhs and 14 lakhs before sending them on to Dunne – 53 lakhs in total. What remained was for Athreya to look at the other set of documents Dunne had scanned and sent – the payment details.

Five minutes later, it was clear. The amounts Adhira had asked for in her draft requests had been split into two roughly equal halves and credited into two bank accounts. The difference between her figures and Dr. Korda's figures had been credited to a *third* bank account.

While these differences might have been due to legitimate reasons, and while Dr. Korda may be able to explain them adequately, chances were that Athreya was looking at a case of misappropriation of funds. Unknown to Adhira and Dunne, Dr. Korda was squirreling away a tidy amount each month.

Athreya decided to not confront Dr. Korda. He didn't want to alarm Dr. Korda and, in the bargain, jeopardise the investigation into Mrs. Markaan's death. As was often the case, a murder exposed other smaller crimes and misdemeanours by people connected with the victim. Occasionally, it also brought to light another major crime.

* * *

Athreya had been waiting impatiently to hear from Bhupinder when his phone rang. It was the inspector. He and his team seemed to have had fruitful day, both in Jhansi and Patna.

"I have updates for you," Bhupinder said. 'We've got some information about Mrs. Markaan from Patna. She was a childless widow. Her husband died over ten years back, leaving all his assets to her. There is nobody close enough in her husband's side of the family to lay any claim on Mrs. Markaan's wealth.

"Mrs. Markaan herself had one brother, who is now deceased. However, the brother had one son, who is Mrs. Markaan's nephew, Sandeep. Sandeep seems to be Mrs. Markaan's closest relative and is therefore her next of kin.

"Sandeep is currently in Kuala Lumpur. The neighbours said that he took up a job there two or three months ago. Unfortunately, none of the people the Patna police spoke to have his contact number, but they are still trying. They will let us know as soon as they make a breakthrough."

"Are they sure that the nephew is her next of kin?" Athreya asked.

"Yes. The Patna police spoke to her lawyer about Mrs. Markaan's will. It's a very short will, in which she has explicitly left all her belongings and assets to Sandeep, her only living relative."

"The will actually states that Sandeep is the only living relative?"

"Yes. The lawyer read out the will to the officer."

"Do we know how wealthy Mrs. Markaan was?"

"Quite well off for an archaeology professor, I must say. She has a pretty large house that should be worth a few crores, and a pretty tidy bunch of financial investments. All in all, she was worth at least ten crores. A good sum to kill for, in my view."

By now, Athreya's right index finger was tracing invisible words on the desk – a sign that his mind was working in high gear. Quite independent of his conscious self, the long finger was busily scribbling and tracing with a mind of its own. Athreya's erstwhile colleagues had said often that had they found a way to decipher what the finger wrote, they would have cracked most cases in half the time.

"Okay," Athreya said. "Do you know Mrs. Markaan's maiden name?"

"No. But I can easily find that out."

"Do that right away. Can you ask the Patna police to send you copies of all of Sandeep's documents they can lay theirs hands on – passport, driving licence, Aadhaar card, etcetera? They should be able to get a phone number from the Aadhaar card."

"I'll do that. Anything else?"

"Once the Patna police complete their preliminary investigation, I'd like to speak to the investigating officer. If possible later in the evening today. I'll be returning to Mr. Sikka's house after interviewing Pratap once more. I'd prefer to speak from there so that I'm not overheard at the base."

"Shouldn't be a problem. Say 8:00 pm?"

"That'll be fine."

"Okay. Want to hear what we found about Pratap?"

"Of course."

"He has been acting strangely. Do you know where his first stop was once he got to Jhansi?"

"Where?" Athreya asked.

"Eshwar Safe Vaults, a firm that hires out safe deposit lockers."

"Aha! Now, it's getting interesting. Was he carrying his backpack when he went in?"

"Yes! He spent forty-five minutes at Eshwar Safe Vaults. After coming out, he left his bike where it was and walked a hundred yards away, until he came to a garbage bin. There, he took out a purple-coloured wooden box from his backpack and dropped it into the garbage bin."

"Your man picked it up, of course," Athreya guessed. "Was it a jewellery box? About a foot long and nine inches wide?"

"Exactly!" Bhupinder chuckled. "And five inches high. It would have fit perfectly into the empty space in Mrs. Markaan's suitcase."

"The box was empty, I take it?"

"Yup. It was empty."

"Fingerprints?"

"We are on it. It got a little mucked up in the garbage bin, but we'll see what we can do. Regardless, we have enough evidence to show that Pratap is a thief."

"Okay. Where did Pratap go after that?"

"From the locker place, he went to meet a man by the name of Jagan."

"Jagan…" Athreya echoed. "Now, why is that name familiar?"

"Have you met him?' Bhupinder asked.

"No, but somebody mentioned him recently … very recently." Suddenly, the penny dropped. "Yes, I remember. Is he a wiry, middle-aged man with close-cropped hair?"

"Yes!" Bhupinder seemed surprised. "How did you know?"

Athreya's mind went back to the dinner at which he had met Sabir for the first time. Sabir had gone over to Jagan's table after chatting with Sharad and Athreya.

"If we are talking about the same person, he is known to Dr. Baig."

"Jagan is known to us, too," Bhupinder said, "but for the wrong reasons. He's never been in jail, but we suspect him of some shady things."

"Is he a fence?" Athreya asked.

"Very likely. He was almost caught a couple of times with stolen goods, but he got rid of them in the nick of time. It's quite possible that Pratap went to him to dispose of whatever he had in his possession. If he stole Mrs. Markaan's jewellery on Sunday night, he would have had no time to get rid of it. The first opportunity he had was this morning, which he utilised immediately. He couldn't run the risk of having Mrs. Markaan's property on him, *especially* after she had been killed. That would make him an immediate suspect."

"Isn't Pratap a suspect now, Bhupinder?"

"He couldn't have killed her if he was stealing from her room when she was on her way to the islet. After stealing, he returned to his room. Ulhas and Mithali saw him."

"Okay. Let's get back to Pratap's adventures in Jhansi today."

"Pratap went to meet Jagan at about eleven o'clock in the morning. Now, this is where we screwed up. My man was watching the front of the building, where Pratap had parked his bike. Till a little after 2:00 pm, there was no sigh on Pratap. My man assumed that he was still inside the building with Jagan.

"But at 2:10 pm, he saw Jagan and Pratap walk down the road to the building. They had left the building by the rear entrance and gone somewhere. We don't know where they went or for how long.

"When they returned on foot, Pratap didn't enter the building. Instead, he started his bike and rode away as Jagan returned to his flat. From there, Pratap returned to the locker place, where he spent twenty minutes before coming out. He took his bike and rode back towards the dig."

"What exactly did Pratap do at the locker place? Did your man check with the people there?"

"He hired a new locker, paying the deposit and a year's rent in cash. After hiring a locker, he put something into it before going to meet Jagan. After meeting Jagan, he came back to Eshwar Safe

Vaults and accessed his locker again. We don't know what exactly he did, but my man thinks that his backpack was empty when he came out of the locker place the second time."

"What do you think of all this, Bhupinder?"

"Well, Pratap's fingerprints are on Mrs. Markaan's suitcase. Although we are yet to have it positively identified, I have little doubt that the purple wooden box was Mrs. Markaan's jewellery box. I'll ask the ladies at the dig if they can identify it. Failing that, we'll try Mrs. Markaan's nephew in Kuala Lumpur. He had lived in her house and might have seen it. In any case, I'm sure that we will find Mrs. Markaan's jewellery in the safe deposit locker at Eshwar Safe Vaults. I am going to get a warrant ready so that we can search it when required.

"To answer your question, sir, it seems clear to me that Pratap is a thief. He stole Mrs. Markaan's jewellery and tried to sell it off."

"Let's be as discreet as we can. We don't want Pratap to get the slightest whiff that you know what he was up to in Jhansi today. If he does, he may flee."

"Understood."

"Excellent, Bhupinder. I'll talk to you later in the evening. I need to go now."

Athreya hung up and hurried out of the room towards the entrance. He had just heard a motorcycle at the entrance and he hoped that it was Pratap coming in.

* * *

An inscrutable Pratap followed Athreya into the temporary office. A subtle change had come over him since the previous night when Athreya had interviewed him – he seemed more assured. On entering the room, he carelessly dropped his backpack on the floor. To Athreya, he seemed to do that with an exaggerated air of nonchalance. Was he indicating that the backpack was empty and held nothing incriminating? It didn't matter. Athreya had decided that he would not speak about Pratap's visit to Jhansi. Instead, he spoke about last night's conversation.

"I wanted to pick up on one point from last night's discussion," Athreya began when they were seated. "Can I?"

Pratap nodded.

"You remember, I had asked you if you had gone out to the veranda after you returned to your room?"

"Yes," Pratap said tersely. "And I had said that I had not been to the veranda."

"That's right. I had then told you that someone heard your door open and close."

"We've been over this, Mr. Athreya. Whoever heard it was mistaken, if not lying outright. You also told me that nobody had seen me on the veranda. I thought that was the end of it."

"Not really," Athreya said. He paused for a moment before continuing in a lower voice. "New evidence has come to light, Pratap. We now have a witness who saw you out on the veranda."

"Who?" Pratap asked harshly. "Show me the witness and I'll show you a liar."

"There is more than one witness."

"Bullshit! They must have seen someone else."

"Did you or did you not come out to the veranda and watch Mrs. Markaan walking away towards the river? She had a torch."

This time, Pratap blanched. He remained silent.

"You were in the veranda for ten minutes from 12:15 a.m. onwards," Athreya went on. "Several people saw Mrs. Markaan with the torch. You saw her too, didn't you? Take your time before answering. You can change your testimony without prejudice, you know. This is not a court. Nor am I the police officer investigating this case."

Pratap shook his head firmly.

"No change," he said decisively. "I don't remember being out on the veranda. I told you that I was pretty drunk – it was a Sunday night, after all. I stick to what I said yesterday. I didn't go out to the veranda. At least, I don't remember going out."

So, that was going to be Pratap's defence – inebriation.

"What if I told you that the police have corroborative evidence?" Athreya persisted. "Not just witnesses who could be mistaken. But concrete, indisputable proof."

"What proof?"

Athreya shook his head.

"I'm not going to play my entire hand, Pratap," he said. "In any case, it's not my hand to play; it's the police's and the prosecution's. I'm only trying to investigate this matter as discreetly as I can. I can't force you to say anything. I can only offer suggestions.

"I believe we are facing a very dark situation here, Pratap. Wicked and macabre. Several things are at play and some of the players are ruthless. The way Mrs. Markaan was killed is warning enough that the forces of evil here are vicious and pitiless. It wouldn't be wise to cross them ... or to threaten them. Come clean, Pratap, and I may be able to help you."

"I'm sorry, Mr. Athreya." Pratap picked up his empty backpack from the floor. "I don't have anything more to say. While I do appreciate your concern, you are barking up the wrong tree." He rose from his chair. "I have nothing to do with the evil that resides in Naaz Tapu. I have not gone there, and I never will. I'm safe."

Athreya remained seated, his face set in grim lines.

"What if ..." he asked Pratap as the young man turned to go. "What if the evil crosses the water and comes here?"

CHAPTER 14

Later that evening, Athreya and Sharad were at the latter's house. Athreya had just made a request that had unnerved Sharad. The two men sat in uncomfortable silence as Sharad contemplated the request, while Moupriya sat in another chair, her eyes shining as she watched her father.

Athreya had just asked for Sharad's permission to take Moupriya to the base the next day to help him with his investigation. While that, by itself, was not a major concern for Sharad, Athreya had added a specific detail that had rattled him – Athreya wanted to take Moupriya to Naaz Tapu.

"I don't like the idea of you going to the islet, Athreya," Sharad finally said. "But your work takes you there. You remember what I told you – if you must go, don't stay on the islet for a second longer than necessary."

Athreya nodded silently.

"But now, you are asking me to send my daughter to the blighted islet. For heaven's sake, why? What is it that she can do that you or the police can't?"

"Mou is approximately the same height and weight as Mrs. Markaan," Athreya replied. "All I want her to do is to retrace Mrs.

Markaan's path across the landing strip. I won't keep her on the islet for a minute more than necessary."

"What do you hope to achieve by her walking on the strip?"

"I have a hunch, Sharad. A hunch that could prove or disprove a vital point in the investigation. And for testing that hunch, I need someone of Mrs. Markaan's height and weight. Mithali, who is next closest, may not fit the bill. Besides, she is a suspect."

"Who else will be going?" Sharad asked unhappily.

"Nazreen and the inspector."

"Nazreen?' Sharad's eyebrows shot up in surprise. "Why?"

"Nobody knows Naaz Tapu as she does. I get the feeling that she knows every square yard and every tree. I would be lost on the islet without her. I will feel far safer with her there."

"Isn't she a suspect?"

"She is … but I can't make her out. In any case, I don't have an option, as I will be exploring deeper after my little experiment with Mou."

"Going deeper!" Sharad was clearly rattled. "For heaven's sake, why?"

"A part of the answer to the mystery lies inside the islet's woods, Sharad. I *must* go there if I am to crack the case. But fear not, Mou will not be coming with me."

"But Uncle, I *want* to!" Mou interrupted. "I want to see how it is deep inside the jungle."

"Mou!" Sharad barked in a mix of annoyance and horror. "Don't be silly."

"It's not without danger, Mou," Athreya reasoned in a softer tone. "I cannot put you in unnecessary peril."

"But you are going in, Uncle."

"Yes, I am. As your father said, that's my job. That's not the case for you. Besides, I don't think Nazreen will permit you to tag along. However, if your father agrees, I'll take you to the edge of the jungle adjacent to the landing strip. You get a good sense of the jungle from there."

"Papa," Moupriya turned on her father. "I want to go at least to the landing strip. Don't say no."

"But Mou—"

"Papa, please! I'll be with *three* adults. I'll be safe. I want to set foot on the islet at least once."

"But the legend, Mou," Sharad countered. "You know all about it—"

"Don't tell me you believe it." She gave him a teasing grin. "You're a lawyer, Papa. You believe only in what can touched, seen and demonstrated. You've told me that so many times."

Just then, Athreya's phone rang. It was the man to whom he had sent several photographs via WhatsApp. He rose and walked out of the room, leaving father and daughter to thrash out their disagreement. He had little doubt that Moupriya would prevail over her father.

"You were right," the caller from Delhi said. "The person in one photo was familiar to the people I contacted. The man you know as Madhav has used other names in the recent past. And as you suspected, he has been around quite a bit in the past two years – Gwalior, Allahabad, Pune, Jaipur, and a couple of other places. He has used at least three names, including Madhav."

"Gwalior, Allahabad, Pune, Jaipur," Athreya echoed. "Do I see a pattern there?"

"You do," the caller confirmed. "These are the places where artifacts have been stolen. Of course, I haven't compared the precise dates of the thefts with the dates Madhav was in these places yet, but there seems to be a prima facie correlation."

"What else can you tell me?"

"Although he has been working at the dig for the past few months, he has been seen several times in Gwalior. As the Gwalior incident is the most recent one, I remember the dates. Madhav was seen in Gwalior just before the failed robbery and was seen again a few days after it."

"Good! Can you get the dates for the other places, too?"

"I'm getting the dates the thefts took place, but it's difficult pin-pointing the dates Madhav was there, because we may have to rely on people's memory. Besides, he used aliases in some of these cities. The curious thing is that we haven't been able to track him down a single hotel. He must have stayed *somewhere*."

"Perhaps not using a hotel was deliberate."

"Very likely. By avoiding hotels, he leaves a smaller footprint of his presence. We've found that art thieves often stay in the houses of associates. Fortunately for us, that has another benefit – that makes it easier for us to trace the network faster once we identify one member."

"Is that how the Bronze Runners work, too? Do they also use the houses of other members?"

"I don't know," the man from Delhi said. "The Bronze Runners are being investigated by another department. That team is very tight, very secretive. Nothing leaks out."

"Maybe you should share your findings with them," Athreya suggested.

"Maybe," the caller agreed. "Let's see what my boss says. It's his decision, not mine. There are always equations and friction between departments that I can never understand."

"What about the video I sent you? Any luck?"

"I'll work on it. Honestly, my focus today has been on Madhav – I had a funny feeling about him."

When Athreya finished his call and returned to the sitting room, he found Sharad and Moupriya at peace with each other. The girl was beaming.

"I'll come with you tomorrow, Uncle," she said when Athreya entered the room. "Papa has agreed."

Athreya's inquiring glance at Sharad made the latter shrug his shoulders.

"Be careful with her, will you," he said gruffly as he struggled with emotion. "I'll never forgive myself if—"

"Don't worry, Sharad." Athreya laid a hand on his friend's shoulder. "I'll see to it that she comes to no harm." He turned to Moupriya. "Now, young lady," he said sternly. "You will do exactly as I say. No arguing, no sweet-talking, no pleading. That's the condition on which I'll take you. Agreed?"

"Yes sir!" The girl threw him an impish salute and ran out of the room.

Athreya resumed his seat and turned to his friend.

"We didn't get a chance talk about Mrs. Markaan's death," he said, changing the topic. "I didn't want to do it in Mou's presence. Now that we are alone, let me hear your views. You've known these people for some time and you knew Mrs. Markaan personally. She's been your client too. What do you make of all this?"

"What foxes me most," Sharad replied, "is a very basic question: *how* was Mrs. Markaan killed? Had her death something to do with the legend of Naaz Tapu? Most locals believe that the spirits of Bhola and his dog killed her because she brazenly desecrated the islet. They can't be convinced otherwise."

"What do *you* think?" Athreya asked.

"Honestly, I don't know what to think. The physical evidence suggests – strongly – that the weapon was a heavy mace wielded by a very tall man. The act seems to have required uncommon strength and height of the kind Bhola had. In addition, there are clear teeth marks and claw marks on the body. These are *physical* wounds that fit in neatly with the legend.

"On the other hand, her death could have been due to far more earthly causes. It could be murder committed by a fellow human being. Now, that would be something up my street." Sharad shifted in his sofa and continued. "But before I launch into my analysis, I have a question for you: Do you think that Mrs. Markaan's death has something to do with the legend of Naaz Tapu?"

Athreya nodded.

"I think so," he said. "As you so succinctly put it, the physical evidence fits perfectly with the legend. Therefore, the legend is very much a part of the answer we are seeking."

"Then, you think that she was killed by Bhola and the dog?" Sharad asked in surprise. "I thought you didn't believe in this kind of stuff."

"It's too early to say," Athreya replied, choosing his words carefully. "I am expecting some evidence to come in over the next twenty-four hours that will help answer that question. But I believe that Mrs. Markaan was struck by a heavy mace or something similar.

"While I wait for additional evidence to come in, let me hear your views on the other scenario you outlined – that it was a murder carried out by a fellow human."

"Well, it's apparent that Mrs. Markaan was disliked by everyone at the dig, with the possible exception of Pratap," Sharad began. "Each person had his or her own reason to dislike her. In other words, each of them had a potential motive. Whether the motives were strong enough to kill her remains to be seen. Let's consider each of them in turn.

"Mrs. Markaan's practise of stealing work done by her juniors and publishing it as her own has affected at least three youngsters in the SBAI: Nazreen, Mithali and Ulhas. For young people, their first few pieces of original work are immensely valuable. They are a source of huge pride and give them a sense of achievement.

"If someone stole their work, they could react very violently indeed – we have seen such cases. If Mrs. Markaan had stolen again, and what she had stolen was an important piece of work, one of the youngsters could have resorted to violence to get it back.

"Let me come to Madhav next. Of everyone at the base, he probably had the most visible and most recent motive – he was unceremoniously and publicly fired by Mrs. Markaan. He admitted that Mrs. Markaan had affected his career. Madhav is a strong young man who has a mind of his own. And he is tall too. As far as height is concerned, he, Ulhas and Dr. Korda are probably the most likely candidates to wield a mace. Madhav is probably the strongest of the three."

"Excellent!" Athreya said. "Your lawyer's mind is a delight when it comes to physical evidence. Go on."

"Reading between the lines of the conversation I had with Mrs. Markaan, she had suspected some sort of financial malfeasance. I don't know what the scale of the misappropriation was. But that is not hugely relevant if we consider the possibility that Mrs. Markaan was contemplating going public with her suspicions – just as she went public with Madhav's firing.

"If she had gone public with accusations of embezzlement, it would have hit two people very hard: Adhira and Dr. Korda. It would have tarnished their reputations and could have ruined their careers. We all know that Mrs. Markaan was quite capable of making sweeping allegations without giving a thought to how it could affect the accused person. One way to stop her from doing that would be to silence her.

"You remember, both Adhira and Dr. Korda were very upset on Sunday when Mrs. Markaan openly asked you about investigating financial misdemeanour? Both were quite stunned, I thought. Thus, Adhira and Dr. Korda also had motives too, and their motives, at least on the face of it, seems stronger than the motives for Nazreen, Mithali and Ulhas.

"As far as Sabir is concerned, he has everything to gain by Mrs. Markaan's death. He has already been appointed interim head of the expedition. Once the paperwork is done, he will replace Mrs. Markaan as the director of SBAI. And if there is anyone in the expedition who has the brains to plan an elaborate murder, it's him. But I must admit that I can't see our erudite Sabir on Naaz Tapu, silently creeping up on Mrs. Markaan with a mace."

"I agree," Athreya said. "He probably doesn't have the strength to lift a heavy mace. But nothing stopped him *hiring* someone who can wield it."

"That leaves Pratap," Sharad concluded. "I find him a dubious fellow, whom I don't trust an inch. I can't pin a motive on him, but I would not at all be surprised if you find something very soon in your investigation. All in all, everyone at the dig had a motive – some had strong motives, others not so strong."

"We have indeed found something about Pratap," Athreya said. "He entered Mrs. Markaan's room in the middle of the night and stole a jewellery box from her suitcase."

"From her suitcase!" Sharad exclaimed. "Wasn't it locked? She wasn't a trusting soul. I don't think she would leave it unlocked."

"It was. With a number lock, though. If he knew the combination, he could have opened the suitcase in a jiffy."

"But why would Mrs. Markaan give him the combination of her suitcase?"

"I can think of one set of circumstances that might have made her do so. I hope to prove or disprove that soon. Perhaps as early as tonight."

* * *

Athreya's phone rang at 8:00 p.m. sharp. It was Bhupinder with the Patna police inspector patched into conference.

"Hello, Mr. Athreya," Bhupinder began. "I have Inspector Choubey on conference."

"Good evening, Inspector Choubey," Athreya said. "Thank you for joining us."

"Good evening, sir," a gravelly voice drawled. "I've heard a lot about you and am very pleased to make your acquaintance. Tell me, sir, how can I help?"

"It would be useful if you could take me through what you have found out about Mrs. Markaan. Inspector Bhupinder tells me that you have inquired into her background."

"Yes, sir. Mrs. Markaan was a widow with no children. Her husband died about ten years ago. When she was in Patna, she lived in her own house, which she and her husband bought in 1998. They bought it at a reasonable price using their savings, which they augmented with a bank loan. The loan was paid off in 2006. Since then, the real estate prices have shot up, and the house is worth a lot of money now.

"While she was not wealthy, she was comfortably off. It is clear that she was careful with money. Over the years, she saved quite a bit and invested her savings mostly in bank deposits. She did not believe in the stock market or mutual funds. She also invested the gratuity and life insurance she received on her husband's death. She was not known to spend money needlessly and she kept a tight control over her financial affairs.

"She was an academician all her working life and had worked in several universities in the archaeology or history departments. Until, of course, she resigned one day and joined the SBAI in Delhi. An internet search reveals that she has authored over seventy papers, most of them on subjects related to archaeology.

"But strangely enough, her erstwhile colleagues do not speak highly of her as far as professional knowledge and competence are concerned. While they did not badmouth her, they also did not say anything complimentary about her, despite my asking them pointed questions. But there was enough to suggest that they did not respect her professionally.

"As far as her neighbours are concerned, they didn't like her very much. Of course, most of them didn't want to speak ill of the departed, but it was quite obvious that she is not going to be missed very much. A couple of ladies told us that Mrs. Markaan was khadoos – ill-tempered, grumpy and generally critical of everyone around her. That's a summary of what we have found out so far."

"Thanks, Inspector," Athreya replied. "One fundamental question first – are you one hundred percent sure that the deceased *was* Mrs. Markaan?"

"Why?" Choubey asked. "Is there any question about that?"

"No. Whenever a person is killed in one place and an investigation takes place in another, I always like to confirm that the deceased was not an impostor."

"Ah! You don't take anything for granted, sir, do you?" Choubey chuckled. "No doubt in this case. We showed a recent photo to the neighbours and the erstwhile colleagues. We have a positive identification.

"I am not sure if you are aware, but we also entered her house. The chowkidar let us in. He is, of course, terrified that he is going to lose his job. Anyway, we found a couple of snaps of Mrs. Markaan in the house, which we photographed and sent to Bhupinder."

"There's no doubt, Mr. Athreya," Bhupinder interjected. "The identity is confirmed."

"Okay," Athreya said. "My next question is about the experience Mrs. Markaan's colleagues had with her. We have been told that she was in the habit of stealing credit from her juniors and publishing their work as her own. Did you hear anything about this from her colleagues?"

Choubey let out another deep chuckle.

"Yes, we did," he said. "More than once. Not directly or in as many words, but there were many oblique references to it. Some even joked about hiding their research papers when she was nearby. When I was speaking about the many papers she had published, one of them said: '*I wonder how much she knows of what is actually written in the papers.*'"

"Did you find nothing amiss in your investigation?"

"No, sir. Nothing. She was not well liked, but there is absolutely no sign of her having done anything wrong, except stealing credit from juniors. But even in that, she doesn't seem to have benefitted financially."

"And what about her reputation around where she lives Patna?" Athreya asked. "Nothing suspicious?"

"Apart from being khadoos, her reputation seems quite clean. She paid her servants on the first day of every month. She never delayed any payments to shops or vendors. She was generally considered a woman who kept her word. Bit of a strict taskmaster, but clean."

"Bhupinder told me about her will. She has left everything to her nephew. Is that right?"

"Yes. A valuable house and a nice little pile of bank deposits."

"What have you been able to find out about the nephew?"

"Sandeep – that's the nephew's name – is her brother's son. Mrs. Markaan's brother died when Sandeep was young – about nine years old. Sandeep's mother was neither a very savvy woman nor a healthy one. So, when Sandeep's father died, Mrs. Markaan took the boy under her wing.

"What is amply clear is that she simply doted over the boy. That's what we heard from the neighbours as well as from her erstwhile colleagues. Sandeep's mother passed away four years after his father had died. Since then, he has been living with Mrs. Markaan."

"It's no surprise that she left everything to him."

"No surprise at all," Choubey rumbled. "He was like her own son, and there is no other close relative."

"Where is Sandeep now?"

"Kuala Lumpur. We're trying to get in touch with him. The neighbours and the chowkidar last saw him about two months ago."

"No phone number with the chowkidar?"

"No. He only had Mrs. Markaan's number – which is the same as the one Bhupinder gave me."

"Have you been able to trace Sandeep's driving licence, passport or Aadhaar card?"

"We are trying, sir. There is a lot of red tape around the Aadhaar card, but we'll get there. As far as passport and driving licence is concerned, we found many Sandeeps – it's a common name. But none of them is in the address of Mrs. Markaan's house. Sandeep must have taken his driving licence more than ten years ago. I am not sure what his address then was. And the passport office is taking its own time."

"Any photos of him in the house?"

"We didn't find any recent photos. There are some old snaps of Mrs. Markaan with a young boy. That could be Sandeep."

Athreya rose from his chair and paced like a caged lion inside Sharad's drawing room. Now was the time to take the chance. He had held back talking about his hunch for twenty-four hours. If his hunch was right, they would take a big step forward in the investigation. If it wasn't, he was going to look silly. Athreya decided to take the plunge.

"Okay, Inspector Choubey," he said. "I'm going to send you a photo. Can you show it to the neighbours or the chowkidar and ask if that is of Sandeep's?"

"Yes." Choubey's response was crisp. "I'll send it to my constable immediately and ask him to check with two or three people. Do you have Sandeep's photo?"

"I just might. Give me a mobile number to which I can send it by WhatsApp."

Once Athreya sent the photo, Bhupinder was on pins and needles, wanting to know whose photo Athreya had sent. But Athreya kept him in suspense, unwilling to talk about his unconfirmed hunch while they waited for Choubey to return. Five minutes later, Choubey was back on the call, brisk and energetic.

"We have a match, sir," Choubey almost bellowed in delight. "The photo you sent is of Sandeep. The chowkidar and two neighbours identified the photo."

"Whose photo did you send, sir?" an impatient Bhupinder demanded. "Who is Sandeep?"

"Inspector Choubey," Athreya asked, "what is Sandeep's full name? Do you know?"

"Yes, sir. It's Sandeep Pratap Yadav."

"You heard, Bhupinder? Sandeep was never in Kuala Lumpur. He is right here at the dig, going under his middle name – Pratap."

"Pratap!" Bhupinder exclaimed.

"Pratap is Mrs. Markaan's nephew, but they concealed the relationship at the SBAI. The doting aunt was trying hard to give her nephew a career in archaeology. And he repaid her by stealing her jewellery box from her suitcase."

"So that's what gave you the idea!' Bhupinder exclaimed. 'He knew the combination of his aunt's suitcase."

"Obvious, isn't it? How often do old, bespectacled people with poor eyesight ask their nephews or nieces to open their suitcase for them?"

"If Pratap is Sandeep," Choubey growled, "the obvious motive is inheritance. He stands to receive crores of rupees."

CHAPTER 15

At 7:30 the next morning, Inspector Bhupinder knocked on the door of Madhav's room. With him was Athreya. After a lengthy delay, during which Bhupinder knocked again, the door was opened by a dishevelled, bleary-eyed Madhav holding a mug of tea in his hand. He was dressed in pajamas and an old-looking sweater that seemed to be a part of his night wear. After staring in befuddlement at Bhupinder for a second, recognition dawned. Even then, Madhav's expression did not become welcoming. Only when his gaze fell on Athreya did the look of annoyance fade. He stepped back and let them enter his room, which had the usual untidy markings of a bachelor's den.

"Late night, Madhav?" Athreya asked conversationally, as they found places among the litter to sit.

"Not really," Madhav replied, scratching his head. "Nothing much to do here, you know. I'm still trying to make new friends after MM fired me."

Athreya said nothing. The plainclothesman shadowing Madhav had reported that Madhav had been out till about 2:15 am. He had first had dinner with two men at Europa Restaurant, after which the three of them had gone to a certain flat. Madhav had left the flat at 2:10 am.

"Ah, that's what I wanted to speak to you about," Bhupinder cut in smoothly. "About your last conversation with Mrs. Markaan. Mr. Athreya tells me that the last time you spoke to her was when you were fired. Is that right?"

"Yes. It wasn't a very pleasant conversation."

"Do you remember what you said?"

"Well, the gist of it. Not every word, obviously."

"I believe you told her that she would regret her decision to fire you. That you would *make* her regret it. Is that right?"

"Who told you?" Madhav snapped.

"Does it matter? You were shouting. Several people heard you."

"Well … I guess so," Madhav mumbled. "I was angry, you know. So would you be if you were fired in that way and for a flimsy reason." His head jerked up as if a thought had struck him. "You don't think I killed her, do you?" he demanded, his eyes darting from Bhupinder to Athreya and back.

"At this point," Bhupinder replied smoothly, "I am only collecting and verifying information. Do you acknowledge that you told her that you would make her regret it?"

"There's no point denying it, is there? Not when multiple people heard me."

"And was that the last time you spoke to her? I believe that's what you told Mr. Sikka and Mr. Athreya."

Madhav nodded briefly but said nothing. His eyes were no longer bleary.

"Mr. Madhav," Bhupinder said as his eyes studied Madhav's face, "that's not true, is it? You saw Mrs. Markaan after being fired. At least twice at Europa Restaurant—alone. And the last time you met her was on Sunday morning – the day she died."

Madhav remained silent, his guarded eyes on Bhupinder's face. For all practical purposes, Athreya might not have been in the room at all. Bhupinder returned his stare, and the two young men locked gazes, neither wanting to be the one to drop it. After a moment, Athreya broke the silence.

"Is that true, Madhav?" he asked. "Is it true that you met Mrs, Markaan on Sunday?"

Madhav's eyes turned to Athreya, but he remained silent.

"You were seen," Bhupinder went on. "On each of the occasions."

When Madhav still didn't answer, Athreya said, "From what I hear, you made no attempt to conceal the fact that you were meeting her. Other than arriving and leaving separately, that is."

"It was a private matter, Mr. Athreya," Madhav said, speaking at last. "I won't talk about it."

"Why not?" Bhupinder demanded.

Madhav shook his head. "Because, I don't want to talk about it."

"Why not?" the inspector asked again.

"We can keep going around in circles, Inspector," Madhav said brusquely. "But that won't get you anywhere. I will not comment on what you said, and I don't want to tell you the reason either. You just have to accept it."

"Not necessarily. This is a murder investigation. You—"

"I know," Madhav snapped angrily. "But what I say or not say is still my choice. You can't force me to talk."

"Your call records show that you spoke to Mrs. Markaan several times in the past week or so."

Madhav shrugged.

"What do you want me to say?" he asked. "The call records show what they show. What I say changes nothing."

"Do you deny that you have been to the dig several times after you were fired?" Bhupinder continued.

"What's the point in denying? Even though it has nothing to do with MM's death. But given where we have reached in our conversation, I choose not to comment on it."

"You were at the dig on Sunday evening too – the day Mrs. Markaan was killed."

"The guard must have told you," Madhav replied. "Yes, I spoke to him." He seemed to finally lose his cool. "For God's sake, man," he thundered, "do you realise I made no attempt to hide the fact that I was there? Would I have done that had I been planning to murder MM? Think about it for a second, will you?"

"Why did you go to the dig?" Bhupinder persisted.

"Because I am interested in the bloody thing, don't you understand?" Madhav yelled. "I have an interest in the excavation and a passion for it. I worked there for months! It's something I'm professionally interested in. MM firing me doesn't change that one bit. I go there to see if they have discovered anything interesting. This cataloguing job at the museum is bloody boring! Now, is that clear?"

Madhav, his face flushed in anger, glared at an unperturbed Bhupinder.

"Madhav," Athreya interjected. The angry young man turned to him. "Madhav, did your meetings and conversations with Mrs. Markaan have anything to do with her death?"

"No, Mr. Athreya. They have nothing to do with MM's death."

"How do you know?"

"Because it was a personal matter."

"Then, why not clear the air?" Athreya asked. "If it's got nothing to do with her death, you will be in the clear. And if it's something sensitive or confidential, be assured that neither the inspector nor I will talk about it."

Madhav rose from his chair and paced around his cluttered room. His eyebrows were drawn down into deep frown as he considered Athreya's suggestion. Abruptly, he halted in mid-step and returned to his chair.

"Alright." He seemed to have come to a decision. "I'll tell you what I was meeting her about. But I want you to keep it under your hat." He drained his mug of tea and set it down. "We were discussing my returning to the excavation. She said that she had discovered something new and was asking if I would be interested in coming back and helping her with it. She needed an archaeologist who knew his stuff and was physically strong."

Unbidden, the conversation with Liam Dunne flashed across Athreya's mind. Mrs. Markaan had said to Dunne: "*I've discovered something. I can't speak to you about it yet, but I'll do so soon.*" Was Madhav referring to the same thing now? And what had Mrs. Markaan been referring to? The bracelet and the ring that she had found at Naaz Tapu?

And then, Mrs. Markaan had gone on to tell Dunne: "*I may have made a mistake, Liam.*" What mistake had she made? Had she begun feeling that she shouldn't have defied the legend by going to Naaz Tapu? Or had she felt that she had erred in firing Madhav?

Athreya forced his mind to return to the present and addressed Madhav.

"What had she discovered?" he asked.

"She didn't tell me. She shared no specifics and said that she'd give the details if I returned to the project. However, she did say that it was a little 'off the beaten track' – those were her words – and she didn't have anyone suitable to pursue the exploration with her. Apparently, she had asked Pratap, but he had refused. Why she didn't want Dr. Baig or Dr. Korda to help her, I can only guess. I got the feeling that she didn't trust Dr. Korda enough. And as far as Dr. Baig is concerned, there was too much professional rivalry between him and MM."

"And what was your reaction to her offer?"

"Honestly, I was desperate to get back. But if she wanted me so badly, I thought that I should extract my pound of flesh – she would have to set right all the adverse publicity I had received when she fired me. It was not my tarnished image at the dig alone. The word was spreading in archaeology circles. I needed that fixed. That's what we were discussing."

"Did she agree to your conditions?"

Madhav nodded. "Finally, on Sunday, she agreed. She said she would send out a message saying that there had been a mistake, and that I had re-joined the SBAI. You see, Mr. Athreya, I had gotten what I wanted – I would return to the project, and my name would be cleared. Why would I want to kill her once that happened?"

Ten minutes later, Athreya and Bhupinder were on their way back to Sharad's house, where they were to pick up Moupriya before proceeding to the base.

"By the way," Bhupinder said as soon as they left Madhav's house. "My men have been inquiring about Jagan. Two shopkeepers on the main road near the dig – one tea seller and a motorcycle mechanic –recognised his photo. He has been hanging around the dig and the base for a few days."

"I'm not surprised. A fence needs to keep himself informed. That's also why he befriended Dr. Baig and Pratap. I wouldn't be surprised if he knows Madhav too – perhaps you can try and unearth a connection there. But I suspect Jagan may only be an accomplice."

"Whose accomplice?"

"That, we need to find out." He turned to Bhupinder with a smile. "So, what do you think of Madhav?" he asked.

"He is lying, sir," Bhupinder snorted. "Lying through his teeth. A cock-and-bull story about Mrs. Markaan wanting him back. She's no longer around to call his bluff. What do *you* think, Mr. Athreya?"

Athreya's right index and middle fingers were rapidly tracing patterns on the car seat, and his brow was furrowed.

"Of course he is lying. But I have a suspicion that he may be telling some truth, too. If Mrs. Markaan was considering taking him back, she might have mentioned it to someone in passing."

"Dr. Baig or Dr. Korda?" Bhupinder asked.

"Or Adhira – for administrative reasons. I will ask them."

Athreya stopped scribbling illegible words on the car seat and turned to the inspector with a beatific smile.

"He's lying about something, Bhupinder," he said mildly. "And that something is big."

* * *

Moupriya stood uncertainly at the edge of the rock shelf overlooking Naaz Tapu's mud strip. A dozen feet behind her, the waters of the Betwa flowed by silently. In front of her was fifteen feet of squelchy mud which Athreya had asked her to cross. He, Bhupinder and Nazreen stood beyond the mud strip, waiting for her to begin her walk across the slippery mud. They had crossed the mud strip at the far end where the police had placed several wooden planks so that they did not have to negotiate the slippery strip each time they came to or left the islet.

Following Athreya's instructions, Moupriya had worn rubber flip-flops – commonly called hawai chappals – that were similar to Mrs. Markaan's. To the extent possible, Athreya was trying to recreate what might have happened on Sunday night. His choice of Moupriya as the person to re-enact was largely due to the girl's similarity with the older woman in terms of height and weight.

Almost sixty hours after the tragedy, Mrs. Markaan's tracks had all but disappeared. The wet, runny mud had filled up the depressions Mrs. Markaan's flip-flops had made. All that remained was a slight difference in texture where the footsteps had been. Moupriya was about to walk parallel to the faint track.

"Ready, Mou?" Athreya called across the strip.

"Yes," Moupriya called back. "Ready."

She had taken a few minutes to overcome her initial trepidation of stepping onto Naaz Tapu for the first time, the islet all her friends considered haunted. Despite her brave words to her father

195

the previous night, she had been distinctly apprehensive when the time for stepping onto the islet had arrived. Eventually, Nazreen's presence—and that of the police inspector—had given her the confidence that matters would not go drastically wrong.

"Remember, Mou," Athreya said. "Walk as naturally as possible. The mud will slip and slide, but you won't fall. Walk parallel to the faint track you can see."

The girl nodded, took a deep breath and stepped off the rock shelf. As soon her right foot pressed into the mud of the strip, it slipped an inch, startling the girl.

"That's okay," Athreya called encouragingly. "You'll get used to it."

With her wide-open eyes riveted to the squishy mud under her, Moupriya took another step. At the movement, her right foot slid a little more, but this time, she was prepared for it. Her confidence rising, she pressed her left foot onto the mud with more assurance, albeit with her arms stretched outwards to facilitate balance. Within a few seconds, she gained enough confidence to walk across the strip unconcerned. Her stride lengthened as she approached the midpoint of her little journey.

"Ew!" she cried out as the putty-like mud climbed the sole of her rubber flip-flops and began making its way under her feet and between her toes.

"Steady, Mou!" Athreya called in response. "The mud can be washed off easily. Don't let it bother you."

The rest of the crossing turned out to be uneventful, and Moupriya soon reached the end of the strip and stepped on to firmer ground where her companions were standing. Her flip-flops were covered with sticky mud and so were her heels, toes and the sides of her feet.

"Don't stamp your feet," Athreya cautioned her in anticipation, expecting the young girl to try and get rid of the mud at the earliest opportunity. "Not yet. I want the flip-flops to be just as they are."

"Ew!" Moupriya complained again. "This is disgusting!"

"Lift your left leg," Athreya said. "I'll take it off."

The girl did as instructed. Athreya held the flip-flop by its strap and slid it off her foot. He repeated the action with the other foot.

"Wait," he said as he pulled out his mobile phone. "Don't stamp your feet."

He took several snaps of her mud-caked feet and then turned his camera to the footwear. Once he was satisfied that he had recorded exactly how the flip-flop looked from every direction, he pocketed the phone and turned his attention to the tracks Moupriya had made on the strip. Moupriya was trying to get the sticky mud off her feet.

Bhupinder was already comparing the tracks with the photographs of Mrs. Markaan's tracks. Athreya stood silently by him and watched over his shoulder. A couple of minutes later, the inspector pronounced his verdict.

"Both the tracks are unevenly spaced," he said. "In both cases, the depressions are far larger than the footwear that made them, although the depressions made by Mrs. Markaan were an inch or so longer. Her feet seem to have slipped back down the slope more than Moupriya's."

"And the depth of the impressions?" Athreya asked.

"Roughly the same – about three-quarters of an inch."

"Okay. Let's have a look at the flip-flops. My impression is that the caking of mud on Moupriya's is very similar to what we saw on Mrs. Markaan's. But please check the photos."

Five minutes later, Bhupinder confirmed that Athreya's first impressions were indeed correct.

"Now," Athreya said as he pulled out his phone, "I'm going to show you photos of Mrs. Markaan's body. I took them as soon as we had discovered the body and sent word to you. Have a look. What do you notice?"

The inspector flipped through several photographs that showed

Mrs. Markaan from different angles. Nazreen stood silently by Athreya's side, her face composed into serene lines. At length, Bhupinder shook his head.

"I'm not sure I know what you are getting at, sir," he said.

"Have a look at Mrs. Markaan's feet," Athreya suggested. "What do you see?"

After scrutinising the photographs once more, Bhupinder shook his head for a second time.

"I see nothing unusual."

"Precisely." Athreya responded cryptically and unhelpfully.

"What are you suggesting? The feet are fine. So what?"

"The feet are clean," Nazreen whispered in Hindi. "Too clean."

Bhupinder's eyes widened a shade as he stared at Nazreen with dawning realisation.

"No mud on Markaan Sahiba's feet," Nazreen whispered. "But her flip-flops are caked in mud."

Moupriya was staring wide-eyed at Nazreen with an intense expression on her face. Nazreen, her face calm and wearing her half-smile, gazed at the inspector with lucid grey eyes that gave away nothing. Bhupinder's face was a mask as his eyes flitted from Nazreen to Athreya. It was apparent that his mind was racing as it tried to fit the new information into a comprehensible pattern.

"There is another key point, Bhupinder," Athreya said at length, preventing the inspector from voicing his speculations about the reasons behind Mrs. Markaan's feet being free of mud. "Let me show it to you. Come here."

Athreya walked over to the edge of the strip where Moupriya's tracks ended and pointed to the ground about a yard from the edge of the mud strip.

"This is where Mrs. Markaan's broken flip-flop lay," he continued when Bhupinder joined him with Moupriya and Nazreen in tow. "Remember, it was pointing toward the trees and *away from the strip*. It was broken."

"Yes," Bhupinder concurred. "We surmised that she met some-body or something as soon as she crossed the strip. In fear, she tried to run into the trees, and her flip-flop broke in her haste. I think we are quite clear on that."

"Exactly." Athreya's voice was abnormally quiet. "She ran into the trees where she was subsequently killed. And she ran *away from* somebody or something."

"What are you implying?"

"When you run from something, you run away from it. Not towards it."

"Yes."

"Then, that something would be *behind* you, right?"

"Right."

"Then, it's logical to infer that whatever chased Mrs. Markaan was behind her when she broke her flip-flop."

"Yes, Mr. Athreya," Bhupinder said a shade testily. "So what?"

"Where was that somebody or something that attacked her when it broke? Remember, she was hardly a yard from the mud strip."

"Behind her—" Bhupinder began as he swung around. "Bloody hell!" He exclaimed. "Bloody, bloody hell! Behind her is only the mud strip."

He stopped speaking and stared at the mud strip.

"Oh God!" Moupriya hissed in realisation. She seemed to have forgotten the annoyance of the caked mud on her feet. "Whatever attacked Mrs. Markaan *must* have been on the mud strip!"

"Yes." Athreya nodded, his face set in grim lines. "It couldn't have been between her and the forest – she wouldn't have run to-wards the forest in that case. Thus, whatever attacked her – crea-ture or human – *must* have been on the mud strip behind her."

"The attacker must have *stood and walked* on the mud strip," Bhupinder hissed.

"Indeed," Athreya agreed. "But where are the attacker's footprints? There are none. We found none on Monday, either."

"Uncle …" Moupriya choked on surging emotion and swallowed hard. "Uncle, what kind of a creature leaves no footprints?"

Athreya didn't answer. Nor did Nazreen or Bhupinder. Moupriya shivered.

"Uncle," she whispered. "I want off this islet. Let's leave now. *Please*."

CHAPTER 16

Back at the base, Athreya gave Moupriya the key to his room so that she could wash and change after her adventure at Naaz Tapu. The girl had regained her equanimity after leaving the islet, and by the time they reached the base, she was her normal self. As he gave her his room key, he spoke to her in an undertone.

"Hang around with Mithali and Adhira after you wash and change," he said. "Women often are more open when they are with other women. They may speak of matters they wouldn't speak when men are around."

Moupriya nodded in agreement.

"I need you to pick up any little pieces of information you may come across," Athreya went on. "I would be interested in your perceptions too, even if you can't substantiate them with concrete observations.

"There is something about Mithali that bothers me, something that seems trivial at this point. But who knows, trivial things can assume vital importance when viewed in the right context. It's happened before. Keep your eyes and ears open for small and big things alike. Anything – even a triviality – that seems odd or out of place might be useful."

"What is it about Mithali Didi that bothers you?" Moupriya asked.

"Her gestures and movements seem to be just a fraction slower than I would expect. A mere fraction. I don't even know if it is just my imagination. There may be absolutely nothing there, but who knows?"

"And Adhira Didi?"

"Nothing specific, but I'm sure there is a lot I don't know about her relationship with others – Madhav and Sabir, for instance. Also with Dr. Korda, who she knows from before this dig began. Adhira is always guarded when she speaks to me. She may just say something when I am not in earshot.

"They are all under pressure and may just want to unburden themselves to someone like you. I think both Mithali and Adhira have taken a liking to you."

"Isn't there something underhanded about this, Uncle?" Moupriya asked. "I feel like a spy or something."

"Look at it this way, Mou – you are playing your part in clearing up this mystery. Once we do that, everyone will be happier for it. Until this matter is resolved, an uncomfortable cloud hangs over all of them. You are helping them become happier."

Leaving the girl to wash and change, Athreya went in search of Dr. Korda. He found the tall man at the paved square in the quadrangle, examining a block of stone with a half-finished carving on one face. As expected, he was wearing his monastic robe and heavy leather boots.

For a moment, Athreya wondered what kind of marks those large, heavy boots would leave on the mud strip at Naaz Tapu. They looked to be size eleven or twelve, against Mrs. Markaan's Size seven. The depressions these boots would leave would be visibly larger than the ones Mrs. Markaan and Moupriya had left. And they would be deeper too, considering that Dr. Korda would be a good thirty kilograms or so heavier than Mrs. Markaan or Moupriya.

Dr. Korda's longer stride would have made depressions farther apart, too. The tall man would have crossed the mud strip with fewer strides. But, of course, he would have had a devil of a time scrapping the sticky mud off those boots. And maybe, the hem of his robe might have picked up some mud. Athreya glanced at the taller man's boots and robe as he approached him. There was no trace of mud.

"Good morning, Dr. Korda," he said aloud. "Can I have a word with you?"

"Good morning," the archaeologist rumbled as he straightened. "Certainly. Here or inside?"

"We can talk here if we can keep our voices down. I don't want to take you away from your work."

Dr. Korda nodded and waited for Athreya to take the lead. Athreya came straight to the point.

"Did Mrs. Markaan talk to you about the possibility of Madhav re-joining the project?" Athreya asked. "Perhaps in the past week or so?"

"She did," Dr. Korda replied solemnly. "She said that she was considering it and wanted my views on the matter."

"And what were your views?"

"I had no objection. In fact, I encouraged it, as I thought that Madhav had been removed without adequate cause. That had impacted the morale of the group too. Adversely."

"Did she say why she was considering bringing him back?"

Dr. Korda shook his head. "No."

"To your knowledge, did she take a decision one way or the other?"

"I'm not sure, but I think she had decided to bring him back. She said nothing to me afterwards, but I think she said something to Adhira."

Athreya thanked him and went in search of Adhira. He found her in her office.

"Yes, MM said that Madhav would be coming back," Adhira said in response to Athreya's query.

"When did she say that?" Athreya asked.

"Sometime on Sunday. I don't remember exactly when."

"Before lunch or after?"

"After."

"What exactly did she say?"

"That Madhav would return the next week, but she didn't know the precise date. Once the date was known, I needed to reinstate his payroll and let him have his room back."

"Were you pleased at that?"

"Of course." Adhira flashed him a smile. "Our relationship is no secret, Mr. Athreya, and I'm no longer a teenager."

There was no trace of embarrassment or awkwardness in her gaze. Here was a woman of the world, who was doing as she pleased, and couldn't be bothered with what others might think of her actions.

Just then, Moupriya walked in. Athreya left the room and returned to the temporary office, where Bhupinder was brooding over some notes.

"So, Madhav wasn't lying," Bhupinder said once Athreya briefed him on the two conversations he had just had. "Mrs. Markaan was indeed taking him back."

"He was not lying about that," Athreya conceded. "But was lying about something else. Of that, I'm sure."

Athreya relapsed into silence as his right index finger began scribbling invisible words and phrases on the wooden arm of his chair. A faraway look came to his face as his eyes seemed to lose focus. A minute passed as Bhupinder, too, sat in silence. Another minute passed. Then, a hint of a smile appeared on Athreya's face. Presently, he blinked at Bhupinder and rose.

"Excuse me for a few minutes," he said. "I need to make a call."

Athreya went out of the room and up the stairs to the terrace.

Bright sunshine was warming the terrace as a gardener tended to a deep-pink bougainvillea at a distance. Athreya ambled past him and went to the rear side of the building where the terrace overlooked the sloping ground going down to the river. He briefly peered over the parapet wall to check if anyone was within earshot.

Satisfied that he would not be overheard, he pulled out his phone and selected a private number in Delhi. It was time to reach higher in the hierarchy. While his contact in Delhi had provided useful information, he had his limitations. For certain types of information, he needed clearance from the top.

"Good morning, ma'am," he greeted the lady who answered the call. "This is Athreya."

After a genial exchange of greetings and inquiries, they got down to business.

"I need your help in finding out a little more about a certain person," Athreya said. "I've been in touch with Department 3, but there some pieces of information that don't cross department boundaries."

"True," the lady answered. "That's by design, as you know."

"Yes, ma'am. I now have a situation that requires potentially sensitive information from across departments. I'll give you a context first, and then send you the details of the person I'm investigating."

Ten minutes later, Athreya hung up and made his way back to the temporary office where Bhupinder was waiting for him. The inspector had just heard from the director of the government museum at Jhansi, who had returned from travel the previous night.

"I spoke to the director – he was the one who had granted Mrs. Markaan permission to use one of their meeting rooms," he began. "Apparently, he had received a call from the ministry in Delhi. The ministry person gave no reasons or explanations. He just said that a man by the name of Khanai would be approaching him the next day, and would need to use a room from time to time."

"Khanai?" Athreya echoed. "Sounds like a Nepali name."

"Don't know," Bhupinder said. "So, the museum followed instructions and made a room available for Khanai. It looks like Khanai has met Mrs. Markaan a few times at the museum. The museum director knows nothing more about the meetings or about Khanai."

"We need to trace Khanai—" Athreya began, when Bhupinder cut him off.

"I've initiated that," the inspector went on briskly. "We'll find out through the police network as soon as I get the name of the ministry person who had called the museum."

"Perhaps," Athreya suggested, "one of the unknown numbers in Mrs. Markaan's call record would be Khanai's."

"Of course!" Bhupinder hissed, annoyed at not having thought of it himself. "I'll have that checked out right away."

He spoke into his phone and issued instructions to hasten the identification of all unidentified numbers in Mrs. Markaan's call record.

"There is one more update," Bhupinder said when he hung up. "Inspector Choubey from Patna called. He expects to get hold of Pratap's Aadhaar card details by tomorrow. This Aadhaar card stuff is a new thing to all of us – we were unsure how to go about getting anyone's Aadhaar details.

"Choubey showed Pratap's photo to Mrs. Markaan's lawyer too. The lawyer identified him at once. Once we verify Pratap's biometrics against his Aadhaar data, we will have an unshakeable identification."

Bhupinder rose and pocketed his notes.

"I'm going to talk to Pratap," he said. "Let's see what he has to say. Meanwhile, I've requested for a warrant or restraining order on Eshwar Safe Vaults. If Pratap has hidden Mrs. Markaan's jewels in a locker, they will stay there."

A minute after Bhupinder went out, Athreya followed him. It was time to go deep into Naaz Tapu with Nazreen.

* * *

Athreya and Nazreen stood at the edge of the forest on Naaz Tapu with the mud strip behind them. Nazreen had expertly piloted the rubber raft across the Betwa to the rock shelf of the islet. With the mooring rope in hand, she had leapt lightly from the raft to the rocks and pulled the dinghy towards the islet so that Athreya could step onto the rock shelf. Once both of them were on the rocks, they had hauled the raft up and tied the mooring rope to an iron stake driven into the rock. They had then crossed the mud strip and reached the edge of the jungle.

Nazreen was attired just as she had been for the past three days – in a light-coloured kameez and a dark churidar. Today, the colour scheme she had chosen was purple. In addition, she was wearing a black sleeveless vest that was unusually long – it reached a good foot below her waist. She had also tied her hair in a ponytail.

As they were hauling up the raft, Athreya saw why she had worn the vest. Concealed under it was a leather belt. From the belt hung two sheathed daggers. Now, as they stood at the edge of the trees, she loosened them.

"Athreya Sahib," she said without looking up, "While we are on my islet, I need you to follow my instructions unquestioningly, especially if it comes to leaving in a hurry."

"*My* islet?" Athreya echoed. "What do you mean—"

"Maybe I'll tell you later, maybe never." She cut in smoothly in her quiet, understated way. "But not now. We are entering a dangerous place where we can't afford distractions. There are perils that you are not aware of. What Habib Mian told you is not the full story. It's imperative that you follow my instructions without hesitation. There may be no time to explain and convince. Your questions may be answered later. Agree?"

"Agree," Athreya replied, running his long fingers through his fine hair. There was nothing else he could say – Nazreen's tone had made that clear.

"Can you please switch off your mobile?" she asked. "Silencing it isn't enough. It can be heard when it vibrates."

As Athreya pulled out his phone and switched it off, Nazreen stood still and listened for a long moment. She briefly closed her eyes and seemed to focus on hearing. The half-smile that usually softened her face was not in evidence. At length, she opened her eyes and nodded.

"Stay close," she whispered. "Don't lose sight of me."

With that, she glided away into the trees on silent feet. Athreya followed as quietly as possible, taking care not to step on twigs or rustle dry leaves. The silence was oppressive and almost physical.

The jungle was as airless and claustrophobic as it had been the last time. But the heightened sense of danger, the need to focus on where he was putting his feet, and having to constantly watch his surroundings left no room in his mind for claustrophobic anxiety. However, within a minute, he again lost his bearings and his sense of direction.

As on the last occasion he had entered the jungle of Naaz Tapu, his imagination flared. Visions of Bhola and his Mastiff returned, as did the imagined scene of attackers closing in on Naazneen and Vanraj. Volleys of arrows flew past his mind's eye as the defenders beat off the attacking force.

Then came a new vision – that of Naazneen wielding sorcery that felled the crown prince's wife and children in faraway Orchha. That act of invoking ancient sorcery, Habib Mian had said, had possibly destroyed Naazneen's body and had forced her into the world of spirits, into which her newlywed husband had followed.

Then, with a start, he realised that Nazreen had stopped. Bringing his mind back to the present, Athreya saw that they were at the hunting lodge. They entered the lodge cautiously to find that nothing had changed. The turned earth lay as it had during the previous visit. The digging tools in the corner were unmoved. Even the cobwebs seemed to be the same as the last time. Athreya wondered if they should go down the steps in the corner. They probably led to a dungeon below.

"There is nothing there," Nazreen whispered, following his gaze. "I've checked. We are not meant to go there."

Before Athreya could respond, she turned and went out of the lodge entrance, back into the jungle. Athreya followed swiftly.

"I'm going to take a winding path that will take us through the center of the islet," she said. "Stay close and follow every turn I take."

For an interminable stretch of time, which Athreya later estimated was twenty to twenty-five minutes, they trekked through dense foliage. Trees and vines blocked their path everywhere. With her daggers, Nazreen could have cut her way through the vegetation as he had seen explorers do in movies. With machetes, explorers would cut their way through dense South American or African jungles. But Nazreen chose to go around thick growth or slip through the gaps between tree trunks. It was almost as if she did not want to hurt the vegetation.

Little light penetrated the canopy above, and not a leaf stirred. The only sounds were the ones he made. Occasionally, he would hear a drop of water fall – perhaps condensation from the thick, moist air. There was nothing to see other than trees, bushes and creepers. No manmade object sullied what seemed to be virgin nature.

Then, without warning, he came to the edge of the islet. At the bottom of a sharp drop of a few feet, bluish grey water flowed rapidly. At the same time, the sound of churning and cascading water registered on his mind.

"We are at the north edge of the islet," Nazreen whispered. She gestured to the flowing water and continued, "This is the middle of the three arms of the Betwa. Across the water is the other islet. It's smaller than the one we are standing on."

Lifting his gaze, Athreya saw that the middle arm of the river was strewn with rocks. The water gushed and roiled as it fought its way past the immovable rocks. Beyond the water was the other islet, looking very similar to Naaz Tapu. Idly, he wondered if it had a name.

"The water here is fast flowing, but it's not deep," Nazreen said. "It you are brave enough, you can wade across."

Looking at the agitated water, Athreya decided that he wasn't brave enough.

"Beyond the other islet is another stretch of flowing water – the third arm of the Betwa," Nazreen continued. "That arm is quite navigable in a raft. As you can see, it's not difficult to reach Naaz Tapu from the other riverbank."

"What's on that riverbank?" Athreya asked.

"Forest. Uninhabited forest. No buildings, no settlements for at least two miles." She turned and re-entered the jungle. "Come, let's go to the shrine."

"Shrine?" Athreya asked as he followed her. "Shrine to whom?"

"To the two people the king of Orchha exiled here."

Before he could ask the next question, Nazreen almost disappeared behind some particularly dense greenery. Dropping his intention to carry on the conversation, Athreya focused on catching up with her. They continued for another few minutes till Nazreen came to a halt before a massive banyan tree.

By the look of it, the tree must have been a few hundred years old. The roots on which the tree had spread outward formed a veritable maze. Some had grown to be over a yard thick. Athreya tried to peer through the forest of roots to find the primary trunk of the tree, but couldn't.

"This way," Nazreen whispered and slipped through a narrow gap between two roots.

Athreya turned sideways and followed her into the maze of vertical pillars of living wood. Nazreen wove her way through the labyrinth and presently Athreya saw a stone structure a short distance away. The structure – presumably the shrine – was more than half-buried under the banyan tree's prop roots, which seemed to flow and drape over the building with loving care. The roots had overrun the building to such an extent that Athreya couldn't see an entrance.

They halted when they reached the shrine. Nazreen went on her knees to pay her respects, and stayed prone for a couple of minutes. Presently, she rose and gazed at the shrine. Her face began to tighten. The calm she'd exuded when she had prayed evaporated. In its place came a certain tautness and anxiety.

"Stay here!" she hissed to Athreya. "Keep your eyes and ears open, but don't go until I come back."

She drew the two daggers from the sheaths and stood for a moment, listening. The dagger in her right hand was held with the ten-inch-long curved blade pointing downwards and her thumb pointing up. She held the other dagger – a slightly shorter one – the other way with both the blade and her thumb pointing forward.

She moved forward noiselessly and disappeared among the maze of living wood. Athreya stood where he was, lacking the confidence to move about on his own in a jungle where he had lost all sense of direction. He couldn't tell which way was east, although he knew that the sun would be in that direction.

How long he stood there, he didn't know.

Then, Nazreen appeared suddenly beside him, her face taut and her body tensed. Her daggers shone menacingly in the gloom.

"Something is not right here," she whispered in his ear. "We must leave. *Now!*"

She hurried past Athreya and stopped when she saw that he

was not following her. He was, instead, staring at a wet patch on the ground as if he had seen a ghost. Whatever he had seen seemed to have paralysed him for the moment.

She slapped his arm with the hilt of her dagger and hissed in his ear.

"Hold my vest," she whispered. "We must go quickly. Hold my vest and follow me. *Now!*"

At last, the urgency of her message filtered into his mind. He clutched her vest with his right hand and hurried behind her. As he went, he cast a backward glance at the wet patch of mud that had stunned him.

In the wet ground was an unmistakeable mark. It was a distinct and a deep impression, and it had been made recently. Very recently.

It was a pawprint. The paw of a very large dog.

CHAPTER 17

As soon as they scrambled into the raft and pushed off from Naaz Tapu, they noticed a knot of people on the riverbank near the base. Two men were waving, trying to attract Nazreen's and Athreya's attention. At that distance, Athreya couldn't make out who they were. But Nazreen's keener vision was up to the task.

"Dr. Baig and Ulhas," she said. "They are calling us … want us to go there quickly." She stiffened. "Something is wrong."

She turned to Athreya and continued as she rapidly piloted the raft back to the base.

"Athreya Sahib, please don't talk about what you saw and did at Naaz Tapu. Or about what I did. Nobody must know about the shrine."

"They won't," Athreya agreed. "I saw something else, too."

"I know … on the wet ground. Now is not the time to talk about it."

"If there is a physical pawprint, there must be a physical dog," Athreya persisted.

"Yes. There were claw marks on Markaan Sahiba, and a bite too. Why does a pawprint come as a surprise?"

Athreya opened his mouth to respond, but Nazreen went on.

"We will have to go back to the islet," she said. "Till then, it's best not to talk about it." She threw a quick glance at Athreya. "Especially to the inspector."

She turned away and gave her full attention to piloting the raft to where eager hands reached out for the mooring rope. The faces of the people waiting for them were grim, and Sabir seemed deeply worried.

Handing over the raft to a couple of workers, Nazreen helped Athreya step onto the rock shelf. Once Athreya was on firm ground, Sabir took him by the elbow and drew him aside.

"There has been another death," he said in a low voice. "They discovered it less than half an hour ago. Your phone was off."

"Who?" Athreya asked as he pulled out his mobile phone and switched it on.

"Pratap," Sabir replied.

"He seems to have died some hours back," Ulhas said as the three men began moving away from the raft. "He was killed sometime during the night."

"Killed?" Athreya asked. "Are we sure?"

"I'm afraid so," Sabir said as Ulhas nodded. "The inspector and the police doctor are there. I have instructions to take you there as soon as you returned."

Athreya turned and looked for Nazreen. But she was nowhere to be seen. She seemed to have vanished.

Ten minutes later Athreya reached the spot about half a kilometre upstream from the base, where Pratap lay among the foliage close to the riverbank. Bhupinder was in discussion with the police doctor as a photographer recorded the crime scene. Sabir and Ulhas halted a dozen yards short and let Athreya go forward to where Pratap lay.

"Nasty business, sir," the inspector said as he came towards Athreya.

He and the police doctor joined Athreya as the latter stood a yard from Pratap's lifeless body and stared down at it. Pratap lay on his back with both arms flung out over his head and his face turned to his left. His eyes were half-open and a grimace contorted his features.

On the right side of his head, which was pointing towards the sky, was a prominent wound. He had been struck by a blunt weapon that had broken his skull. But what was gorier was his throat. It had been savagely ripped out.

"Good God" Athreya exclaimed. "How were the wounds inflicted?"

"By the same things that inflicted the wounds on Mrs. Markaan," the doctor said. "He was struck twice on his head, but neither of the blows are as powerful as the one that killed Mrs. Markaan. The one on the side of his head – the one you can see – was fatal."

"And the throat?" Athreya asked.

"Caused by the jaws of a large animal. It clenched the whole throat and bit it out."

Athreya turned to the doctor and spoke in an undertone.

"Did you do the analysis I requested?" he asked.

"Yes," the doctor replied equally softly. "I did it yesterday but didn't get a chance to call you. There was no animal saliva on or around the bite wound on Mrs. Markaan."

"A physical bite, but no saliva? Are you sure?"

"Positive."

"Are you sure that the wound was inflicted by a dog?"

"Well, it was caused by the jaws of a large animal. The perforations made by the canines are unmistakable – deep punctures that are the hallmark of carnivores. There were other tooth marks as well. The spacing and depth of the punctures clearly suggest a large set of jaws."

"Could it have been caused by some another animal?"

"You mean other than a dog? Possibly … quite possibly. I'm not sure I can distinguish a panther's or a leopard's bite from that of a large dog."

"What about the claw marks on her back?"

"Inflicted by three very sharp and short objects. Consistent with a bared claw of a predator. I can't say if it was a dog, a wolf or one of the big cats."

"The three long cuts," Athreya mused aloud. "They ran parallel to each other for about a foot, right?"

"Yes."

"Were they clean cuts or ragged ones?"

"Quite clean, I think. I can have a look again."

"Will you, please? And did you find any dirt or mud in the claw marks?"

"Not that I recall."

"Can you check that too?"

"Sure." The doctor looked at him quizzically. "What do you have in mind?"

"I'll tell you after you complete your examination." Athreya smiled benignly. "I don't want to bias you." He gestured to Pratap's lifeless body. "No claw marks on him?" he asked.

"None. But there was no need – the teeth rendered the claws redundant."

"I see … I wonder what the locals are saying."

"What else!" Bhupinder snorted. "Bhola and his Mastiff crossed the water and came after Pratap. He too must have desecrated the islet, they say. Now that Bhola and his Mastiff have crossed the water – something they have not done for two hundred years – nobody here is safe any longer. Panic is the order of the day. They are cursing the day the archaeologists came here."

Athreya blinked. All of a sudden, he recalled the last words he had said to Pratap: *"What if the evil crosses the water and comes here?"*

* * *

Athreya stood at the centre of Pratap's room and watched the forensic team go about their business of collecting fingerprints and samples. He was not optimistic that they would find anything useful. If the killer had entered the room, he or she would have been extra careful about not leaving any signs that could be traced back.

The situation had been different when Mrs. Markaan had been killed – Pratap and Ulhas had opportunistically entered Mrs. Markaan's room when she was away. They had probably not known that she was going to be killed.

Athreya paused for moment to reflect on his latest surmise. If Pratap and Ulhas had known of Mrs. Markaan's imminent death, they wouldn't have left fingerprints in her room. The fact that they had left prints suggested that they had not known of her impending death. Did that rule them out as suspects? At least as far as Mrs. Markaan's murder was concerned?

He filed that thought away in his mind and resumed his scrutiny of Pratap's room. It was untidy as he had expected it to be – clothes and other things were scattered around, and on the desk was a jumble of books and papers. Pratap had left his suitcase half open on the floor, with a few clothes hanging out of it. That suggested that he had not stored anything of value in it. That further meant that the jewellery he had stolen from his aunt's room was in the locker in Eshwar Safe Vaults. However, a search of Pratap's room had not yielded the locker key.

Whatever was in the locker was safe for the time being – Bhupinder had acted as soon as he heard about Pratap's death, and had obtained a judicial order to prevent the locker from being opened. Two policemen were watching the entrance to Eshwar Safe Vaults, and one plainclothesman had been positioned inside, posing as a new clerk. If anyone approached with Pratap's locker key, he would be apprehended.

"The front door of Pratap's room was locked from the inside," Bhupinder said as he came and stood by Athreya. "But the door to the veranda was unlocked. Shut but unlocked. Anyone could have entered the room through it. I'm hoping that he has left just one tiny clue for me."

"Bhupinder," Athreya asked, "what is the estimated time of death?"

"Between 2 a.m. and 3 a.m.; give or take half an hour on either side. From the marks on the ground, we are fairly certain that he was killed where we found his body."

"Did you find any signs of a dog? Pawprints, for instance?"

"No." the inspector shook his head firmly. "The ground is dry. Broken bushes and disturbed soil suggest that Pratap was killed there."

"Mace this time, too?" Athreya asked.

"Can't be sure. The first injury was from a glancing blow. But we think it was powerful enough to knock him down. The second blow that broke his temple would have been fatal. Don't know if it was the same mace that killed Mrs. Markaan, but it was a blunt weapon for sure."

"Then, what was the bite to the throat for? Abundant caution? To make sure that he was indeed dead, or could not call out for help?"

"This is eerie, Mr. Athreya," the younger man said. "I don't mind telling you that this second death has unnerved me a little. The legend of Naaz Tapu seems to be coming alive."

"Despite the fact that the doctor found no animal saliva in or near the bite wound?"

"A ghost dog wouldn't be dripping saliva, sir, would it?"

"Guess not," Athreya agreed. "Did the security guard hear any-thing?"

"No. But Pratap was killed half a kilometre away."

"Any sounds of a boat or a raft this time?"

"No, sir. No sounds at all. Which reminds me, you need to ask all the archaeologists whether they heard any veranda door sounds last night."

Athreya nodded absently and asked, "When was Pratap last seen alive?"

"Lunchtime, as far as I have been able to find out. He was not at dinner – apparently he had gone out on his bike."

"Bike?' Athreya asked. 'Where is his bike now?"

"Don't know. The security guard says that it isn't where it is usually parked, and it wasn't there when he came on duty at 8 p.m. Pratap had gone out sometime after lunch and hadn't returned. He had apparently been saying that he was leaving the project very soon. That's one of the reasons nobody raised an alarm when he hadn't returned for dinner. They assumed he was busy winding up his matters in Jhansi."

Athreya was about to ask another question when his phone rang. It was a number he didn't recognise.

"Hello," he said, answering the call.

"Mr. Athreya?" a crisp male voice asked in a matter-of-fact way.

"Yes."

"Good morning. My name is Khanai, Colonel Khanai. I have just learnt about the inquiries you have been making in Delhi. I have been instructed to meet you."

"Wonderful!" Athreya replied. "Where are you now?"

"In Jhansi. At the government museum. Are you at the SBAI's project location?"

"Yes."

"How quickly can you get to the museum?"

"Half an hour? Can I bring along the police inspector handling this case? We are working together."

Colonel Khanai hesitated for a moment.

"If you can assure me of his discretion, yes. I leave it to you. We will be discussing classified information."

* * *

Colonel Khanai turned out to be a clean-shaven, trim man with hair as straight as Athreya's but not as fine. His features and complexion confirmed Athreya's guess that he was from the north-eastern part of the country. Inquiries had revealed that the colonel, who was in his early fifties, was an officer in the military intelligence. He had been deputed to an investigation that was being conducted jointly by three ministries including the ministry of culture. Looking at the colonel's face, Athreya would have estimated his age to be a little over forty. Except for the beginnings of grey at his temples, there was little sign of aging.

The room Athreya and Bhupinder entered was bare, save a table and four chairs. Colonel Khanai was alone. He rose swiftly from his chair and came forward to shake Athreya's hand with a firm grip. Once the two older men had shaken hands, Bhupinder threw the Colonel a salute, which was crisply returned. Though he was not in uniform, there was no mistaking that Khanai was a military man.

"Please sit," he said briskly, gesturing to the chairs as he resumed his own.

Once all three were seated, Khanai began.

"I was briefed about you, Mr. Athreya," he said energetically. "I must say that I am very pleased to meet you. Your name was not unfamiliar to me in the first place, as I have been in military intelligence for many years now. I believe you have worked with at least two of my colleagues."

"It's a pleasure to meet you too, Colonel," Athreya replied. "I have had the privilege to work with some very sharp people from your department. I am not sure if you are aware, but I had been deputed to military intelligence for two years. That was quite a while ago."

"Excellent!" The colonel smiled affably. "That makes my job easier. Having worked with us, you would appreciate that in our line, what we share is driven by the need to know."

"Yes, I do."

"Then, why don't we start by your telling me what your interest in this matter is. I would like to understand what you need to know from me and why."

"Okay, let me start with this: I believe you have been meeting Mrs. Markaan during the past week or so."

"That's right."

"Are you aware that she is dead?"

"Dead?" Khanai's face remained expressionless, as would be expected of a seasoned intelligence man. "Give me the details, please."

Athreya summarised the events of Sunday.

"Naaz Tapu?" the colonel asked. "I haven't heard that name. Where is it?"

"It's an islet in the Betwa; a river island," Athreya replied. "It is right across the water from the base. Didn't Mrs. Markaan mention it?"

"No. This is the first time I am hearing of it. What was Mrs. Markaan doing on the islet?"

"That is one of the things I intend to find out. Even if she hadn't used the name, didn't she mention an islet or a river island?"

"No. She said nothing of that nature. But what is this you say about a legend? Surely, you don't suggest that Mrs. Markaan was killed by a ghost or some sort of a mythical creature."

Khanai looked from Athreya to Bhupinder.

"We don't know who or what killed her, sir," Bhupinder replied. "The locals, of course, believe that she was killed because she dared to disturb the peace of the islet."

"Surely, we know better, Inspector?"

Bhupinder didn't reply.

"Did Mrs. Markaan talk about a bracelet?" Athreya asked.

Khanai nodded. "She talked about it at length," he said, "but she wouldn't show it to me – she didn't want to risk bringing it away

221

from the base. A new find, apparently."

"Then, you haven't seen it?"

"No."

"Not even photo or video of it?"

The colonel shook his head. "All I know is what the museum director told me – that it was an eighteenth-century design, perhaps from the south."

"A pity," Athreya murmured. "I was hoping that you could tell me something about the bracelet. I have a short video of it here. Let me show it to you."

Athreya pulled out his mobile phone and played the twelve-second clip that Dr. Korda had given him. Dr. Korda had shot the video holding his phone in his right hand while his left hand held the bracelet. During the twelve seconds, he turned the bracelet around so that all parts of it were captured in the clip.

"A fine piece," Khanai said after watching the clip twice. "Must be worth a minor fortune. No wonder Mrs. Markaan was reluctant to bring it here. Can you share the video clip with me?"

"Certainly." Athreya forwarded the clip to Khanai's mobile.

"Thanks," the Colonel said. "By the way, the museum director was surprised at Mrs. Markaan's lack of knowledge in certain areas. She was supposed to be a very senior archaeologist."

"Others have said that, too," Athreya said. "She seems to have built her reputation by riding on work done by her juniors. Coming back to the bracelet, here's one more piece of information – marks on Mrs. Markaan's palm suggest that she had been clutching the bracelet when she was killed. Whoever killed her took it."

"She took the bracelet to the islet in the middle of the night?" the colonel asked incredulously. "Whatever for?"

"We don't know yet."

"She was so reluctant to bring it to Jhansi and show it to me. She was scared that she might be waylaid and robbed. Yet, she sneaks away in the dead of the night with the bracelet and takes a raft to the islet? Only to have the spectral guardians of the islet kill her and take away the bracelet? It sounds like a horror movie, Mr. Athreya."

"Doesn't it, Colonel?" Athreya smiled wryly. "The wounds that killed her match the weapons wielded by the spectral guardians of the islet. And the phantom dog left no trace of saliva in the bite wound."

"Phantoms wouldn't drip saliva, I suppose," Khanai said briskly. "But I see what you are getting at. What would you like from me?"

"Mrs. Markaan's meetings with you were clandestine in that she told nobody else—"

"That was by design," the colonel interposed. "I told her not to speak of our meetings to anyone."

"There is a lot she seems to have kept to herself," Athreya continued. "If you could tell us what your conversations were about, it may help us get to the bottom of this matter. There is more here than is apparent on the surface, Colonel. For instance, we discovered last night that one of the archaeologists in her team was her nephew. He and Mrs. Markaan had kept that fact from everyone else. In fact, the nephew used his middle name rather than his first name to hide his real identity."

"Who is the nephew?"

"Pratap."

"I see. I wonder why they concealed the fact."

"As I said, Colonel, there is more here than meets the eye. That is not all. Last night, Pratap too was killed."

Khanai stared at Athreya. "He, too, went to the islet?" he asked.

"No. He was killed half a kilometre from the base in much the same manner as his aunt. In addition to being struck on the head by something like a mace, he seems to have been mauled by a large-jawed animal. The legend has repeated itself within two days."

The colonel smiled thinly. "That must have set the cat among the pigeons, as far as the locals are concerned, eh, Inspector?"

"Yes, sir. They are convinced that the evil from the islet has crossed the water and come to the bank. They are terrified."

"Thanks for the briefing," the colonel nodded. "That gives me a picture of where things stand. I'll tell you what I can. Please let it stay with yourselves only. As you will see, what I will be sharing is classified and sensitive. If word leaks out, all our efforts will come to a naught. I need you both to treat what I say as top secret."

Athreya and Bhupinder nodded.

"You see, Mr. Athreya," Khanai went on in a low voice, "I am a part of a multi-departmental team that is investigating the recent spate of art and antique thefts."

"The Bronze Runners?"

"So, you have heard of them. We have reason to believe that Jhansi and Gwalior are somehow involved with the thefts. We don't know how or why, but several disparate indications seem to point towards Jhansi, Gwalior and Bundelkhand in general. And if you draw a map of all the art and antique thefts that have taken place over the past couple of years, you'll find that Bundelkhand is at the centre of the map."

"Colonel," Athreya asked, "what can you tell me about the Bronze Runners?"

"I am not sure how much I should, but let me say this ... the Bronze Runners are well organised and very swift. More often than not, they seem to have had prior inside knowledge of the place they hit. Once they orchestrate a theft, the stolen goods disappear *very* quickly. Sometimes, they reappear far away, often overseas. However, many stolen articles have not reappeared as far as we know.

"How they do this, we are not sure, but we have some preliminary ideas. Unfortunately, I can't talk about them. Based on what we currently know, we've stationed people at different places, including at Gwalior and Jhansi. That is what brings me to this town. I really don't want to go into any more details. I'm sure you understand."

"Yes, I do," Athreya replied. "Thank you for telling us this much. But I am not clear about where Mrs. Markaan fits into all this."

"Ah, of course! I should have told you that. The SBAI's dig is the only one near Jhansi, and therefore an obvious draw to thieves – a low-hanging fruit, as the Americans would say," Khanai said. "We believe that the dig is being watched by the Bronze Runners. Once the SBAI start finding valuable artefacts, the dig will become a target. I was talking to Mrs. Markaan in this context, and my intent was two-fold. Firstly, I wanted to prevent a theft if possible. Secondly, I wanted to apprehend the thief."

"I can understand that," Athreya said. "What was Mrs. Markaan's role in this endeavour? What did you talk about? And what did she do as a result?"

"Some time back, without her knowledge, I placed one of my operatives in her team—"

"One of the workers, sir?" Bhupinder asked.

"Let's leave the identity aside for the moment, Inspector," Khanai said. "As I said, one of my operatives was inserted undercover into the dig. This gave us everyday inside information, and in addition, we had a trained operative close at hand to counter any attempted theft, should that materialise.

"But as the dig yielded nothing of value all these months, my person had little to do, except to send periodic reports. But all that changed eleven days back – Saturday before last, to be precise. Mrs. Markaan came to meet the museum's director and showed him the bracelet she had found. The news reached me and I decided to come down and speak to Mrs. Markaan right away.

"In my first meeting with her on Monday, I told her what she needed to know, and impressed upon her the need to be vigilant. I suggested that she not announce the finding of the bracelet until I could make the arrangements I needed to. If the Bronze Runners were to hit the poorly defended dig, I wanted to catch the thief."

"What was Mrs. Markaan's response?' Athreya asked.

"She thought about it for a couple of days and agreed to go along with my plan. That was on Wednesday." Khanai paused for a moment to press a button on his desk. "But my problem was that my undercover person was no longer in place at the dig. I had to put him back there at the earliest."

"Put who back, sir?" Bhupinder asked. "Who is your undercover man?"

There was a knock on the door.

"I believe you know him," the colonel said and gestured towards the door. "Here he is, now."

The door opened, and in came Madhav.

CHAPTER 18

Madhav stood with an uncertain smile on his face as his eyes flitted between Athreya and Bhupinder. He was neatly turned out, quite unlike the dishevelled, bleary-eyed man they had surprised early that morning.

If Madhav was uncertain, Bhupinder was positively stunned. Surprise, annoyance and disappointment vied for dominance on his face as he glared at Madhav with his mouth partially open. Athreya knew what was going through the young inspector's mind.

Bhupinder was annoyed that the man he had confronted that very morning—and who had lied to him—had turned out to be an undercover agent of the government. He was disappointed because the past two hours had knocked off the top two names from his suspects list—Pratap and Madhav. Suddenly, Bhupinder found himself with no real suspects.

As he watched the expressions on the two young men's faces, the humour in the situation struck Athreya and he burst out laughing. Relieved, Madhav broke into an answering grin, while Bhupinder regained his composure and snapped his mouth shut.

"So, this what you were lying about!" Athreya chuckled.

"Lying?" Khanai asked, puzzled.

"We confronted Madhav early today about his meetings with Mrs. Markaan, which he had denied. It was apparent that he was lying to us, but we didn't know why he was concealing the fact that he had met Mrs. Markaan in the past few days."

"I hope you didn't meet her at the museum," the colonel said, his gaze snapping to Madhav.

"No, sir." Madhav shook his head. "We met at a restaurant to discuss details of my return to the dig."

Khanai frowned. "Was that necessary?" he countered. "Couldn't you have done it over phone?"

"We could have, sir, but MM insisted on meeting personally before she allowed me back. I took precautions to ensure that we were not seen together in public."

"What about the two men you met late at night?" Bhupinder asked, cutting in. "Who were they?"

Madhav's geniality vanished and he turned to look at the colonel for guidance. Khanai gestured him to the empty chair and continued in a low voice.

"I didn't want to talk about it, but I guess we have no choice," he said. "There is one other thing we are trying to do, Inspector … we are trying to infiltrate the Bronze Runners. Madhav has been meeting men whom we think are connected to the gang in some way. That's the reason I didn't want him to meet Mrs. Markaan openly or in the museum, lest the gang suspects his real intentions.

"As you can imagine, this is *absolutely* confidential. You must not speak of this to *anyone*, Inspector, including your superiors. Over the past year or two, Madhav has gradually been gaining the gang's confidence. If word leaks out now, not only will everything come to a naught, but some lives – including Madhav's – would be at risk."

"So, that's what took you to Gwalior, Allahabad, Pune, Jaipur, and other places over the past two years," Athreya mused aloud, gazing at Madhav as his long fingers drummed a slow beat in his chair's armrest. "But why did you have to use aliases?"

"Because it demonstrates his willingness to be … er … flexible," the colonel replied. "It builds confidence in the minds of the Bronze Runners."

"Have you also been meeting a man named Jagan?" Athreya asked Madhav. "A wiry, middle-aged man who is also Dr. Baig's friend?"

Madhav nodded. "I have been meeting a number of shady characters, sir."

"Let's leave it there if you don't mind, Mr. Athreya," Khanai interposed. "We've already said more than I am comfortable with. As you know, information is shared only on a need-to-know basis."

He pulled out his mobile phone and turned towards Madhav. He touched his phone's screen a few times, and then passed the phone to Madhav.

"Mr. Athreya gave me a video of the bracelet," he said. "What do you think?"

Madhav watched the video clip for a minute or two as it looped and played repeatedly.

"A nice piece," he said as he handed the phone back to Khanai. "Loads of rubies and emeralds without complicating the pattern with diamonds. Looks a classic … and heavy, too." He looked up at Athreya. "Where *exactly* did MM find it?"

"We don't know," Athreya replied. "She confided in no one."

That Mrs. Markaan had excavated the hunting lodge and had explored parts of Naaz Tapu was something he had preferred to keep between Nazreen and himself.

"From what the guard said, she seemed unusually excited the week before last. That's when she must have found it."

"The guard at the dig?" Athreya asked.

Madhav nodded and chuckled under his breath.

"I might have been booted out of the project, but I kept tabs on what was happening there. I went to the dig a couple of times a week when MM wasn't around."

"Did you learn anything from the guard or anyone else that might be relevant to our investigation into Mrs. Markaan's death?"

Madhav frowned and thought for a long moment before shaking his head.

"I guess you already know by now that nobody at the base liked MM. And for good reason, too. When you steal credit from your juniors, you can't expect to be liked or respected. As a result, she resorted to terrorising people. She had her knife into Adhira, too, and Dr. Baig made her insecure."

Athreya nodded. "Anything else?"

"Well, you also probably know that she hired the raft a couple of weeks ago. I had no idea why she did that. I guess it was one of those excesses she indulged in from time to time."

"Excesses?" Athreya asked.

"You know, one car exclusively for her and another car for everyone else; a fancy laptop for herself; stuff like that. Maybe, she hired the raft for taking pleasure trips down the Betwa. Nobody else at the base used the ruddy thing."

Madhav ran his fingers through his hair and looked up at Athreya.

"But what really beats me is why she went to the cursed islet in the middle of the night," he said. "Was she bonkers or what?"

"Madhav," Athreya said. "You spent several months at the base and the dig with your ex-colleagues. Did you notice anything peculiar about any of them?"

"Well," Madhav began, rubbing his chin thoughtfully. "It depends on what you consider to be peculiar. Let me answer your question another way – where there unanswered questions in my mind about the people at the dig? Yes, there were."

"Tell me. We don't know what could be useful. Why don't you start from the top?"

"Sure. MM was at the top, and I've already spoken about her.

The biggest question I had early in my stay was about her incompetence as an archaeologist and her lack of knowledge. But that has been answered since – she plagiarised and stole her juniors' work.

"Coming to the next in command, Dr. Baig, I think he is probably the most authentic and knowledgeable person at the dig. Quite a gentleman who keeps very regular working hours, and has interests outside archaeology. But I do have unanswered questions about him. Why has he lately become sure that he would soon replace MM as the director? Had MM's ineptitude been noticed by Liam Dunne, or was there something else?

"Why does he prefer to go alone to Jhansi most of the time? We often go in twos or threes, sharing the one car that we were allowed to use. But Dr. Baig often walked to the main road and hitched a ride to Jhansi or took a passing autorickshaw."

Athreya didn't respond. Both the questions had possible connections with the anonymous letters.

"Coming to Dr. Korda," Madhav continued, "he is one unfathomable guy, and there is something sinister about him. I am sure he has secrets, but I don't know what they are. He plays his cards very close to his chest. By the way, he carries a pistol. Says he has been in some god-awful places where a gun is a life-preserver.

"Next is Nazreen – the lovely Nazreen on whom no man has ever made an impression. She is an enigma, Mr. Athreya. I know nothing about her. She is supposed to be a local, but I don't have the faintest idea where her family lives. She walks as silently as a ghost. And those eyes! They look like they know everything. The one thing I know about her is that her knowledge of Bundelkhand's history is encyclopaedic. Nobody comes closes to her in that, not even Dr. Baig.

"Then comes the curious couple – Mithali and Ulhas. Why does she work so hard? She puts in twelve hours a day, day after day. She is always messing around in her lab. Seldom takes a break.

What drives her? Some secret project she is working on? If so, I hope she kept it away from MM's clutches!

"Ulhas is the most doting husband you could find. So caring that it's sometimes sickening. He does all the shopping for her at Jhansi, and even gives away her stained and scarred clothes. He wouldn't have to do that if she remembered to wear her apron while working.

"Then my friend Pratap. The basic question is this: why is he there? He has no skill, knowledge or interest in archaeology. Why then did MM pick him? There would have been dozens of better candidates to pick from. Quite frankly, he doesn't pull his weight, Mr. Athreya. But MM pays him more than she pays Ulhas or Mithali or Nazreen. Why?"

"That question seems to have been answered," the colonel interrupted. "It appears he was Mrs. Markaan's nephew."

"Nephew!" Madhav exclaimed snapping his head around to his boss. "Who told you that?"

"Mr. Athreya."

Madhav turned his intense gaze to Athreya. "Is that true, sir?"

"It is. We established that last night."

"Pukka?"

"Very pukka."

"Bloody hell!" Madhav swore. His face looked as if a long-pending question had been answered "That explains it! That explains everything."

"He used a different name at the dig," Khanai said, looking at his watch. "His middle name became his first name."

"The little rat—"

"You better get back to your work," Khanai interrupted, cutting the discussion short. "Don't want you in this room for longer than necessary. There's only Adhira left to talk about, and I don't think you'll say anything negative about her. In any case, you are conflicted as far as she is concerned.

"Lend Mr. Athreya a hand if he needs it, Madhav. But only if it doesn't jeopardise your work. Your work is far more important than a murder investigation."

"Two murders, sir." Madhav rose to go.

"How did you know?" Bhupinder asked at once.

Madhav just smiled.

"Adhira?" Athreya asked.

Madhav's smile broadened. He turned to the colonel.

"Can I have a copy of the video, sir?"

"I'll send it to you."

Madhav nodded goodbye to Athreya and Bhupinder and went out. Athreya also rose. The other two men followed suit.

"There is also a small ring that Mrs. Markaan's killer did not take, Colonel," Athreya said. "I'll send you a photo of it. I suggest you send it and the video clip to your central team. I suspect that the ring and the bracelet hold the key to this mystery."

* * *

Bhupinder had been brooding for fifteen minutes when Athreya patted him on the shoulder. They were in the car, returning to the base after meeting Khanai and Madhav.

"Cheer up," Athreya said. "Things are getting clearer."

"Clearer?" the inspector retorted. "They have never been murkier. My top suspects are out the window. Who do we have left – Dr. Korda and Dr. Baig?"

"You are ignoring the ladies, my friend."

"Could any of them wield a mace, sir?" He reflected for a second and continued. "But you are right. Pratap was lured out of his room. He was the kind of guy who is easily attracted to women."

"None of the three ladies at the base had the slightest interest in him, Bhupinder. Besides, meeting half a kilometre away would be

233

far too suspicious when their rooms are a few yards apart. Pratap must have been lured by someone from outside the base. Perhaps for a clandestine meeting that was scheduled sufficiently late in the night and sufficiently far away from the base so that nobody could see or hear them."

Bhupinder's head snapped around to Athreya. "Jagan?" he asked.

Athreya nodded. "There is more to Jagan than we have been willing to admit. I hope you have a tail on him?"

"Twenty-four hours, but only a single tail at a time. Sorry, short-staffed."

"Check with your man if Pratap met Jagan yesterday."

Bhupinder picked up his phone. Five minute later, he had the answer. Pratap and Jagan had met for three hours from 4 p.m. onwards, after which they had left on Pratap's bike. Jagan's whereabouts after that were unknown until he returned at around 6 a.m. the next morning.

"There, you are," Athreya chuckled. "You have a new top suspect. Find out all you can about this man."

"I'll do that right away, and I'll pull men from elsewhere to tail Jagan. We won't lose sight of him next time. Incidentally, didn't you tell me that Jagan is a good friend of Dr. Baig?"

Athreya nodded absently. His mind was elsewhere, and his long fingers had begun scribbling invisible words on the car seat. Seeing that the older man had lapsed into deep thought, the inspector began making phone calls to initiate a background check of Jagan.

***

Half an hour later, they were back at the base, where Athreya found Moupriya waiting for him.

"I didn't find anything out of the ordinary with Mithali Didi or Adhira Didi," she said once they were seated in the temporary office. "Except some little things, which I don't know are relevant at all."

"It doesn't matter," Athreya replied. "Tell me anyway."

"Well, Adhira Didi has a gun."

"A gun?"

Moupriya nodded. "A pistol or an automatic or something of that sort. Like what you see in the movies."

"She showed it to you?" Athreya asked.

"We were talking about a second death taking place within forty-eight hours, and all of us were scared. That's when Adhira Didi said that she was going to start carrying her gun with her as protection. She pulled it out of her bag and showed it to us. Apparently, the JBF issued guns to her and Dr. Korda after some nasty incident elsewhere."

"I see … did she happen to say anything about Dr. Korda?"

The girl shook her head.

"She went away after that, and I spent time with Mithali Didi in her lab. She was telling me about her work. Very interesting."

"What did you pick up about Mithali?"

"I'm not sure if I am just imagining things, but I wonder if she has some sort of a skin condition."

"Why do you say that?"

"My mother always says that if I didn't go outdoors, I'd become pale and my skin wouldn't get the nourishment it needs – vitamin D or something. Apparently, sunlight is good for us. You see, Uncle, Mithali Didi works so hard that she hardly ever goes out into the sunlight. She is *so* pale skinned."

"So?"

"Didi changed her T-shirt when I was there because she spilled something on it. I saw that her skin seemed a little loose and slightly wrinkled in a couple of places. Not like an old woman's or anything like that. It just seemed a *little* loose in two places. I am not sure if it is somehow related to the lack of sunlight she receives. I am not even sure if I just imagined it."

Athreya sat up. All of a sudden, the penny dropped. He now sat with a pleased expression on his face, smiling affectionately at the girl across the desk.

"Mou," he said to a surprised Moupriya, "you'll make an excellent detective. You have just solved a part of the case for me."

"Really?" Moupriya flushed pink in delight. "Really, Uncle?"

Athreya nodded, beaming at the girl.

"You notice small things, Mou. Little things that others don't. Your parents are going to be proud of you."

"What did I solve? Tell me!"

Athreya's face grew serious.

"Not now, Mou," he whispered. "We are dealing with dangerous people here. You are better off not realising the significance of what you saw. Let it stay that way for now. Meanwhile, don't speak to *anyone* about what you told me, okay?"

"Okay." She nodded, her eyes large and round.

Athreya rose and so did the girl.

"Now run along and mingle as you have been doing all day," Athreya said. "You've done your part, Mou. You can return home when you want to. I'll have a car drop you."

"Can I go now, Uncle? I'm tired and I have already pestered people enough. I'll say goodbye and leave in two minutes."

Five minutes later, Athreya had tracked Bhupinder down.

"I'm going to interview the residents of the base," he said. "I need to record some conversations. Do you have a recorder?"

"Yes, sir."

"Excellent! After the interviews are over, I need to send parts of the recorded conversations to a friend."

* * *

The first thing Bhupinder did was to pull out his phone and call the security guard who had been on duty the previous night when Pratap had been killed. Yes, the guard had done his hourly inspection around the base, and he had done it at the top of each hour as was his routine. No, he had not heard any unusual sounds during the night. Nor had he seen anyone on the veranda except Dr. Korda, who had risen from his chair and returned to his room when the guard had come around for this midnight round. As far as the guard could recall, all lights were off during his midnight round, the last person to switch off his light being Dr. Korda.

The most important piece of information the guard provided was that Pratap had returned to the base a little after 11:30 pm. He had just walked in without his bike because the bike had broken down, and had to be left at a mechanic's. The guard, who had been dozing inside the closed double-doors at the entrance, had been awakened by Pratap knocking on the double doors. The guard did not recall hearing a vehicle drop off Pratap.

After speaking to the guard, Athreya and Bhupinder began interviewing the residents of the base. They began with Dr. Sabir Baig, who had newly been appointed as the head of the project.

Sabir had gone to bed a few minutes short of 10 pm. He had read in bed for about fifteen minutes, after which he had fallen asleep. He hadn't heard any sounds, and the morning had seemed normal. As Pratap's motorcycle was not in the parking lot, he and the others at breakfast had assumed that Pratap hadn't returned.

Sabir hadn't been surprised at Pratap's absence, as Pratap had announced his intention to leave the project, and wanted to be relieved at the earliest possible date.

"Do you know if Pratap was related to any other member of the project?" Athreya asked.

"Related?" Sabir blinked in surprise. "How do you mean?"

"Was any other member Pratap's relative? You know – cousin, aunt, uncle, etcetera?"

"No." Sabir shook his head firmly. "I don't think anyone here is related to anyone else. Why did the idea cross your mind?"

"Would you be surprised if I told you that Pratap was Mrs. Markaan's nephew?"

Sabir's mouth fell open.

"You're serious?" he asked.

Athreya nodded.

"Of course, I'm surprised," Sabir exclaimed. "Stunned, actually. I had no idea—" Sabir suddenly leaned forward. "Look here, Mr. Athreya, you're not pulling my leg, are you?"

"Not in the least, Dr. Baig. Pratap was the nephew who was known as Sandeep. Pratap was his middle name – Sandeep Pratap Yadav. He used his middle name here and hid his relationship with Mrs. Markaan."

"I see."

Sabir sat back, his cultured face darkening in anger. Nothing needed to be said – it was apparent that Mrs. Markaan had indulged in nepotism. She had misused her position as the director of the dig and given very remunerative employment to her incompetent nephew.

"Please don't mention this to the others until we complete the interviews," Athreya requested.

"Sure. I understand."

"Thanks. I know you have just started taking charge, but would you know how many bank accounts SBAI operates?"

"Oh, yes. I'm an authorised signatory for the bank accounts. We have two accounts – one in Delhi and another in Jhansi. The salaries and other regular payments are made from the Delhi account. The Jhansi account is used mostly for local payments at the project here – worker salaries, rent, expenses, cars, and the like."

"That's it? Only two accounts?"

Sabir nodded. "Why would we need more?"

"One last question, Dr. Baig," Athreya said. "Do you know why

Mrs. Markaan hired the rubber raft?"

"No." Sabir shook his head. "She didn't confide in me. I came to know of it from Dr. Korda only a couple of days before her death."

After Sabir came Dr. Korda.

He too hadn't heard any sounds of doors before or after going to bed. Being the furthest away from Pratap's room, it was unlikely that he would have heard Pratap's door. He confirmed that he had risen from his chair at the sight of the security guard doing his midnight round, and had returned from the veranda to his room. He had switched off his light almost immediately and had gone to bed.

He too was stunned and angry to hear that Pratap had been Mrs. Markaan's nephew, and insisted that Liam Dunne be informed immediately. On Athreya's assurance that Dunne would hear of it in the morning, he relented and agreed not to speak of it to the others until the next morning.

"Would you know how many bank accounts the SBAI uses?" Athreya asked.

"Two." Dr. Korda's eyes were steady as they gazed at Athreya. "Why do you ask?"

"Routine," Athreya replied noncommittally. "Are you an authorised signatory to any of them?"

"No. MM, Sabir and Adhira are the signatories."

"Were you aware of her plans to hire a rubber raft, Dr. Korda?"

"No," the tall man said ponderously. "I came to know of it after the fact."

"Do you know why she hired it?"

"She said that she wanted to survey the entire stretch from the river. She felt that it would help her identify other potential archaeological sites."

"Did she hire someone to pilot the raft?"

"I'm not sure. She was quite adept at it herself. Has been doing that from a young age, I believe."

Adhira, who came in next, confirmed what Sabir and Dr. Korda had said about the bank accounts. She too was stunned that Pratap had been Mrs. Markaan's nephew. But in hindsight, she said immediately afterwards, she shouldn't be surprised – both MM and Pratap had been that sort of people. Adhira had heard nothing at night, and was unaware that Pratap had returned around 11:30 pm.

None of the other three residents – Mithali, Ulhas and Nazreen – knew anything about bank accounts, and very surprised to know about the relationship between Pratap and Mrs. Markaan. Mithali and Ulhas had heard no sounds during the night. Nazreen, on the other hand, had heard Pratap's front door a little before she had fallen asleep, but was not sure what the time had been. Thereafter, she had not heard Pratap's veranda door.

Nazreen's discussion concluded interviews. When Bhupinder left the room for a moment, Nazreen came over to Athreya.

"Tomorrow morning," she whispered, "we'll go to Naaz Tapu again. This time, you'll see something."

* * *

Athreya lay awake in his bed, listening to the beat of the watchman's stick as he made his 11 p.m. round. The residents of the base had retired to their rooms after dinner and a brief conversation. He wondered if Dr. Korda was in the veranda smoking his pipe.

Athreya was waiting for a phone call, which he hoped would come soon. He had sent to his contact in Delhi excerpts from the six interviews Bhupinder had recorded earlier in the evening. One of the six voices, he hoped, would find a match among the dozens of eavesdropped telephone conversations his contact had.

If that happened, one of the mysteries would be cleared up. His gut told him he was right. What he needed now was corroboration.

When his phone buzzed at 11:15 pm, Athreya almost leapt out of his bed to pick it up.

"Yes?" he asked as soon as he answered the call.

"We have a match," the voice at the other end said.

"Excellent!" Athreya whispered. "And the solitary thumbprint?"

"That matches too. Your hunch was right."

CHAPTER 19

The overnight mist was yet to clear when Athreya and Nazreen climbed into the rubber raft. Athreya had donned a jacket as a protection against the morning cold. Attired completely in green, Nazreen was once again wearing the extra-long vest that concealed her daggers. For the first time, Athreya saw her wearing shoes – she had swapped her habitual leather sandals for black, rubber-soled, slip-on shoes, which she wore without socks.

Nazreen expertly piloted the rubber raft into the river, and to Athreya's surprise, she turned right and pointed the raft upstream. He looked at her quizzically.

"Aren't we going to Naaz Tapu?" he asked.

"We are," she replied. "But we are going somewhere else first."

He didn't question her further as she took the raft to the centre of the river, glancing repeatedly at the islet and the riverbank. Athreya too studied the dark and still islet, which was as enigmatic as ever despite his having visited it thrice.

When the raft reached the end of the islet, Nazreen turned left and took it around the tip of the islet. Just as he began wondering where she was headed, she pointed it into the turbulent waters of the middle arm of the river.

For the first time, Athreya found himself between Naaz Tapu and the other smaller islet. A moment later, he lost sight of both the riverbanks. The gloomy, sinister woods of the two islets closed in from either side as the raft bounced along the increasingly choppy waters. His active imagination, which was easily provoked by proximity to Naaz Tapu, flared. But before it could take flight, he clamped down on the untameable creature and suppressed it for the time being.

Meanwhile, Nazreen's attention was entirely on piloting the raft. She took it closer to the smaller islet, taking care to avoid rocks and eddies. Athreya remained silent, not wanting to distract her at such a time.

Now that they were moving downstream with both the engine and the river pushing in the same direction, they went swiftly towards the unknown – too swiftly for Athreya's comfort. Ahead of them, the river was strewn with rocks to an extent that it looked unnavigable. The river was rock-strewn for as far as he could see, except for a stretch in the middle. In that stretch, the roiling waters seemed to pause and catch their breath before crashing into the rocks beyond the calm stretch.

Finding himself being thrown one way and the other as the churning waters buffeted the raft, Athreya held on tightly to the ropes. Nazreen, however, remained apparently unconcerned on her feet, swaying with the raft and maintaining her balance with feline grace. Apprehension was building in Athreya's mind as he watched the rocks come closer by the minute. Soon, they were no more than a hundred feet away.

Just as he was about to voice his concern, the pitch of the raft engine changed, and the boat's bow swung slowly towards the smaller islet and began approaching it. A few moments later, Nazreen pulled the rudder again, and the raft swung once more till its bow pointed upstream, the way they had come.

Keeping the boat pointed upstream, Nazreen adjusted the

throttle of the engine. Gradually, the raft came to near standstill, except for an occasional drift. Nazreen had adjusted the throttle such that the engine was cancelling out the flow of the waters. The rocks were no more than a dozen feet from the raft.

The raft began drifting towards the smaller islet. Nazreen picked up one of the two mooring ropes, which she had coiled in preparation. Just when the raft's side bumped into a flat rock at the edge of the islet, she let go of the throttle and leapt onto the rock with the coiled mooring rope in her hand.

Landing perfectly on her two feet, she deftly uncoiled a length of rope and pulled the raft towards her. At the same time, she stepped backwards till she reached a tree. She quickly wound the rope around the tree trunk and knotted it. She then asked Athreya to throw her the second mooring rope. Once she had tied that to an adjacent tree, she gestured to Athreya to join her.

"We call this Chota Tapu," she whispered. "Chota" meant small in Hindi. "It's not as dense as its bigger brother. Come."

As soon as Athreya entered the woods, he saw that the trees were further apart than in Naaz Tapu and the undergrowth was less too. Vines were plentiful but not as ubiquitous as on the larger islet. As they walked deeper into the woods, he noticed brown and dry creepers hanging here and there as if someone had hacked them with a machete to cut a path for themselves.

As they went in silence, it seemed to Athreya that Nazreen was looking for something. She had not yet told him why she had brought him here, nor had he asked. Shortly, they reached the far side of Chota Tapu, and Athreya got a panoramic view of the expanse of water stretching from Chota Tapu to the riverbank on the other side of the Betwa from the base. This arm of the river was broader than the middle one. And it was free of rocks.

"It's easy to come from the far riverbank to Chota Tapu," Nazreen said. "The gentle flow makes it a nice swim, too."

After gazing at the river for a few moments, Nazreen resumed her search, walking parallel to the edge of the islet and a few dozen feet from it. She went slowly, studying the undergrowth and pausing ever so often to poke it with the stick she had picked up.

"Ah," she exclaimed softly, staring at what seemed to be a large pile of scattered leaves. "You see, Athreya Sahib?"

For a moment, Athreya didn't understand what she meant. Then it dawned on him – what he was looking at was not a pile of scattered leaves. It was a thick camouflage net into which were sewn hundreds of artificial leaves. It was of the kind that the army used to camouflage their vehicles and artillery to hide them from peering eyes in the sky or on the ground.

That begged the obvious question. If there was a camouflage net, it was camouflaging something. What?

After searching for a minute, Nazreen found a corner of the camouflage net and lifted it. Under the net lay a mass of black rubber.

At first, Athreya couldn't make out what it was, but when Nazreen lifted the whole thing, he recognised the shape. Before them lay four deflated rubber tubes. Two tubes, a foot in width and seven feet in length, lay parallel to each other. Their ends were connected by two more tubes of similar girth but only three feet long. Together, the four black tubes enclosed a rectangle that was seven feet long and three feet wide.

Four sturdy handles were embedded on the inside of each of the longer tubes. Within the rectangle was a pile of black rubber. It turned out to a large rubber sheet that was ribbed with long flat pieces of nylon-enclosed foam. Under this foam-ribbed rubber sheet lay a much thicker rubber base.

"A raft," Athreya breathed. "An inflatable raft from which air has been removed."

"It's too narrow for people to sit in," Nazreen whispered. "And there is no plank to sit on either."

Nazreen was right. The raft was unsuitable for transporting living people. There was no place to sit, stand or row. It was clear that the raft was used to transport something else. What?

His surging imagination, which he had been restraining, broke free. In his mind's eye, he saw a long narrow box, six feet long and two-and-a-half feet wide. A coffin.

Even as the thought flashed through his mind, he saw Nazreen going down on her haunches at one end of the raft and peering at it. Embedded there were two large handles – towing handles. Darting to the other end of the raft, Athreya saw two large towing handles there, too.

"This raft isn't a transport on its own," he said. "It is towed."

"Yes," Nazreen agreed. She returned to the centre of the raft and lifted foam-ribbed rubber sheet that lay within. "This is a covering for whatever is transported in this raft. The cargo is tied down to the small handles by these." She pointed to four rolls of thick nylon belts. "Then, the cargo is covered by this foam-ribbed sheet before it is towed."

She dropped the rubber sheet and began covering their discovery with the camouflage net. Two minutes later, the deflated raft lay under the net, which looked as it had been fifteen minutes ago.

"It is as I feared," Nazreen whispered as she rose.

"Coffins," Athreya whispered in a strangled voice.

"What?" Nazreen's gaze snapped to his face.

"Coffins," he repeated. "Have coffins been seen anywhere around here?"

Nazreen's grey eyes bored into him, seeming to peer into his mind. Gradually, her face grew grimmer.

"Come," she finally whispered. "Let's go to Naaz Tapu."

* * *

Half an hour later, Athreya and Nazreen were on the islet. Nazreen had skilfully piloted the raft out of the angry waters between the two islets and taken it upstream. As she had controlled the throttle and the rudder, Athreya had untied the mooring ropes and leapt onto the raft. Once they were out of the middle arm of the river, Nazreen had let the current take them to the rock shelf of Naaz Tapu. There, she and Athreya had hauled the raft onto the shelf and made their way into the woods of Naaz Tapu.

When they had been on the islet less than twenty-four hours ago, Nazreen had been tense and wary. She had loosened her daggers before entering the woods. But today, she seemed her normal self and at ease. Though she had brought her daggers and they hung inside her vest, she didn't seem to anticipate a need to use them. Even on Chota Tapu, where they had seen clear signs of clandestine human activity, she had not felt the need to be on her guard. Athreya wondered what had changed in less than a day.

As had been the case during his earlier visits to Naaz Tapu, Athreya lost his sense of direction within minutes of entering the woods. But he sensed that they were going towards the shrine under the giant banyan tree. He followed Nazreen closely, but she didn't seem anxious or in a hurry. He found that he was getting used to Naaz Tapu, and his claustrophobia was far less evident. But he could feel it lurking at the back of his mind.

Presently, they came to the far edge of Naaz Tapu, where they stopped and gazed at Chota Tapu across the water. Athreya realised that the point they were standing at was adjacent to the calm stretch of water he had earlier seen from the raft. Though flowing swiftly, the water was not agitated. Far to his right and left were plenty of rocks.

It occurred to him that Chota Tapu was not far from where they stood. If he was able to manage the swift water, this would be a good place to cross from one islet to the other.

Nazreen hadn't said a word since they had left Chota Tapu. She now silently turned and made her way back into the woods with Athreya following her. Soon, they reached the fringes of the old banyan tree that was surrounded by the maze of roots.

Unhesitatingly, Nazreen plunged into the labyrinth. Athreya hurried in after her. A couple of minutes later, they were standing at the same spot where Nazreen had asked him to wait the previous day when she had gone to inspect the shrine with her daggers drawn. Athreya recalled vividly how she had returned in haste and how they had fled the spot.

But today, she seemed relaxed and assured. She sank to her knees and stayed there with a bowed head, offering her respects or prayers or both. Presently, she rose and looked towards where the prop roots were the thickest.

"Wait here as you did yesterday," she murmured. "I'll be back soon. Today, I'll show you the shrine."

"Do you come here often?" he asked her before she had a chance to walk away.

"Yes." Her voice was low and reverential. "I pay my respects regularly. But we enter the shrine only once in three years, unless there is a pressing reason to do so."

"Will we be entering it today?"

Nazreen nodded.

"We must. We have an urgent reason to do so."

With that, she walked away, and her bottle-green dress was soon lost to sight. Left with little to do, Athreya's mind and imagination began wandering. Habib Mian's tale of Naazneen and Vanraj rose in his mind, and he wondered how much of it was true and how much had been fabricated over the years. Myths tended to grow and expand with time.

He then thought about their guardians, Bhola and Moti. One of the pieces of information Nazreen had let slip the last time they were at Naaz Tapu, was that the Bola's gigantic dog had been an uncommonly large Mastiff called Moti.

As soon as he thought of Moti, his mouth went dry. He recalled the large pawprint he had seen yesterday at this very spot. Instinctively, he swung towards where he had seen the moist patch of soil that had held the pawprint. The patch was still there, but the pawprint wasn't.

He walked cautiously toward the patch with his eyes riveted on it. As he went closer, he grew certain. No, the pawprint wasn't there. It had vanished.

Just as he began wondering if he had imagined the pawprint the last time, he sensed a faint movement out of the corner of his eye. He swung around and stared. At first, he saw nothing other than the forest of brown and grey roots of the banyan tree.

Then, as his eyes grew accustomed to the low light in which the brown pillars of living wood stood, a different shape – also brown – grew visible. It was far shorter than the prop roots and it was stout. It had a massive head with heavy, black-edged folds of flesh handing over its mouth. And it had a tail.

Standing there, watching him was the largest dog he had ever seen. It was a Mastiff.

CHAPTER 20

Athreya stood rooted to the spot. Every muscle in his body had frozen, and his gaze was locked on the Mastiff's huge head. The massive dog stared stonily at him through unblinking eyes. No sound, not even a low growl, came from it.

This was no illusion. The dog stood there, as real as the roots around it, as real as the beads of sweat that were forming on Athreya's forehead and palms despite the cold. The creature's barrel chest was heaving gently and rhythmically, sending translucent puffs of condensed moisture into the air in front of its face. It was less than twenty feet away – a distance it could cover in two leaps.

Although Athreya's body was incapable of movement, his mind was wasn't. It quickly assessed his options and came up empty-handed. Physically, he was no match to the Mastiff. Even as it stood on its four legs, its head came up to his chest. If it were to rear up on its hind legs, it would easily tower over him.

Its massive jaw, which seemed eminently capable of tearing out Pratap's throat with one bite, could clamp over any part of his body without difficulty. Its teeth were hidden behind the hanging folds of the upper lip, but Athreya had no illusions about the size of its fangs.

In essence, there was no getting away. If this was Moti, the legendary guardian, could Bhola be far away?

Even as this thought flashed across his mind, a brown-clad figure materialised beside the Mastiff. It had emerged from behind a thick root and had taken its position beside the Mastiff.

Surprise plucked his taut nerves as he shifted focus to the new arrival. This was no Bhola, no mace-wielding giant. It was a young man with fair skin and sharp features that showed through his wispy beard. This dark-haired man was no taller than Athreya, but there was no doubting his wiry strength. He had dark eyes, but there was a striking resemblance with someone Athreya knew.

The young man's hands were empty, but from underneath his long vest, the tips of two daggers were visible. As Athreya watched, the man lifted his left arm and placed it on the Mastiff's shoulder. At once, the dog's face seemed to soften. It opened its mouth and began panting with its tongue hanging loose. There was no doubt about the size of the Mastiff's jaws – they were massive.

The dog glanced sideways and its tail moved ponderously in a slow wag as a figure in bottle-green appeared on its other side and patted its head.

Nazreen.

She wore the same benign half-smile Athreya had come to know well in the past few days. Studying the faces of the two figures standing beside the Mastiff, the resemblance became obvious.

"My brothers," Nazreen said purred.

"Brothers?" Athreya asked, finally finding his voice. Was she referring to the Mastiff as a brother, too? She had used the plural.

Her smile widened as her grey eyes flickered to Athreya's left. Athreya snapped his head that way. Less than ten feet away, stood a slightly younger man, looking very much like the one beside the Mastiff. This younger man was clad in a shade of green lighter than Nazreen's churidar kameez.

How had he come so close to Athreya without the latter realising it? He must have moved as silently as his sister.

With a shock, Athreya realised that the younger brother also was flanked by huge dog. It was a brown Great Dane – an erect, long-legged, pointy-eared creature with a black face. Its imperious gaze contemplated Athreya as it stood rock-still. Athreya noticed that the younger brother's hand was on its shoulder.

"Come, Moti," Athreya heard Nazreen say in Hindi and turned his eyes to her.

Nazreen was coming toward him with the Mastiff. The massive dog's gait reminded him of a tiger's. A few seconds later, he was face-to-face with the Mastiff.

"Hold out your right hand," Nazreen said. "Palm up."

Slowly, taking care not to alarm the Mastiff with sudden movements, Athreya held out his hand. The dog lowered its massive head and sniffed it. It then looked up at his face and contemplated him. Athreya stood still. It lowered his head again, gave a brief lick to his palm and turned away to return to its master.

"Churi," Nazreen called, turning to the Great Dane.

Clearly younger than Moti, Churi darted forward eagerly, making Athreya freeze in apprehension. It came up and smelled his arms and chest, while keeping its eyes on his face all the time. Athreya stood still with his arm thrust outwards. The Great Dane smelled his hand, nuzzled it briefly and returned to its master.

Athreya let out a silent breath of relief and turned to a smiling Nazreen. So, this was why she had been at ease today. Her brothers and the dogs had arrived at Naaz Tapu earlier and had surveyed the islet for any potential threats.

"Adaab, huzoor," the younger of the two brothers said as he brought his palm towards his face in greeting. "I have been looking forward to meeting you," he said in Hindi.

"Adaab." Athreya returned the greeting. "Churi is a lovely name for your dog. Is he as sharp, too?" "Churi" meant knife in Hindi.

"He is, huzoor. And swift too. He can catch a man on a motorcycle and bring him down."

"Adaab arz hai," a deeper male voice spoke beside Athreya. The elder of the two brothers had joined them.

"Adaab," Athreya replied. "I don't think I have seen a larger dog than Moti."

"He is special," the older brother said. "He is a direct descendant of the original Moti."

"Really?"

Athreya turned a quizzical face to Nazreen. Clearly, there were things she hadn't told him.

"Later," she said in response. "I will tell you some things if you promise not to breathe a word of it to anyone."

"The full story, which Habib Mian did not tell me?"

Nazreen nodded. "Only if you promise not to repeat it to anyone. It is history nobody knows, and we wish to keep it that way."

"I promise," Athreya responded.

"Very good. We'll talk about it later. We have other matters to attend to first. Remember, I said that I was going to show you something?"

"The shrine."

She nodded. "Come."

Nazreen turned and went deeper into the banyan tree, with Athreya and her brothers following her. Soon, they came to the stone structure that was overrun by the banyan tree's roots. The stone of the building was old and seemed to have struck an equilibrium with the roots of the ancient tree.

Nazreen went around the stone structure and squeezed through a gap between two prop roots. Athreya followed and found himself staring at the other side of the root-shrouded stone structure. In front of him was a narrow opening between two roots.

The opening was about five feet high and triangular in shape. Two roots curving away from each other formed two sides of the triangle, while the stone floor formed the third.

"Have you smoked out the shrine?" Nazreen asked her brothers.

"We have," the elder one replied. "Surprisingly, there was nothing inside. But we'll do it once more."

He pulled out a length of cloth that had been soaked in a grey mixture and then dried. His brother lit a match and held the flame under the cloth for a few seconds. The cloth began smouldering, and soon caught fire. The elder brother crouched at the opening and threw the burning cloth into the shrine. The younger brother let out a soft whistle. The next moment, Churi came running. They sat down on the grass and waited for the cloth to burn itself out.

Athreya eyed the narrow opening with growing apprehension. The original doorway had been much larger. But now, it was little more than a triangular slit between the banyan tree's roots. The ancient tree had covered the rest of the stone building that was the shrine. There would be no other opening. He knew what it meant to enter such a chamber.

He dreaded entering the airless, lightless shrine that lay beyond the narrow entrance. His claustrophobia stirred. Anxiety flared. The demons in his mind awoke. This was not something he had bargained for.

His mind went back to the time when claustrophobia had made him botch up a critical case. He had not been able to rein in his fears that day, and rising panic had prevented him from seeing what he would have otherwise observed. It had led to an embarrassing failure.

The subsequent dressing down he had received from the IG had been humiliating. He had had no option but to admit to his weakness; a weakness a police officer could not afford to have. He had been told to seek medical help if necessary, but such a failure wouldn't be tolerated again.

"As I told you," Nazreen said, breaking into his thoughts, "we usually enter the shrine only once in three years. Between visits, it's possible that crawling, creeping and other sorts of creatures enter the shrine. We need to drive them out before entering. My brothers have already done that, but as twelve hours have passed since the last smoking, we are doing it again. We don't want our guest to be bitten."

"What is in the shrine?" Athreya asked, trying to supress the fears in his mind.

"You'll see."

Fifteen minutes later, by which time the smoke had dissipated, the younger brother rose. Churi too stood up, looking lean and long-legged, waiting for his master's order. When he patted the dog's side twice, Churi approached the opening.

It first explored the shrine's entrance with its nose. Satisfied, it thrust its head in. A few moments later, Churi entered the shrine.

They waited for the dog to complete its scrutiny of the shrine. A few minutes later, the Great Dane stuck its head out of the opening. The younger brother stooped, switched on a torch and disappeared through the five-foot-high opening. A minute later, he called out, saying that it was safe to enter.

Next went Nazreen, who asked Athreya to follow her. The elder of the two brothers remained seated outside. As Athreya prepared to enter the shrine, Moti ambled up to its master and sat by his side.

Claustrophobia hit him like a physical blow as soon as he entered the dark, low-roofed, windowless chamber. Panic knifed through his mind.

This time, he was prepared. He knew what to expect and was determined to not let it get the better of him. He clenched his jaw and breathed slowly and deeply. He forced his arms and legs to stay still. He opened his eyes wide and confronted the daunting, low-roofed, dungeon-like chamber he was in.

Bit by bit, panic receded and his rational half asserted itself. He stood rooted to the spot as he gained control over himself. Fortunately, Nazreen and her brother had their attention focused entirely on the shrine and were taking no notice of him. Knowing that the best way to conquer his fears was to engage the mind intellectually, Athreya threw himself into studying his new surroundings.

He would *not* falter this time.

The shrine turned out to be a twenty-foot square, rough-hewn chamber with three short passages running away at right angles to each other. In one corner of the chamber was a raised platform on which two stalagmites stood. One was about five feet tall and the other about a foot taller. Except for the conical head onto which water dripped, both seemed to have a vaguely human shape.

The shorter one was slimmer and lighter in colour than the taller one. Athreya needed no explanation. These stalagmites represented Naazneen and Vanraj. The shorter, slimmer one was the lady and the other the disinherited prince.

Nazreen and her brother were down on their knees, praying. Athreya waited silently, studying the chamber and celebrating his victory over his fears.

One of the three passages seemed to lead downwards into darkness. The second was about twenty feet deep, but was bare and empty. The third passage, also bare, was much shorter. It ended abruptly in a grey stone wall.

Athreya wondered what purpose the passages served, but was unable to come up with a satisfactory explanation. Having explored the shrine with his eyes, he waited for Nazreen and her brother to finish their prayers.

They rose in unison ten minutes later. Nazreen came and stood beside Athreya, while her brother went to inspect the shortest passage along with Churi.

"That is an underground passage that goes to Chota Tapu," Nazreen said, pointing to the passage that led downwards. "But it got flooded about forty years ago. You can still go to Chota Tapu through it if you can hold your breath long enough."

"Swim?" Athreya asked in horror. Visions of swimming through a narrow, flooded tunnel unnerved him. What if he ran out of air? What if he couldn't turn back?

Nazreen nodded calmly. "I've done it a few times. My brothers have done it more often."

"Isn't it dangerous? What if you get stuck?"

"We won't. The shrine protects us. The same cannot be said for intruders."

A grating sound interrupted the conversation. Athreya and Nazreen turned towards the short passage into which her brother and Churi had gone. To Athreya's surprise, he saw Nazreen's brother moving the stone wall at the end of the passage with ease.

Athreya watched in amazement as the wall fell away as if it were lighter than wood. Only when it lay on the floor did he realise what it was – a fake wall made of fibreglass. He had seen similar ones on movie sets. It had been put there to conceal something that was hidden further into the tunnel. He glanced at Nazreen and was stunned to see the fury on her face.

"Desecrators!" she hissed and switched on her torch.

She strode into the passage and halted where the fibreglass barrier had been. She stood still, glaring into the passage that was now lit by her torch beam. Athreya walked up and stood beside her, looking into the passage in astonishment.

Five feet from him were nine rectangular wooden shapes, stacked in three rows of three each. Each of the boxes were six feet long and two feet square. They were precisely the size and shape that would fix the black inflatable rubber raft they had seen at Chota Tapu.

Athreya's imagination had not misled him – he was looking at nine coffins.

* * *

Athreya and Nazreen sat in a small clearing a few dozen yards from the shrine. The Mastiff sat by her side as she absently scratched its massive head. The Great Dane, far more inquisitive than the older Mastiff, was sniffing around the maze of prop roots. Nazreen's brothers were beginning the exercise of shifting the nine coffins to the hunting lodge as Athreya had instructed. Four men, who had arrived swiftly after one of the brothers made a phone call, were receiving instructions from the elder brother.

"This is why we had to leave the islet in a hurry yesterday," Nazreen said. "Armed strangers were here, and I didn't know who they were. All I knew was that they had desecrated the shrine. I didn't know about the fake fibreglass wall they had installed to hide their coffins."

"But now, your brothers have been here since last evening with their dogs. You knew that the islet was safe."

Nazreen nodded.

"Now, I'll tell you some history that is not publicly known," she said, taking care that her voice didn't carry to the shrine. "I'll begin where Habib Mian left off. He would have told you that Naazneen invoked ancient sorcery to fend off the crown prince's men, and that effort killed her. She and Vanraj then entered the world of spirits. Is that how Habib Mian ended his tale?"

"Yes," Athreya confirmed. "After that, Naazneen and Vanraj were never seen again."

"This is what really happened," Nazreen whispered almost reverentially with her eyes on the shrine, "Naazneen invoked sorcery, but she didn't die. She and Vanraj lived for many more years and raised a family.

"Within days of Naazneen and Vanraj's rumoured deaths, a small settlement sprang up on the riverside that is closer to Chota Tapu. Some of the staunchest followers of Vanraj had decided to make their homes as close to their beloved prince's islet prison as possible.

"Very soon, a chieftain emerged amongst them. Though young, the chieftain had a wife. They were reclusive and seldom left the settlement. They were none other than Vanraj and Naazneen, who were now living their married lives incognito.

"The queen knew about this and made sure that the fiction about Vanraj's and Naazneen's deaths was spread and repeatedly reinforced. The notion that Bhola and Moti guarded the now-haunted islet was buttressed with a dozen hair-raising tales that are told even today. The queen also ensured that paintings of Naazneen and Vanraj were destroyed, so that people forgot their faces. But, in secret, she frequently visited her youngest son and daughter-in-law.

"Eventually, the queen told the king the truth. By then, the king had grown remorseful, and was ruing the hasty banishment of his youngest son. He received with great delight the news that Vanraj was alive and was with his beloved Naazneen. In joy, he gifted Naaz Tapu and Chota Tapu to the chieftain's family.

"By that time, the fading memory of their faces aided by their changed appearance, they were able to go about unrecognised. They even visited the king in his private chambers without the knowledge of the courtiers or servants.

"They went about their lives as ordinary people, except for their chieftainship within the settlement. The crown prince and his ministers never discovered the truth, and by then, all records of Naazneen and Vanraj had been erased. Before long, the secret died with the king and the queen. History soon forgot the youngest prince of Orchha and his bride. It was as if they had never existed.

"Naazneen and Vanraj went on to live full lives and had three children. Their progeny lived on and kept the family secret to themselves. For the children of their small group of followers, this secret became a myth that lives to this day. The descendants of the followers still lay a table for Vanraj at the wedding feast. Occasionally, one of Vanraj's male descendants attends a wedding in regal attire to keep the legend alive."

"Let me guess the name Naazneen and Vanraj took when they moved into the settlement of their followers," Athreya asked.

Nazreen's half-smile widened a trifle as she encouraged him with silence.

"It was Vaziri, was it not?"

Nazreen nodded.

"Your name is Nazreen Vaziri," Athreya continued. "You are Naazneen's descendant. That explains the remarkable resemblance."

Nazreen nodded again.

"In our family, we worship our ancestors – Naazneen and Vanraj. That is what this shrine is about. We visit it once every three years because Naazneen and Vanraj had to stay hidden for three years before they had changed their appearance sufficiently to go out into the world.

"It is our belief that Naazneen returns in every alternate generation of the Vaziri family," she said. "She usually does so as the eldest daughter. The surest sign that she has returned is the colour of the daughter's eyes. She is the only one who will have grey eyes. Everyone else will have brown eyes."

"So," Athreya whispered, "you are both Nazreen and Naazneen."

Nazreen smiled beatifically.

"The daughter with grey eyes is always given a name that begins with 'Naaz' or 'Naz'," she said. "My grandmother was named Nazaquat and her grandmother was Nazeera."

"You were speaking the truth when you said that Naaz Tapu was *your* islet."

Nazreen nodded.

"These two islets are the property of the Vaziri family. You will find that the land records confirm it. This is private property, even if it isn't commonly known."

"You are the lady in white bridal dress people see from time to time," Athreya said.

Nazreen smiled.

"After all, this is private property, Athreya Sahib. We would like to keep people away from it. The best way to do it is to keep the myth alive. Once or twice in a generation, we float a rumour of someone being mauled or killed by the spectral guardians of the islet."

"There is more here than just the hunting lodge and the shrine, isn't there?" Athreya asked.

Nazreen didn't answer. She dusted her bottle-green dress and made as if to rise.

"I have another question," Athreya said. "Will you answer it?"

A bewitching smile played on Nazreen's lips.

"That depends on the question," she said.

"You are a local. You and your brothers have grown up close to the two islets. Yet, nobody in Jhansi knows about you."

Nazreen remained silent for a long moment, thinking. At length, she turned to him and looked into his eyes.

"Can I trust you with the answer, Athreya Sahib?" she asked. "If you betray my confidence, you will hurt me and the Vaziri family."

"You can, Nazreen." He gazed back into her grey eyes. "I give you my word."

"Alright." The grey eyes wandered away. "I'll tell you a little. We live a dual life, Athreya Sahib … we all use dual identities. Vanraj was Hindu and Naazneen was Muslim. Everyone in my family has a Hindu identity as well as a Muslim one. You know me by my Muslim identity. But the people of Jhansi know me by another name, a Hindu name.

"We live as a joint family in an isolated place surrounded by a large farm. We are self-sufficient, and don't interact very much with the people of Jhansi. While the Hindu name of our family is known in Jhansi, the people of Gwalior know it better. And all of us make it a point to study outside the state."

Nazreen fell silent. Athreya waited. He was wondering if she would tell him the family name. A minute passed. She didn't. Athreya decided to respect her decision. His interest was limited to solving the puzzle of how nobody in Jhansi, including Mrs. Sikka, had known about a local Muslim girl called Nazreen. That puzzle was solved now. Her Hindu identity was not important.

Nazreen rose. So did Athreya. All was clear in his mind now. It was time to bring the case to a close.

He pulled out his phone and made two phone calls – one to Inspector Bhupinder and the other to Colonel Khanai. He would get the residents of the base together at 10 a.m. the next day, he said. They had twenty-four hours to do a number of things.

He asked Bhupinder to raid three places including Jagan's house, and described what he was expecting to find in one of them. He wanted the places to be raided late at night, when he expected Jagan and some others to be away. On Jagan's return to his house, he was to be arrested.

Colonel Khanai and his men had the most to do. Based on two people Athreya named, Khanai's team was to trace as many connections to the Bronze Runners as they could. Once the murderer was disclosed the next morning, it was only a matter of time that the gang went underground.

Finally, he summoned Nazreen's brothers and told them what needed to be done. The rest of the day was going to be busy for a number of people.

When he finished, he noticed that he had received a message from his contact in Delhi. From Dr. Korda's video, the contact had identified the bracelet that Mrs. Markaan had found. He opened the message and smiled as his suspicions stood confirmed.

The message read: *The bracelet is not an archaeological artifact. It was stolen recently from a museum in Mysore.*

CHAPTER 21

The lounge was full at 10 a.m. the next morning. Athreya stood at one end of the room and surveyed the dozen faces in front of him. The residents of the base were scattered around the lounge in their usual seats. Khanai and Madhav had taken seats at opposite ends of the room while Dunne and Sharad sat together in the middle. As usual, Moupriya was close to Adhira, while Bhupinder stood at the opposite end of the room from Athreya. Khanai and Bhupinder were in full uniform.

The previous evening, Athreya had spent an hour with Dunne after the latter had confronted Dr. Korda and extracted a confession in private. Dr. Korda had confessed to opening a bank account named "SBAI Associates" – a name very similar to the SBAI in an abbreviated form, except for the "Associates" added at the end. He had used a morphed SBAI letterhead to open the account with himself as the sole signatory. Whether he was to be publicly prosecuted or dealt with in some other quiet way, was now up to Dunne and his lawyer. Athreya's job was done as far as Dr. Korda was concerned.

However, Athreya had requested that he be present at the gathering, as he had a contribution to make. The tall man now sat motionless and silent in a corner.

"Good morning," Athreya began. "I called all of you here to conclude this mystery that has been puzzling us for the past few days. Let me begin with where we found Mrs. Markaan's body.

"As you know, she was found lying face-down at Naaz Tapu, with the back of her head crushed. Her broken flip-flop was found at the edge of the strip behind her, pointing towards the trees and *away from the strip*. The obvious interpretation was that she had been running away from her attacker when she was struck *from behind*.

"If that was the case, her attacker *must* have been behind her. But behind Mrs. Markaan was the squelchy mud strip, which you cannot tread without leaving a footprint. But there were no footprints. Then, was the attacker some sort of ghost that didn't leave footprints?

"A short distance in front of Mrs. Markaan was another clue – her torch. It was broken, as one would expect from the fall that it had suffered when she was killed. But the killer had made a mistake – the torch had not been switched on. Why not? Probably because a glowing torch would have attracted unwanted attention in the dark of the night.

"The third inconsistency that clinched the issue was this: *Mrs. Markaan's feet were virtually free of mud.* Anyone who has walked the squelchy strip knows that the wet mud oozes up your footwear and sticks to your feet like glue. If Mrs. Markaan had indeed walked across the mud strip as the tracks suggested, why was there no mud on her feet?

"Therefore, it was apparent from the very beginning that the whole set-up at Naaz Tapu was a tableau, an elaborate arrangement designed to convince us that Mrs. Markaan had gone to Naaz Tapu in the dead of the night, where she was killed by Bhola and his Mastiff.

"But the truth was very different. Mrs. Markaan had been killed elsewhere. Thereafter, her body and the evidence were arranged on the islet in the manner we saw the next day."

"What about the wound on her head?" Sabir asked. "It was clear that the blow had been delivered from a great height."

"Another piece of deception," Athreya replied. "The blow needed to be delivered from a great height *only if she had been standing* when the blow was struck. If she had already been killed or rendered unconscious with a smaller weapon, she could have been laid out on the ground before the larger blow was struck."

"Did the doctor discover two wounds?"

"He didn't at first. That's because the second blow was so powerful that it all but obliterated the first one when it crushed her skull. However, on re-examination under x-ray and after closer inspection, a straight, vertical crack grew apparent. When reassembled, her scalp, too, showed a straight, vertical tear.

"The width and length of the crack and the tear were consistent with the injury an iron rod would inflict. After being struck by a rod, she was transported to Naaz Tapu, where the second blow was struck and the tableau arranged."

"But the tracks on the mud strip were made by Mrs. Markaan's flip-flops," Sharad protested. "You said so yourself. There was mud sticking to them, too."

"Indeed!" Athreya agreed. "But the feet wearing them were not Mrs. Markaan's. Remember, there was no mud on Mrs. Markaan's feet.

"As you know, I got Moupriya to wear flip-flops similar to Mrs. Markaan's and walk across the mud strip. We then compared Mrs. Markaan's tracks with the tracks Moupriya made, we found some interesting things.

"The depressions that were supposedly made by Mrs. Markaan were an inch or so longer than what Moupriya made. Mrs. Markaan's footwear had slid back down the slope more than Moupriya's had, even though both of them were similar in build and weight. That meant that the person wearing Mrs. Markaan's flip-flops was considerably heavier than Moupriya. That's why they slid back a little more before they gained purchase on the slimy mud.

"The other interesting aspect was the depth of the impressions made in the mud."

"But they were the same!" Moupriya objected. "The inspector measured them – both were three-quarters of an inch deep."

"Exactly, Mou!" Athreya agreed. "They were the same depth, but Mrs. Markaan's were *fifteen hours older* than yours. Depressions on the squelchy strip fill up with time – you saw that, didn't you?"

Moupriya nodded vigorously.

"Which means that Mrs. Markaan's prints must have been deeper when they were made!" she said breathlessly.

"And that, in turn, meant that the person wearing those flip-flops was considerably heavier that you," Athreya confirmed, "They must have been worn by the person who carried Mrs. Markaan's body from the rubber raft to firm ground. That brings me to the rubber raft – it offered us yet another clue."

"What clue?" Sabir asked. "It just lay there on the rock shelf. There were no fingerprints in it."

"Indeed. As you say, the raft had been pulled up onto the rock shelf. When Nazreen and I went to the islet, it took the two of us to haul it onto the shelf. How had a sixty-year-old woman done it by herself in the middle of the night?"

"Of course." Sabir breathed. "How stupid of me! Then, she was killed somewhere behind this building and then transported by the raft to the islet."

"Correct. Remember, more than an hour elapsed between Mrs. Markaan's going out through the veranda and the guard hearing the raft's engine. Mrs. Markaan went down to the river at 12:11 a.m. but the guard heard the raft's engine only at 1:25 a.m."

"But why did MM go out in the first place?"

"To meet someone and show him or her the bracelet. I suspect it was someone she trusted and believed to be an expert. Remember, she was desperately trying to find out as much about the bracelet as she could. But at the same time, she was afraid to carry it to Jhansi, for fear of being waylaid and robbed. When a trusted person offered to bring an expert to meet her clandestinely behind the base, she agreed."

"She was killed by a person she trusted?'

"Yes. Someone she knew well. The mere possession of the bracelet led to her death."

"Come on, Mr. Athreya," Sabir countered. "The bracelet was not some ancient religious relic of an obscure tribal god that MM had desecrated and had therefore to be put to death. It was a mundane archaeological find, for God's sake. There has to be a saner explanation."

"To find the explanation, Dr. Baig, we must digress a little and talk about Pratap. Being Mrs. Markaan's nephew, Pratap was unlikely to kill her. Why would he kill his golden goose? Especially when he was not a particularly competent archaeologist and the goose was giving him a lucrative job. And as her only relative, he would anyway inherit her wealth.

"I was convinced that Pratap had not known of Mrs. Markaan's death when he stole her jewels from her suitcase. He merely took advantage of her leaving her room unlocked. The next day, he tried to sell the stolen jewellery to Jagan, who is the fence."

"Jagan?" Sabir exclaimed. "An erect, wiry man with close-cropped hair? The man I met in the restaurant last Saturday?"

"The same," Athreya confirmed. "You found him knowledgeable about history and artifacts for the simple reason that he is a dealer in them. He buys and sells stolen artifacts."

"Good lord!" Sabir sat back, stunned. "Good heavens!"

"As Pratap had stolen the jewels from Mrs. Markaan's suitcase, the natural assumption was that he had stolen her *personal* jewels.

But was that really the case? Why would he be killed merely for selling his aunt's personal jewels?

"On reflection, I began seeing it differently. Mrs. Markaan possesses the bracelet and she is killed. Pratap possesses another piece of jewellery, and he too is killed in a similar fashion. What was it about those pieces of jewellery that was getting people killed?

"Once I thought about it, the answer grew apparent – Pratap had tried to sell what *somebody else* had stolen in the first place ... perhaps something the Bronze Runners had stolen from some museum. Yesterday, the police opened Pratap's safe deposit box in Jhansi and discovered a jewellery set of eight pieces. They also discovered that two pieces were missing from the set – a bracelet and a short necklace.

"This ten-piece jewellery set had been stolen by the Bronze Runners in Mysore. Somehow, it had come into Mrs. Markaan's possession. When the gang learnt about it, they had to kill her immediately. She had already shown the bracelet to one person at the museum. It was only a matter of time that she discovered that the bracelet was hot. And the fact that she had found the bracelet also meant that she knew where Bronze Runners' stolen cache was hidden. That was unacceptable.

"The Bronze Runners lured her out that night and killed her. They then put her body at Naaz Tapu and set up the tableau such that it reinforced the legend of Bhola and his monster dog.

"Imagine their consternation when Pratap lands up the next day at Jagan's doorstep and tries to sell another piece from the same set – the one they had stolen from Mysore. The immediate assumption was that Pratap too knew of the gang's hiding place. He had to be terminated. Pratap too was lured out and killed."

"Is Jagan a member of the Bronze Runners?" Sharad asked.

"I believe so. But as far as the two murders are concerned, he is an accomplice. The mastermind is someone else. Someone Mrs. Markaan knew well and trusted."

"Another Bronze Runner, Athreya?"

"More than one, Sharad. You haven't realised it, but you know more than one Bronze Runner."

"In this room?" Sharad demanded.

Athreya didn't reply. Instead, he turned to Adhira and Moupriya.

"Remember, you told me about a lady from the Bronze Runners who tried to sell a Nizam's dagger to an American?" he asked Adhira.

"Yes, I do."

"If I remember right, this is how you described her: chubby and busty, long and straight black hair, dressed in a saree with an ethnic print and wearing heels. She was the very picture of a chic, modern socialite. Is that correct?"

"Correct." Adhira nodded.

"Now, let's do a little exercise, Mou. If not for anything else, just to demonstrate how imagination can help solve crimes. Shall we?"

Moupriya nodded.

"Let me break up the description into six smaller pieces … chubby and busty … long hair … black hair … straight hair … ethnic attire … chic and modern. Now Mou, imagine that you are that woman. You have been seen trying to sell the dagger, and you need to change your appearance so that you are not recognised. Assume that you can go away somewhere to do that, and that you have sufficient time. What would you do?"

"Let's see." Moupriya frowned as she concentrated on the problem. "I'll take each of the six pieces and answer you.

"Busty and chubby – I'd lose weight like crazy, and very quickly. Long hair – I'd cut it short, very short. Black hair – I'd colour it brown or something acceptable, as I wouldn't want to stand out. Straight hair – I'd use a curler and curl it. Ethnic attire – I'd stop wearing Indian clothes and wear only western ones. Chic and modern – I'd try and do something that makes me look traditional."

"Excellent, Mou! Well done! One last question: you are a woman and can't grow a beard to hide your features. How would you disguise your face?"

"Glasses?" Mou responded immediately. "Large glasses?"

"Wonderful! Let me repeat what you have just said. You will become a woman who is thin, has short, curly hair that is coloured, wears only western clothes, wears large glasses and – let me contribute here – wears a nose stud."

An abrupt silence fell. Eyes widened. They began stealing glances at one person in the room who shrank into her chair.

"Do we know such a lady?" Athreya asked in the pin-drop silence. "If such a person is here at the base, she would not go out very much because she is in hiding. She would immerse herself in her work to give herself a pretext for not going to Jhansi."

"Uncle," Moupriya asked in a hushed voice, "it this true?"

"You know, Mou," Athreya said with a sigh, "when a person loses weight too quickly, her skin tends to sag a bit in a few places. It takes time for the skin to contract after an abrupt loss of mass in the limbs and the torso.

"You may have also observed that chubby people tend to move their limbs a tad slower than thinner people do. When a chubby person suddenly becomes thin and loses muscle, her movements might appear slightly slow for her new girth. And her gait may seem awkward for a thin woman."

Athreya turned to Mithali.

"Are those plain glasses you are wearing, Mithali?" he asked. "Or are they prescription?"

Mithali had blanched. Ulhas had frozen.

"The outside of the Nizam's dagger had far too many fingerprints," Athreya went on. "But the inside did not. You left a clear thumbprint on the blade."

He turned to Ulhas and continued, "Your voice sample matched with the voice of the man who had negotiated the sale of the Nizam's dagger over the phone with the American buyer."

Colonel Khanai had stood up and was glaring at Mithali and Ulhas in silence. Madhav, too, was facing them squarely. The other residents of the base were in shock. Mithali began sobbing.

"We didn't kill her," Ulhas said in a strangled voice. "By God, we didn't kill MM. We have nothing to do with her death or Pratap's."

Silence reigned for half a minute.

Ulhas spoke again. This time, his voice was a wail.

"You must believe me," he pleaded. "We did not kill MM or Pratap. I am speaking the truth!"

"I know," Athreya said.

Every head in the room snapped towards him.

"You were associated with the Bronze Runners," he said to Ulhas. "But the network is so partitioned that you did not know another Bronze Runner when you saw him."

"A *fourth* Bronze Runner?" Sharad demanded. "In this room?"

Athreya nodded.

"The two murders have a lot more to do with the Bronze Runners than with Naaz Tapu," he went on. "The legend of Naaz Tapu was a convenient tool that lent itself admirably to the gang's plans. But first, let me tell you what we found at Naaz Tapu yesterday.

"We found nine wooden coffins. Not full-sized adult coffins, but rectangular wooden boxes that would pass as coffins. In these coffins, we found a huge cache of stolen artefacts – statues, sculptures, busts, figurines, jewels, jewelled weapons, etcetera. A cursory scan suggests that the coffins hold most of the Bronze Runners' loot that has not appeared in the market.

"The legend of Naaz Tapu was tailor-made for the Bronze Runners' purposes. It ensured that the locals remained terrified of the islet. So terrified that they wouldn't set foot on the islet. Nobody, save a rare brave or inebriated man, would go anywhere near it.

"And with the islet shrouded in thick greenery, it was the perfect hiding place. Naaz Tapu was where the Bronze Runners hid their cache. To keep their secret from being discovered, they reinforced the legend – mostly through rumours, but also by murder. They even killed a man named Ranvir who had ventured onto the islet.

"When Mrs. Markaan began exploring the islet, she stumbled upon a ruined building that was overrun by the roots of a banyan tree. Inside the ruin, she found a box that had not been adequately concealed by the gang. Perhaps, they inadvertently left it in a corner on the shrine's floor and didn't realise it. Remember, it's pitch dark in there, and they couldn't risk using much light for fear of being discovered.

"Mrs. Markaan opened the box and found the ten-piece jewellery set from the Mysore museum. Not realising that it was stolen property, she picked it up and brought it to the base, where she hid it from the others. That is where the bracelet came from. I suspect that's also where she found the ring she was wearing when she was killed. Once the Bronze Runners came to know of Mrs. Markaan's find, they killed her."

Athreya nodded to Bhupinder, who opened a large bag resembling a cricket kit. From it, he retrieved a crude weapon – an oversized sledgehammer. To its fearsome head, a hollow half-sphere of iron the size of a football had been welded. From the way Bhupinder lifted it, it was clear that the weapon was heavy.

"Bhola's mace," Athreya explained. "Heavy enough to crush an elderly woman's skull in one blow. The inspector found it in Jagan's house. He also found some other things, including Pratap's locker key. Jagan, incidentally, is behind bars."

Bhupinder put down the modified sledge hammer and pulled out a metal contraption from the bag. Thin steel rods had been shaped and welded to form the jaws of a large animal. Four large steel canines protruded menacingly from among two rows of sharp metal teeth. The two jaws were hinged, and from the hinge, two long handles protruded backwards.

Bhupinder held the handles and operated them like a pair of garden shears. When he brought the handles together, the massive jaws closed, simulating an animal's bite. He repeated the action a couple of times to make the jaws open and shut repeatedly.

"That is how Pratap's throat was ripped out and Mrs. Markaan's shoulder was bitten. Metal jaws, obviously, leave no saliva. And the final weapon is this."

He reached into the bag and pulled out a large artificial paw with three metal blades.

"This was supposed to be the dog's claws," he said. "But unlike real animal claws that leave skin torn and the flesh with ragged edges, these blades leave clean cuts. It was a clear giveaway. Nevertheless, these are the tools with which the Bronze Runners kept alive the legend of Naaz Tapu's spectral guardians. They found a convenient legend and turned it to their advantage."

"You said that the Bronze Runners killed MM as soon as they knew that she had found the bracelet," Adhira asked in a hushed voice. "How did they find out? MM told no one."

"Dr. Korda," Athreya said, turning to the tall, sombre man brooding in a corner. "Perhaps you can help us. When did you shoot the video of the bracelet?"

"Sunday before last," Dr. Korda rumbled tonelessly.

"The Sunday before the one I came here to the base?"

"Yes."

"Thank you. Did you share the video with anyone?"

Dr. Korda hesitated. His eyes flickered to Adhira. A moment later, he spoke.

"With Adhira," he said.

"When?"

"The next day … Monday."

Athreya turned to Adhira, who had turned ashen. Her lips were quivering. She was terrified of what was coming.

"Did you share it with anyone, Adhira?" he asked.

Adhira nodded. Her eyes brimmed with tears.

Madhav, who had been watching intently, began walking towards her. On the way, when he was close to the lounge door, he turned towards the door.

"Madhav," Nazreen called from her seat near the door. In the silence, her voice rang clearly in everyone's ears. "I wouldn't go out if I were you. There is a large dog there, and he won't like seeing you."

She whistled softly. The next moment Churi stood just outside the lounge door. Erect and long-legged, the fierce-looking Great Dane's sudden appearance drew startled gasps.

"There is no way a man can outrun him," Nazreen continued almost nonchalantly. "Take my word for it … he kills. If I were you, I'd stay inside the lounge where I would be safe from Churi."

"Adhira," Athreya asked again. "With whom did you share the video?"

"Ma … Ma … Madhav." Her voice was a whisper.

"When?"

"Tuesday … the day after Dr. Korda shared it with me."

Adhira broke down and buried her face in her hands, weeping bitterly. Moupriya wrapped her arm around the disconsolate lady.

"But Madhav didn't share it with Colonel Khanai, his boss," Athreya went on. "For eight days, he kept it from the man who was running the investigation into the Bronze Runners. And when Colonel Khanai showed him the video the day before yesterday, Madhav acted as if he was seeing it for the first time.

"The first time I interviewed him, Madhav inadvertently let something slip. He knew that Mrs. Markaan had been exploring Naaz Tapu. When I questioned him about it, he said that someone had mentioned that in the lounge. But nobody else had even a suspicion that Mrs. Markaan had been visiting the islet. Besides, Madhav had not shared his knowledge with Colonel Khanai.

"These, by themselves, *prove* nothing. That's why we set up a trap for you at Naaz Tapu yesterday, Madhav. We installed cameras in the shrine, and Colonel Khanai told you to organise a raid on Naaz Tapu today. That gave you only last night to retrieve your coffins. But when you reached there, you discovered that the coffins were no longer there.

"Your midnight trip to Naaz Tapu along with Jagan is on record, Madhav. The cameras inside the shrine began rolling the moment you switched on a light inside. Before and after that, night cameras outside the shrine entrance made their own recordings. In addition, we have two witnesses.

"For those of you who don't know, Madhav is a government investigator who is *supposed* to be investigating the Bronze Runners as a part of Colonel Khanai's team. He had been planted at the dig because the colonel expected this project to be targeted by the Bronze Runners.

"When Mrs. Markaan spontaneously fired him, the colonel had to confide in her so that Madhav could return to the dig. Once Mrs. Markaan knew that Madhav was a government agent, she began implicitly trusting him. The doubts she had earlier harboured vanished. On Sunday morning, he introduced Jagan to her as an expert who was willing to come to the base that night and give his opinion on the bracelet.

"Trusting Madhav unreservedly, Mrs. Markaan agreed. He killed her with Jagan's help. The next day, Pratap unknowingly put his head into the noose by approaching Jagan for selling the short necklace from the same set the bracelet had come from. Pratap too was lured out, perhaps with a promise of payment, and was killed."

"Madhav was supposed to be infiltrating the Bronze Runners on our behalf," Khanai said bitterly as he pulled out his pistol and pointed it at Madhav. "Little did we realise he had infiltrated *us*. He was supposed to bring us actionable intelligence that would prevent theft and help apprehend the thieves. Instead, he misled us into looking in the wrong direction whenever the gang struck. He passed on our plans to the Bronze Runners so they could get away every time. He is a double-agent and will be treated as one."

He glanced at Nazreen, who called Churi to her and made the dog sit beside her. Four armed and uniformed men entered the lounge and took the three Bronze Runners away.

* * *

"You've solved every mystery except one," Sharad said as they were driving back from the base. "Who wrote those anonymous letters to Liam Dunne?"

"Serious criminals usually don't engage in petty misdemeanours like writing anonymous letters," Athreya said. "It needlessly raises the risk of exposure without adding any benefit. With Dr. Korda and the Bronze Runners excluded, it left only Nazreen, Adhira and Dr. Baig as the possible authors of the anonymous letters.

"Nazreen has her secrets, but this is not one of them. Dr. Baig would have been uncharacteristically foolish to write those letters. It was rapidly becoming apparent that Mrs. Markaan was not as competent as Dunne had thought her to be. It was only a matter of time before Dr. Baig replaced her as the head of the SBAI. In any case, Mrs. Markaan's contract would come up for renewal in a year.

"Which left Adhira. I confronted her privately, and she confessed. I decided not to ruin her career by telling Liam Dunne. Yes, it was an indiscretion on Adhira's part, but everything that she wrote in those letters was also true. She deserves a second chance."

"You are a kind person, Uncle," Moupriya said in a small voice. "I agree that Adhira Didi deserves another chance. By the way, I had a question of my own. What did Nazreen Didi tell you before we left the base?"

"Oh, nothing," Athreya replied with a smile. "A small matter of detail between her and me."

What Nazreen had said was in reply to Athreya's question. There was more to the shrine, he had thought. The Vaziri family was protecting something far more valuable. Athreya had asked Nazreen what that was.

After a full day's consideration, Nazreen had let him in on the secret. Hidden in the shrine were artefacts belonging to Naazneen and

Vanraj, which the Vaziri family didn't want to fall into the hands of strangers and museums. The most precious of the artifacts the shrine concealed were the jewels Vanraj's mother had given to Naazneen before they fled to Naaz Tapu. Worth a fortune, that treasure belonged to the Vaziri family.

About the Author

After a corporate career spanning three decades and four continents, RV Raman has moved away from full time roles to pursue his interest in teaching and writing. He now teaches business strategy at an IIM, mentors young entrepreneurs, advises select clients and writes. In an earlier avatar, he led KPMG's Consulting Practice, and was a partner with A.T. Kearney and Arthur Andersen. He writes crime fiction set in India. His first Harith Athreya novel, *A Will to Kill*, was selected as a *New York Times* Editor's Choice.

Visit him online at www.rvraman.com